TIME IN A BOTTLE

For Ginnie,

Best wishes and hopes that we'll meet again soon —

MARJORIE KLEIN

Marjorie Klein

Black Rose Writing | Texas

The author grants the final approval for this literary material.

First printing

This is a work of fiction. Names, characters, businesses, places, events, and incidents are
either the products of the author's imagination or used in a fictitious manner. Any
resemblance to actual persons, living or dead, or actual events is purely coincidental.

ISBN: 978-1-68513-142-5
PUBLISHED BY BLACK ROSE WRITING
www.blackrosewriting.com

Printed in the United States of America
Suggested Retail Price (SRP) $21.95

Time in a Bottle is printed in Old Style

*As a planet-friendly publisher, Black Rose Writing does its best to eliminate unnecessary waste to
reduce paper usage and energy costs, while never compromising the reading experience. As a result,
the final word count vs. page count may not meet common expectations.

For my children, Allison and Ken,
and grandsons Joshua and Bennett:
There's no time like the present.

PRAISE FOR
TIME IN A BOTTLE

"*Time in a Bottle* is a story so delightful, so exquisitely told, and so exhilarating that you'll want to stand up and cheer when you've finished. Marjorie Klein is always fun to read, and here she is at the top of her game. She's breathed life into her characters, into Lorelei, Sharleen, and Juan, into the irascible Corabelle and the preternatural Winona, and these irresistible folks breathe life into us. Lorelei thinks she's found the fountain of youth but may have found something more important—herself."

–John Dufresne, author of *I Don't Like Where This Is Going*

"Once again the fans of Marjorie Klein can celebrate as she brings a magical elixir of whimsy and gravitas to a tale that is spelling-binding in more ways than one. The city of Miami is a willing accomplice, providing a pitch-perfect backdrop to what is a wise meditation on youth and aging, disguised as a romp. A non-trigger warning: readers will revel in knowing nods of recognition and happy tears of laughter."

–Madeleine Blais is a Pulitzer-prize winning journalist and author of *Queen of the Court: The Many Lives of Tennis Legend Alice Marble*

"In this novel, Marjorie Klein bottles water from the Fountain of Youth with wacky humor, pop culture, sexy lingerie and an alluring sense of place (southeastern Florida). The magical water may be elusive, but the promise of a second chance at life and love will sustain readers long after they finish the book."

–Heather Newton, author of *The Puppeteer's Daughters* and *Under the Mercy Trees*

"What do Florida, lingerie saleswomen and The Fountain of Youth have in common? *Time In A Bottle,* a book with enough lace and larceny to keep the hilarity flowing. Watch out readers, this one's hard to put down!"

　　–Maryedith Burrell, Emmy-award winning writer and producer

"Time in a Bottle is audacious and touching and comic and wonderfully written. It's an adventure, one that relies on a fountain of youth, Ponce de Leon, and present-day characters who are frayed by time, then re-invigorated. You'll be taken inside a world that is both magnetic and charming, a world you'd never be able to experience except here, in these pages."

　　–Judy Goldman, author of *Child: A Memoir*

"Marjorie Klein is a teller of tales. Her colorful characters are exaggerated versions of people we recognize. It's a glorious ride! But, make no mistake, there's a lesson to be learned: the desperation to be forever young is very real."

　　–Susan L. Brooks, *Changing the Face of Aging*

"Marjorie Klein has written a terrific book! *Time in a Bottle* is a page-turner that begins when a fountain of youth is discovered in the Miami backyard of a 60-something lingerie store owner. Nuanced characters, real wit, and an engrossing, original plot make this modern-day *Tuck Everlasting* a novel to savor and enjoy. I loved it."

　　–Dan Elish, author of *Nine Wives*

ACKNOWLEDGEMENTS

I am deeply grateful to fellow writers who read my novel in its earlier incarnations and provided me with insights and wisdom that enhanced the story I wanted to tell. The Flatiron Writers, my writing group in Asheville, were supportive throughout, and I give special thanks for extensive comments from Maggie Marshall, Heather Newton, Maryedith Burrell, Kim Mako and Jude Whelchel. Editing kudos to Allison Klein, and much appreciation to Ken Klein for his cover design assistance.

Time in a Bottle

ONE

Lorelei kicks up dust as she walks, frosting her new white Reeboks with a rusty haze. She walks briskly, head high, arms pumping, breathing deeply. Her lungs burn from the parched air, sun-sizzled despite the early hour. Melaleuca Lakes slumbers in post-dawn ennui, a pastiche of pink, blue and yellow houses. Subdued in this light, the delicate pastels will become garish as the sun climbs higher, exposing their true colors in its unrelenting glare.

Corabelle, her elderly neighbor, is up as well, perched on her porch rocker, surveying all as the self-designated neighborhood watchdog. "Hot enough for ya?" Corabelle hollers.

Lorelei nods her head once, accelerating past Corabelle. She does not smile. Smile, and people want to stop and talk, and she has no patience for that. A glance at her watch shows there's just enough time to make another lap around the block, a quick shower, then off to work.

She is chief fitter and part owner of Ladybug Lingerie. This is not a flighty profession, despite the proximity to fluff. Admittedly, times have changed since she first entered the field. Whereas once brassieres were designed as objects of containment, they have evolved into frivolous bits of enticement, the purpose of which she sometimes questions. Nevertheless, fit is as crucial in trashy styles as it is in the truly supportive, and Lorelei is a professional.

She can see Corabelle from her bathroom window, opened just a crack to release the humidity of the shower. Corabelle has descended from her porch rocker and set forth on the first of her neighborhood patrols, tiny feet scurrying beneath a baby-doll body. A dust cloud envelops her as she shuffles past Lorelei's house. Lorelei ducks beneath the window before Corabelle can spy her and holler another greeting.

Her shower is more of a dribble. The water pressure has diminished over the past week or so, but she's too busy to do something about it. She wonders if Corabelle's pressure is low, too, but past experience has proven any communication with her to be a mistake, resulting in no information other than Corabelle's skewed interpretation of whatever gossip she has picked up in her excursions around the neighborhood.

Lorelei dries off and dresses quickly, having laid out her clothes the night before. She is a person who likes things just so. Her pantry is organized according to food groups, her closet according to color. She dusts daily, vacuums nightly, makes her bed while it's still warm. She keeps no pets.

Vanity left her long ago, and when she knots her hair into a tight French twist, she doesn't linger over her image. It's been said that she's a handsome woman — never pretty, but at 60, she's aged fairly well. She takes care of herself: vitamins, fiber, exercise. Her body is trim, but always compressed within the boundaries of support: a practical brassiere, a girdle.

Some forgo such fortification as bras and girdles in this climate, using the heat and humidity of Miami as an excuse. Lorelei says nothing is an excuse for slovenly dress, and yet she lives in an increasingly sloppy world. Her business partner, Sharleen, who once took such pride in her dress when they were in high school together, has devolved into a wearer of thongs.

Uh oh. It's late. She always makes a point of getting to the shop before Sharleen, not ordinarily a problem since Sharleen will usually wander in after Lorelei has organized the merchandise for the day. But there was one morning when Sharleen arrived first, and despite knowing that Lorelei preferred that the panties be displayed in a symmetrical manner on the front table, Sharleen just dealt them out like cards. Lorelei had to hastily rearrange the table before the first customers arrived. Fearing the worst, Lorelei rushes out the door, berating herself for not drying the breakfast dishes before she leaves.

• • •

UPS has arrived with boxes. "Sharleen!" Lorelei calls, alerted by the return address, VaVoom Bazooms. "Did you order these?"

Sharleen skitters out from the back on little spike-heeled feet, digs long acrylic nails into her piled-up hairdo, and giggles, the sign that she knows she's done something naughty. "I know. They're trashy." She grins at the UPS man, who seems to be in no hurry. "But they're so *fun*."

"I thought we agreed not to order from this company," Lorelei says, exasperated, as always, with Sharleen's judgment when it came to buying. Although their understanding as equal partners was that merchandise would be decided upon together, Lorelei's decisions usually prevailed. But every so often, Sharleen would go gaga over the X-rated catalog from some smutty company or another and sneak in an order that Lorelei would ultimately veto. Case in point: VaVoom Bazooms.

"This is their new line," Sharleen says. "I couldn't resist." Expertly avoiding the use of her nails, she tears open the first box before Lorelei can protest, then dives into the layered nest of tissue paper. "Oooo," she sighs, "look." She dangles from two fingers what seems to be the outline of a bra: a cup-free, breast-baring bit of red lace. The UPS man stares, speechless but clearly appreciative as he moves closer for a better look.

"'Trashy' isn't the word," Lorelei says. "That is obscene."

"Yeah. Isn't it fabulous?" Sharleen reaches into the box once more.

"Fabulous," the UPS man says. He gasps at the next specimen, a sheer nude number with red hearts over the nipple area, and nearly convulses at the wispy black crotchless panties that Sharleen holds up to her hips.

"See?" she says. "They're practical, too."

"Oh yes, oh yes," agrees the UPS man. "Practical. Fabulous. Definitely fabulously practical. What else you got there?"

"Don't you have other deliveries?" Lorelei opens the door and points the way out. "The world is waiting."

He reluctantly makes his exit. Lorelei sees him standing at the storefront window, fogging the glass with his breath as he tries to catch a last glimpse. Ignoring him, she turns to Sharleen. "What in the world are you thinking when you order something like this?"

"That I like it and I want it." Sharleen holds a ribbon-trimmed corset up to her curvy little body. "Don't you love it? It's so sexy."

"We are not about sexy," Lorelei corrects her. "We are about support. We are about fit. We are about providing elegant undergarments to discriminating women. We are not about ticky tacky trash."

"I like ticky tacky trash. Ticky tacky trash sells. It's so fun." Sharleen pouts, her mouth constricting tiny and red as a spark. "I don't know what you've got against fun. Isn't that why we're in this business, anyway?" She gathers the boxes to her breast and teeters past Lorelei on her way to the back. "We're keeping them. Just because you want to be a fuddy duddy old fart doesn't mean I have to." Sharleen turns suddenly and, mouth now a defiant hyphen, glares at Lorelei. "You know, it wouldn't kill you to get yourself a boyfriend or something."

Fuddy duddy? Old fart? *Boyfriend?* Lorelei turns and sees multiple Lorelei's in the shop's mirrors, staring, shocked, at one another. And then notices, in the same mirrors, that the UPS man is still pressed against the window. She feels strangely gratified when he gives her a big wink.

The word "boyfriend" vanished from Lorelei's vocabulary long ago, at least in relation to herself. Even when she was young and opportunity was there, opportunity rarely knocked. Few men stepped foot in her shop, and when they did, it was with, or for, a wife or girlfriend. The rare man who was available was invariably attracted to Sharleen, who never had a shortage of male admirers. Lorelei had cultivated an appearance and attitude that said "Keep away" for all those years. That wasn't about to change now.

Sharleen's perky persona has mutated with age. What was at one time perhaps adorable and sexy was devolving into a caricature of her younger self. She wears the same big blonde hairdo and bright makeup she wore at 20, and squeezes her curvy body, now succumbing to sags, cellulite, and a major muffin top, into miniskirts, tight jeans, and towering heels that threaten to topple her daily.

Despite their differences, it's worked all these years. Sharleen, Lorelei has to admit, is the shop's mainsail, while Lorelei is what keeps it afloat. In that sense, they make good partners. Sharleen's upbeat, wacky charm brings the customers in and keeps them coming; Lorelei's practical, business-like demeanor gives them confidence in the merchandise. But times are changing, along with the economy.

Some months they just scrape by, barely making enough to pay the rent and cover their expenses. The internet has not been their friend, and Lorelei doesn't want to hear it when Sharleen shows her what's available online, and how, if they don't keep up with this competition, they'll be doomed. Until recently, business had been steady and profitable, but bringing in younger, hipper customers—the Victoria's Secret crowd—has gotten harder as the number of their older clientele declines. While the dimensions and proportions of their loyal, more mature customers may have waxed and waned over the years, those same women remain faithful to Ladybug Lingerie, knowing that, while styles may change, the proprietors do not. Sharleen will always be zany Sharleen, and Lorelei, sensible Lorelei.

WATER, OR THE LACK OF IT

Sometimes when the wind blows hard, you can smell the salt of the sea. But here in Melaleuca Lakes, that hint of nearby ocean is smothered by aromas from the neighborhood strip mall where Bucket o' Beans and La Casa de Pollo duel for fast food dominance. Behind the mall lies Melaleuca Lakes, a dusty suburban Miami grid of streets set with rows of houses as blocky and predictable as a Monopoly game.

The development was named after the trees planted on each tiny square of lawn. The melaleuca, a thirsty tree that sucks water from the ground, was imported in the early 1900s from Australia to South Florida in the belief it would reclaim the swampland of the Everglades. Its unusual peeling trunk, wispy branches and tenacious hardiness in the tropical climate made it popular with homeowners as well. Later, it was discovered that those very melaleuca trees were to blame for the plague of stuffy noses, sneezing fits and blotchy red rashes now indigenous to the neighborhoods. By then, their proliferation was out of control.

But allergies have taken second place to the most recent worry for the residents of Melaleuca Lakes: drought. The ground water that feeds the twin lakes has slowed to a trickle. The lakes, formed long ago when limestone was blasted to build homes in nearby Coral Gables, have sunk to the level of puddles.

Winter has been dry. Summer was wet, the sky stacked with thunderheads, underbellies hung dark and low each morning, rumbling in anticipation. In late afternoon, the clouds would detonate with crashing booms and terrifying flashes, dumping torrents of rain in a deluge. By fall, the clouds appeared only at sunset, skimming the horizon in puffs of lavender and orange. Now the winter sky is unblemished, clear and dry, an ethereal powder blue.

Ground water, which usually flows through the porous coral rock as if it were a colander, now seeps as slowly as sweat, dropping the water table to record depths. The city has ordered rationing: no sprinklers, no car washing, no water glasses filled in restaurants. Neighbors spy on neighbors to report illicit lawn watering. Dogs go unbathed, kiddie pools are empty, Publix has run out of Perrier. Between the ocean and the Everglades, the land rolls on, flat and dry as parchment.

TWO

Lorelei is preparing her bath. It is a luxury she allows herself after a day on her feet. Today was stressful, what with the whole VaVoom thing, so the need to submerge herself seems particularly urgent at the moment. While the tub fills with iridescent bubbles, she steps out of her dress and hangs it on one of the satin hangers ordered through the shop.

She unhooks her sensible bra (Playtex, style #2325), 34-B, the same sturdy brand and size worn when she was young and weighed the same as now, give or take a few pounds. The proportions of her body seem to have shifted, hips wider, shoulders narrower than they once were. She lets the bra drop and gazes at her breasts in the bathroom mirror. Her doctor is the only other person who has seen them since Itzy Morganstern bared them over 40 years ago in the back seat of his mother's Chevy wagon.

She never dwells on the brief tryst that changed her life so much. But sometimes, in her dreams, she feels the weight of Itzy's body on hers, the tickle of his crewcut beneath her chin, the feel of his zipper on her cotton-clad crotch. She hears herself saying "No no Itzy" but when he stops, the desire remains for even more. She wakes with a start, then lies blinking in the dark, trying to reassemble pieces of her just-forgotten dream.

Lorelei peels off her control top pantyhose (Donna Karan, natural beige #4). Her skin is the translucent ivory of the shade worshipper, a rare breed in this sun-struck city. She hasn't had a tan line since she was twenty, after she noticed something about a customer she was measuring. The skin of the woman's face and arms was the color and texture of a cured tobacco leaf; the skin of her breasts was like milk. Sun. It was a lesson. Lorelei never went to the beach again.

Yet, despite her vigilance, time is toying with her anyhow. She turns her nude body this way and that before the mirror, criticizing as she goes. The pale blue veins that map her legs are becoming thick and twisted routes. Something strange is going on beneath her chin, as if skin had detached from bone and then accordion pleated its way down her neck. Her butt and thighs have lost their tone and become as dimpled as bubble wrap.

Her hair, once her secret pride, thick and wavy and black, is fading fast to gray beneath the Eternal Ebony color applied monthly at her salon, thinning at the temples where she pulls it back into a neat and tidy French twist. She reaches back and releases her hair from its prison of pins, lets it fall around her angular face, notices how violet the area beneath her eyes has gotten, how crepey, how dark. How sad.

Kazunk. She whirls, startled at the sound coming from the tub. *Kazunkity-zunk.* The faucet seems to vibrate. And then the water stops. Just like that.

The bubbles glisten and wink at her with rainbow eyes. "Well?" they seem to say. "What's going on?" They float lazily upon the few inches of water, waiting for life to resume.

Lorelei fiddles with the faucet, turning it on, then off, then on again. Hot. Cold. Nothing.

Damn. She tries the sink. Nothing there either. She wraps a towel around herself and stalks to the kitchen sink. The faucet hums a little, splats out a few drops, then shudders and quits.

She'll need a plumber.

It's after hours. She gets the answering service at Flush'em Plumbing. Is it an emergency? Yes, it's an emergency, Lorelei answers irritably. I don't have any *water*, implying but not adding,

You idiot. Yes m'am, says the answering service lady, I'll give them the message.

Lorelei goes into the bathroom and stares at the tub. The bubbles have dissipated, leaving a few shrunken survivors floating here and there. She drops the towel and sighs. This may be the only opportunity she'll have to bathe tonight, so she eases into the now cool water and lies down. Her goose-pimpled breasts, pink nipples like periscopes, float above the shallow water. Shivering, she soaps herself rapidly, sloshes around to rinse, and hops out of the tub, rubbing herself briskly with the towel. Damn damn damn. She's been looking forward to her nice hot bath all day and now this.

She dials the plumber again and leaves the same message. She does not disguise her annoyance. Neither does the answering service lady. "They'll get back to you as soon as they can," she says tightly. "Please be patient."

"Easy for you to say," Lorelei says before she's disconnected. "*You* don't have to flush my toilet."

• • •

It's late. Lorelei still has not heard from the plumber, and now, teeth unbrushed, face unwashed, and toilet unflushed, she is preparing for bed. She's still hungry; she was unable to prepare the brown rice for the Tofu Bean Surprise she had planned for dinner and had to run to Bucket o' Beans for takeout. When she returned to her car, she noticed a blue flyer clamped beneath the windshield wiper. She almost tossed it, but one word caught her eye: "Water."

WATER WATER EVERYWHERE, INC.

Need a well? Call "Juan"!

Specializing in well drilling for home water systems.

"Quality" residential and irrigation wells.

24 HOUR SERVICE. CALL ANYTIME!!

"JUAN" at (305)555-WATR (305-555-9287)

She has a well. What she needs is a plumber, but she had stuffed the flyer into her purse and forgot it until now when preparing for bed has become a water-free challenge. She unrumples the crumpled blue page and smooths it out to read once more.

24-hour service. Call anytime!!

Wells. Plumbing. They're all connected, aren't they? But this "Juan" isn't a real plumber. Did she really want to call someone who needs business so badly he leaves flyers under windshield wipers?

Lorelei tries the faucet again, willing it to spurt water on her Crest-laden toothbrush. The only response is a death rattle.

Juan. He's probably Cuban. That means he'll be here whenever.

She's desperate. She dials the number and leaves a message.

• • •

Lorelei is deep in the dream again. Itzy's crewcut is prickly beneath her chin. She hears him whispering into her ear, please please please. She hears him knocking, knocking, knocking...

What? She springs up in bed. Who's that? Someone at her door? What time is it?

She fumbles for the glasses on her nightstand and squints through bleary eyes at the digital clock. 6:02. Who is banging on her door at 6:02 am? It's still dark out. She throws on her bathrobe (pink terry Natori #3498, size M), and shuffles to the door. "Who is it?" she calls.

She flicks on the porch light and squints through the peephole of the door. An amber eye stares back. Now she's scared. "Who are you? What do you want?"

"You wanted a plumber?"

"Yes!" she cries. At long last, that idiot woman at Flush'em Plumbing has sent someone, albeit at 6 am, but this is no time to complain about scheduling. He's here. She throws open the door in relief. "Flush'em?" she asks.

"Nope," he says, stepping out of the shadows and into the circle of porch light. "I'm Juan."

"Juan?" The name drifts somewhere in the fog of her awakening mind. Oh, yes. The well digger.

"You left a message. Help. Emergency. At this address. I called. No answer." He shrugs. "You sounded kinda…panicked."

"Panicked? I don't panic." Of all the nerve. Who does this guy think he is, with that ridiculous silver gray ponytail and that smirk of a smile. "I need a plumber. Not a well-digger. I've already got a well."

"I've got a plumber's license. Wells are my business, but I know my way around pipes." He digs into the back pocket of his jeans and pulls out a battered card. "Here's my card," he says, and points to a number on it. "License number. You can check it out."

He's a plumber. She needs water. She could wait a week for Flush'em to show up, and Juan is here on her doorstep. She's annoyed that she finds him attractive despite the pony tail and the John Lennon glasses held together at the bridge with electrical tape. She chalks it up to leftover dream and asks, "Can you fix it?"

"I don't know. I just got here," he says, his slight accent hinted at by a skipped consonant or stretched vowel. "Want me to take a look?"

She lets him in and leads the way into the kitchen. When he crouches to check under the sink, Lorelei notices two things: that the design on the back of his T-shirt is the same as on the front–a single water drop, white on black, curved highlight to one side– and that as Juan's T-shirt inches up, his jeans slide down his slim hips, making real the cliché about plumber's crack.

She fights a sudden desire to touch the downy patch of fuzz above his butt cleavage–lightly, softly, maybe he won't notice. So strong is this impulse that she clutches her hands together to keep them under control. What is wrong with her?

Metallic clanks and hollow clunks are coming from beneath the sink. Juan climbs out. He has bad news: there's nothing wrong. He checks the bathroom and laundry room. "*Nada*," he says. "Where's your pump?"

It's been so long since she's needed to know that she's not sure. "Out back, by the garbage cans?"

"That may be your problem." Juan hitches up his jeans with his thumbs, stuffs his T-shirt back into them, and unhooks a flashlight from his belt. "I'll check it out," he says, and heads out back. She hears clanks, clunks, then sighing sounds coming from the pump.

He's gone a long time. Lorelei tries to peer out the kitchen window to see what Juan is doing, but sees only her own reflection, face still pasty with night cream, hair undone from its twist and hanging loosely about her shoulders. Appalled at her appearance, she rips a paper towel from its holder and wipes the goo from her face, then rakes her hair back with her fingers.

Oh, what's the difference. He didn't even look at her.

Why does she care?

She doesn't care. This is ridiculous. Vanity is Sharleen's thing, not hers. Sharleen is the same age as Lorelei but denies it. Sharleen preens like a cockatoo whenever a male is around, reads *Cosmopolitan* for sex tips aimed at 20-year-olds, keeps an autographed picture of fat-days Elvis in her night table drawer—this, Lorelei knows for a fact.

Not that Lorelei snoops, no no. But she and Sharleen have exchanged house keys in case of emergency. Who else would check if one or the other has fallen and can't get up? That commercial once struck her as funny when she was young and single. Now that Lorelei is old—well, not old, just mature—and single, its message seems a scary premonition. She has used Sharleen's key, not to see if Sharleen has fallen, but at her request to water her plants and feed her cat when she goes away for a weekend with her latest fling. On those occasions, Lorelei can't help but notice how

Sharleen lives. Of course it's none of her business, but she does wish Sharleen would throw out the fuzzy blue food in her fridge, or make her bed now and then, or hand-wash the lovely lingerie she gets wholesale from the shop instead of throwing it in the machine like a bunch of rags.

Juan taps on the window, motioning for Lorelei to open it. "It's not your pump," he says. "I think it's something else. I'll need more time to see what's going on. I've got another job waiting. I'll have to come back tomorrow."

"What's wrong?"

"I think your well's run dry."

"What does that mean?"

"No water."

"I *know* that." Lorelei closes her eyes, summons up the patience she tries to exercise with particularly dull people. "What's wrong, what has to be done and how much will it cost?"

"Not sure yet. I'll know tomorrow. I may have to dig a deeper well."

Oh no. No digging. Not if there's some alternative solution, which had better happen soon. Sharleen has offered to let her shower at her place—a prospect, given Sharleen's housekeeping deficiencies, Lorelei doesn't anticipate with joy. "We'll talk about it tomorrow." By then, she hopes she'll have gotten a real plumber.

• •

The next morning, still no callback from Flush'em. Lorelei is brushing her teeth with Syfo Seltzer when the doorbell rings. She peers out the window. It's Juan. Behind him is a giant drilling rig on a truck that blocks the street.

She opens the door. "What are you doing?"

"If you'll get your car out of your driveway, I'll have room to pull this around back."

"Why?"

"I got a hunch."

"Look," she says, "I need a second opinion."

"You calling a doctor?"

"No, a plumber. A real plumber," she adds with what, she feels, is just the right touch of dignity. After all, she is the boss.

"Fine with me, but I'll tell you this: whoever dug your well in the first place didn't dig deep enough. You got a twenty-foot well, and it's supposed to be at least forty feet for drinking water. With this drought, your well is dry."

"It's only twenty feet deep?"

"Yup. I just measured it. Somebody got lazy. You're lucky you haven't gotten sick. Water that shallow can be contaminated."

"Twenty feet? Why isn't it deeper?"

"I dunno. I'll see if I can punch it deeper, but I got a hunch there's a reason it's short." He kicks at the dirt with a dusty boot. "May have to dig a new one."

She hesitates. Maybe this guy Juan is a con man, wanting to dig another well just to make a buck. She trusts no one. "I got a hunch, too," she says. "I want a second opinion."

"Be my guest. But if I leave, I'm not coming back with this rig. It's a butt pain to get it here, and I'm only doing it once."

"As you wish." She goes inside to dial Flush'em's number, which she has committed to memory. By Lorelei's third call, the answering service lady recognizes Lorelei's voice at the first panicked syllable, disconnects her and blocks her next call. Now what? She's going to be late for work.

Juan is still outside, fiddling with the pump. "Okay," she concedes, resigned to settling for second (and only) choice. "Can you do this without digging? I don't want a mess here."

"I'll try to pull up the casing from the old well to see what's what," he says. "Maybe I can punch through and make it deeper. But I can't make any promises."

"Do that," she says, irritated that her morning is getting off to such an annoying start. "Pull up the casing, whatever. Just don't make a mess."

•

When Lorelei returns home after work, there is indeed a mess. The rig that was around front is now around back, and there is a hole in the ground. Her neighbor Corabelle is standing guard, tiny features squinched together in defiant disapproval. "What's going on here?" Corabelle demands. "What you digging for?"

Lorelei ignores her, as she has for most of the 30 years they've lived across the street from one another. Corabelle, in her zeal for uncovering crimes and misdemeanors, has zeroed in on what clearly is a major felony occurring in Melaleuca Lakes. "You got a permit?" she yells at Juan.

Juan reaches into his back pocket and waves a paper at her. "Permit," he says.

"Humph," Corabelle says, and having nothing to add, returns to her porch where she resumes the neighborhood watch.

Lorelei glares at the heap of slurried rock ejected by the drill. "I told you, Don't make a mess!"

"I could tell it was useless to pull up the casing from the old well," he says. "At twenty feet, the rock's like steel. I figure we might have better luck over here, where I've started to dig. But there's no telling how deep we need to go. So far, it's bone dry."

Lorelei peers into its depths. "How deep is it?"

"Still twenty feet. Not a drop. You got some kind of rock under here, I'll tell you that. Now I know why whoever dug your well gave up. I hope it's just a freak layer of bedrock and I can punch through it to hit the aquifer, where the ground water is. I'll find out tomorrow if my drill can handle it."

"Tomorrow! I won't have water until tomorrow?" Lorelei was cheated out of a good hot soak yesterday. She wants a bath, and she wants it now.

"Can't promise you'll have water tomorrow, either," Juan says. "I know there's got to be water under there somewhere, but how long it's gonna take to get to it, I can't say."

"Tomorrow," she says, glaring at Juan. "That's my deadline."

"I've never run into anything like this," Juan says, arms folded over the water drop on his T-shirt, looking hot, sweaty and cranky. "It's like rock from Planet X. I think I'd have better luck finding water on the moon. Two days I've pounded away at this rock and I'm only down another ten feet."

Lorelei is on her hands and knees, peering into the borehole in the ground. She struggles to her feet, modestly clutching her skirt over knees now scuffed and dirty as a child's. When she left home this morning for work, she had assumed the well would be dug, Juan would be done, and that would be that.

He takes off his glasses and, avoiding the taped-over bridge, gingerly cleans the lenses with the bottom of his T-shirt. He puts them back on, where they rest lopsided on his nose.

"Well, now what?" She'd ask Sharleen if she could shower at her place, but Sharleen had mentioned something about a hot date tonight, meaning Sharleen and Hot Date might be in the shower themselves for all she knew. What's the alternative? The Y? No no. Too many people. Too many germs. "You've got to do something," she pleads, her voice rising in panic.

"I dunno. This may take a rotary drill, not my cable tool drill. If so, that means you gotta call another company, because I'm a one-man operation. A rotary drill's a whole other animal. It's fast, but it's complicated and expensive and needs at least two people.

Problem is, I'm not even sure they could get that monster truck into your backyard."

"Oh, God," Lorelei moans, and plunks herself down on the step to the patio. "Why is everything so complicated? It's just a well, for God's sake."

"Wells are complicated." The tip of Juan's nose quivers with perceived insult. "You think it's just a hole punched in the ground, then POW and there's water like magic? It's a *science*."

Lorelei, startled at first by his pugnacious response, recognizes herself in his defensiveness. She's done that, too, on those days when she wonders where she would be if only she had gone to college. "Sorry," she says, "but I was really looking forward to a nice hot bubble bath after today." Overwhelmed by frustration, she blathers on. "Nothing went right, the Bali bras all came in wrong—who needs six boxes of 38 DD's?—and then Sharleen had a hissy fit because I told her for the hundredth time *don't put the thongs in the same drawer as the hip huggers*." Lorelei rests her head on her knees. "I just don't think I can face the shower at the Y tonight."

Juan kicks at the dirt, wipes his forehead. "Well," he says after a moment, "I have a bathtub. You're welcome to use it."

Oh God. That's all she needs. Taking a bath in her plumber's bathroom. "I think I'll just sponge off with some Handi-Wipes and call it a night."

"Your choice," he says. "But it's a whirlpool. And I have Laura Mercier bubble bath."

"Laura Mercier?"

"Lavender Harvest."

"Lavender Harvest?" If it's possible to salivate through one's pores, she's doing it.

"Yeah," he says. "My ex left it. When she left." He pauses, as if to say something, but doesn't, and instead adds, "It's not even opened yet."

Not even opened.

The thought of sinking into a warm tub of lavender-scented foam makes her sigh with longing before she snaps back to reality. Bathing in a stranger's bathtub? Certainly not. Even if he does have warm brown eyes with a little twinkle. And a charmingly lopsided smile. And a nice...

She must be delirious from stress. No water, no bath, and now no well in her immediate future. Plus the whole thong/hiphugger aggravation with Sharleen. Life is not good at the moment.

"If it would make you more comfortable," Juan says, "I'll disappear. I need to pick up some things from Home Depot, so you can give me a call when you're done."

Well, that would resolve one of her considerations: Privacy. But why would she trust this plumber to disappear while she bathes? People have to earn her trust, and not many have passed that test.

"Listen," he says. "If you're concerned, I'll meet you there, give you my key, and you can let yourself in and out. Just leave the key under the mat. You don't even have to see me when you're done."

Oh, she really really wants this bath. She can almost feel the caress of those yummy bubbles, the surrender of a hot water meltdown, the feeling of total escape. Temptation is crowding out the common sense on which she prides herself, so she counters that impulse with another barrier to cross: how far is she willing to travel for the sake of a bath?

"Not that I'm seriously considering this," she begins, "but I'm just curious. Where do you live?"

"Little Havana. Just a couple of blocks off Calle Ocho. Not far."

Not far indeed. Calle Ocho—8th Street—is nearby, stretching from the Everglades through Coral Gables to downtown, and is part of her usual route to the shop. One of the reasons she bought her house so many years ago was the convenience of zipping to work via 8th Street – not such a zippy ride any more, given the sludge of traffic clogging streets once lightly traveled.

"Twenty, twenty-five minutes, tops," he adds. Timewise, close, by Miami standards.

How can she resist?

• • •

Juan's house is a surprise. Lorelei expected calendars of nude women on the walls, beer cans on the floor, dirty dishes piled in the sink. Instead, when Juan opens the door, she's dazzled by a glow of fluorescent blue light that shimmers around him as if he were underwater. Upon entering, she realizes that the living room walls are lined with fish tanks.

The room undulates with the movement of the fish, the surrealistic glow, the musical burble from the filters in the tanks. A red and yellow flame of a fish flickers inside a miniature coral castle, seeming to set it on fire. Another tank holds a tiny shark, ferocious as a toy poodle, and another, a slithering, smoky swirl of octopus. She's mesmerized by this translucent world of blue, spinning in an aquatic universe. Juan hands her his key, and before she can thank him, he's gone.

Juan's bathroom is a pleasant surprise as well, clean and tidy, soap and shampoo lined up on a shelf, an orchid arching down from the windowsill. She runs her bath in his big white tub—oh, so lovely, warm and fragrant with Lavender Harvest bubbles that froth in transparent towers. She lowers herself into the airy foam. It takes her a moment to adjust to a foreign tub, like trying on someone else's clothes, but soon she's lulled into the soporific state her bath never fails to induce, a dream state she took for granted until the day her well ran dry.

Some people take drugs; Lorelei takes baths.

Sharleen says she takes them to escape. Sharleen prefers showers: quick, brisk, invigorating. Lorelei understands the convenience and practicality of a shower, for she takes a quick one after her morning walk. However, the luxury of sinking into a comforting hot bath at the end of the day is one of the few vices she allows herself. The other is watching "Project Runway" on TV.

When she's immersed, her mind is a blur of dreams, a confetti of memories that disappears in a poof when she emerges. It's a kind of renewal that she looks forward to all day. If she could bottle that pleasure, she'd be rich.

WATER, IN ALL ITS ABUNDANCE

Deep in the earth, the water waits. Above, there is chaos, the percussive pounding of metal, the pulverizing of stone. The water waits, deep and still, cradled in a reservoir of rock.

Fed by an undiscovered source, the water is virgin and plentiful: pure, clear, pristine. It has never seen daylight. Not a drop has been recycled, either by nature through the process of rain and evaporation, or by man, through the process of plumbing. Never frozen, boiled, desalinated, vaporized or chemicalized, the water is the essence of purity. It waits without stagnation, the gradual leaching into the surrounding rock constantly refreshed by a steady infusion from its clandestine source, the surface never disturbed by so much as a ripple.

Until now. Like fearful intakes of breath, the water quivers reflexively as the pounding above escalates to a roar. In one explosive moment, an avalanche of rock heralds the penetration of steel, ending the quiet slumber of the ancient spring.

THREE

Juan's drill breaks through just when he's ready to quit. Lorelei runs out of her house when she hears his yelp of joy. "Two hundred feet! I've never dug a well two hundred feet deep. I didn't know if my new drill head could handle it, but it worked! Worth every penny." He's dancing a little rhumba around the drill, and she does a little jig herself, that's how happy she is.

Juan had decided, since a rotary drill was unworkable in her tiny yard, to give it one more try, this time with a diamond drill head. It was an investment, but, as he explained to Lorelei, a challenge to his expertise he was eager to accept. It will be another two days before the pump is installed and the plumbing hooked up, but this delay is anticipated rather than dreaded. It means Lorelei can make two more visits to Juan's bathtub—visits she finds herself looking forward to, not just for the luxury of a hot bath, but because she and Juan talk, if briefly, before he leaves. She doesn't want him to leave when he does, and is sorry those visits will end. The work is done.

There is a ceremonial turning of the tap in Lorelei's kitchen sink. After a tense moment, the faucet shudders, then burps as the first flow of water gushes out in a silvery stream. They hold their hands beneath it as if it were a sacrament, letting the water pour over their palms, between their fingers, all the way up to their elbows. They shudder with its delicious iciness, surprised that tap water in Miami could ever be this cold.

Lorelei takes down her very best stemware, the Baccarat she bought herself for her 60th birthday. She washes the glasses carefully before filling them from the tap, then examines the water as she holds it to the light. The water looks different from the way it had before. It's not merely that it's clean instead of tinged with yellow and sprinkled with tiny particles she had learned to accept as normal in the old tap water. No, this water is different. It's clean, yes; cold, yes; crystal clear, yes yes. But there is something more, something undefinable. It's almost as if it glows.

Two stemmed glasses of crystal water clink in celebration.

"To water," says Lorelei.

"To the irresistible power of steel," says Juan.

The water goes down like liquid silk, smooth and sweet as honey. They sip and savor it as if it were wine; they've never drunk anything like it. They fill their glasses to the brim and drink them down again. They are giddy, whether from intoxication or relief, it doesn't matter. They are saturated with pleasure.

"I think I'll have another drink," she says.

"Me, too." Juan holds his glass out for a refill. And they clink again.

"Water is life," he pronounces. "Without water, there would be no tomatoes."

"No tomatoes?"

"No tomatoes. They're 95% water. And no chickens. 75%."

"No chickens?" Lorelei says in mock horror.

"And...no people. We're 65% water. Remove water from a human being, and you get Lot's Wife..."

"A pillar of salt and a story whose moral is 'Don't look back,'" she finishes.

Lorelei drains the last water from her glass, seeing Juan through its crystal curve. She lowers it and her eyes catch his in a Velcro moment before she looks away. "Refill?" she asks, not knowing how to react to this ocular spark. It's something she hasn't experienced since...never.

"Sure. I haven't hit my limit yet." He hands her his glass and she escapes with it into the kitchen.

What was that all about? she wonders, oblivious to the fact that the stemware beneath the faucet is now overflowing and soaking her hand. Is she attracted to this...this plumber? It's like the opening scene of a porno movie she once saw—purely by accident, of course—when she was channel-surfing and came upon it: *Well, hell-o-o-o Mr. Plumber, I need a big strong man with a plunger.* All that's missing is the negligee (Natori black satin #1356 could work)...

Good grief—where did that thought come from? She shakes her head at such nonsense, dries her hand and marches back to the living room.

"I have to get up early for work," she announces, briskly handing him his water. "I didn't realize it was so late. I'm sure you have places to go. Things to do. People to..."

Juan drains it quickly and hands it to her. "Sure. Sorry I hung around so long, but I'm glad we solved your problem."

"Wait, wait," she says, not knowing what for, and then thinks of a reason. "I haven't paid you yet."

"I'll send the final bill in the mail," he says. "You're paid up to now."

He charged fairly, so she can't complain. And now he's leaving. "Wait," she says again. He turns, questioning, but receiving no follow-up, gives her a small salute. "Have a great bath," he says, and he's gone.

•   •   •

Lorelei turns the tap of her tub, watches with deep satisfaction as the gush of water performs its alchemy upon the sprinkling of

Jojoba crystals. The bubbles heap high upon one another in an Everest of foam, and she sinks into her bath with a sigh.

What a strange week it's been. The trauma of the dry well, the appearance of Juan, the mess of drilling, the miraculous discovery of water. She should be pleased that it's ended so well, but she's oddly depressed that it *is* at an end. She lowers herself even farther beneath the bubbles until her hair is underwater, drifting about her head like a seaweed cloud.

The water swirls, invading every orifice—ears, mouth, nostrils, and all points south. As she soaks, she feels, not the usual release and relaxation of slipping into nirvana, but a feeling, almost electrical, of invigoration. Her hands move lightly over her body, as if discovering it for the very first time. She tingles all over with a sensuality she remembers only from dreams and the distant past.

What time is it? Past her bedtime, she's sure. She rises from her bed of bubbles with a sudden splash, annoyed at herself for wallowing in such an unseemly exploration of flesh. What has come over her? She got through The Change fairly painlessly, bearing the hot flashes and moodiness with what she considered grace, and has now settled back into routine. But—what is this nonsense? Is she going through some new life crisis, where her mind has taken leave of its senses and taken her body with it? After all, she is a person who likes things just so, and this isn't part of the plan.

She quickly dries her hair, then checks the color, recently refreshed by Clarissa the Colorist. Lorelei has maintained the same shade of black she has had since birth when it sprouted from her head in a dandelion fuzz, then multiplied into the mane she tames in a French twist. She hasn't given it a chance to go gray; once her hairline begins to betray her, it's Clarissa to the rescue.

As she brushes her teeth, her eye catches the glint of the bottle of Shalimar Sharleen had given her for her birthday. She had dabbed it on once, politely, for Sharleen's benefit, and never wore it again. Too heavy. Too earthy. Too sensual. Scent of that nature appeals to men's basest natures, and she has no intention of doing such a thing. Shalimar. It's nothing more than bottled sex.

She reaches for the thick crystal bottle. Removes its glass stopper. Pours the fragrant liquid into her palm. Splashes it behind her ears, over her wrists, between her breasts.

FOUR

It's the sensible thing to do, Lorelei thinks as she fills an empty Crystal Creek five-gallon bottle with water from her sink. Compared to what now comes out of her faucet, the Crystal Creek water delivered to the shop has been tasting off to her, so she canceled the delivery in favor of bringing her own from home. Nothing equals the clear fresh taste of the water from her well, and if she has to lug it from home herself, that's what has to be done. She brings her own lunch since none of the nearby restaurants has any takeout comparable to the healthful food she can prepare at home, so why not bring her own water?

"What now?" Sharleen asks as Lorelei wheels the big bottle into the shop on her luggage cart. "Aren't you carrying this health nut bit a little too far?"

"Not when I can see the results." Lorelei struggles to get the bottle off the cart, but, to her delight, manages to lift it onto the cooler before Sharleen makes the offer to help. "See?" Lorelei says. "I don't think I could have done that a couple of weeks ago. Eat right, exercise, and drink lots of pure water. It makes a difference."

Sharleen gives her an eye-roll, her usual reaction to Lorelei's pronouncements on healthy living. "Whatever."

Lorelei fills a paper cup of the newly-installed water. "Here." She hands Sharleen a sample. "Tell me this isn't better than Crystal Creek."

Sharleen peers into the paper cup. "It looks a little weird. Like it's lit up or something. Are you sure it isn't radioactive?"

"You're just not used to pure, clear water," Lorelei says. "I think this cleans out your innards. I feel lighter after drinking it."

"Miralax works for me." Sharleen takes a tentative sip. Then another. Then gulps the rest down and refills her cup. "I must be thirsty."

"Good, isn't it? Makes me feel energized, too," Lorelei adds.

"Maybe it's caffeinated," Sharleen says. "Are you sure it's not some water version of Red Bull?" Then she has another cup.

• • •

Lorelei mourns the decline of girdles. Not the imitations that abound now, those so-called "shapers" which, she complains, do little to truly compress the abundance of flesh so visible in today's skimpy clothes. She herself wears a style which some may call old-fashioned, but which she prefers to call proper: the truly structured, front paneled, high waisted, thigh hugging girdle which she wears when she wants to look her best. The shop, at her insistence, still carries a few of those, and she has stashed several away in case of a future shortage. Although she has retained the slimness of her youth, she still avoids any hint of jiggle.

So the reason she's taking home one of the VaVoom bra-and-panty sets is research. When she mentions this, Sharleen just looks at her and says "yeah." Sharleen fails to appreciate the effort Lorelei puts into evaluating the merchandise that goes into their stock.

Once home, Lorelei studies the bra first for structural weaknesses. It, like the panty, is silver-colored lace with demi-cups designed more as platforms than cups. Now how practical is that? About as practical as the matching thong panty, a tiny triangle of lace. She has never understood the theory behind the thong. The only word that comes to her mind is "ouch."

Having thoroughly examined every aspect—architecture, stitching, quality of fabric—of both garments, it occurs to her that she cannot perform a complete evaluation without a trial run. For the sake of research, she must try them on.

Hmf. This bra is not designed for comfort. The underwire cuts into her flesh, the spaghetti straps are flimsy, and you call these cups? Why, they barely cover her nipples. If she were fitting this to a customer, she would have to say no no no, this will never give you the support you need. And as far as the thong goes, the common analogy of dental floss is well deserved.

So. Comfort aside, how is the style? She turns to the mirror, dreading the sight of herself decked out in this ridiculous regalia.

Um. Not bad. *Really* not bad. Actually, Wow-wow, as Sharleen would say. Lorelei is shocked. Not only do these two little wisps of silver look good, they seem to have performed a miracle. Her breasts are firmer, her abdomen flatter, her butt has risen to new heights. Is her membership at the Y finally paying off—all those hours on the treadmill, the interminable counting of abdominal crunches? Would that be the reason the blue map that patterned her legs has diminished, as well as the bubble-wrap texture of her thighs? Well, there are no miracles. It's either exercise or the new halogen bulb she put in the lamp. She loosens her hair and lets it tumble. Odd. Her hair seems as lushly black as it was in her youth with no trace of gray, yet she's overdue for her monthly application of Eternal Ebony at the salon. Clarissa the Colorist may be using a new, longer-lasting formula. Or it might be the light.

She decides to keep the VaVoom set for further study, maybe bring home a few more. Its effects are indeed a mystery, but perhaps this line could be the key to attract a younger generation of customers.

•   •   •

Sharleen and the UPS man rejoice with each new delivery from VaVoom. Today he hovers expectantly as Sharleen slices through the tape of the latest box of merchandise. She parts the rustling tissue to reveal a rainbow nest of silk teddies, bras and panties. "Ooo-eee," breathes the UPS man as Sharleen extracts a thong, sheer and pink as the membrane of a flower.

The shop has bloomed with such previously forbidden ticky-tacky tidbits. Lorelei shuffles through the new VaVoom catalogs with the expertise of a blackjack dealer.

"Nice choice," Sharleen says as Lorelei, still intent on quality in merchandise, examines each newly arrived item of fluff. Lorelei attempts to disguise her fascination with this hitherto scorned line of lingerie, but she really can't wait to get home and try on the pieces she's claimed for herself. Her collection is growing, and every now and then she wears a piece to work beneath her conservative dresses. She finds the discomfort of push-up pads and thongs to be strangely erotic. Where are these new feelings coming from, these disturbing thoughts that intrude wherever she may be—in the shop as she does the books, in the tub as she soaks in bubbles, in her bed as she slides into sleep? Maybe it's not a good idea to wear such provocative reminders of her nascent sexuality, but...

She plucks a petal-smooth teddy for herself from the froth filled box, and tells Sharleen to add the rest of the merchandise to the stock. She's sure it will sell.

FIVE

Juan has crept into Lorelei's dreams. He's replaced Itzy, who in that dream kisses her and touches her where no one has since then. Now that Juan has taken his dream-place, she looks forward to going to sleep. She has foregone her usual granny gowns in favor of the negligee (yes, the Natori black satin #1356) that she slips into after her bath.

She thinks of Juan whenever she touches water: brushing her teeth, washing her clothes, making iced tea—but especially when she's soaking in her bath. She can't get him out of her head.

Which is why now, on impulse, she calls him. Picks up the phone before leaving for the shop, and calls him with the excuse that there's a strange noise in her pipes. He'll be right over, he says, and suddenly her work outfit seems drab: the dress with the shoulder pads, the Lilyette #324 bra, the Rago #6210 girdle, the slate gray Hanes Business Sheer pantyhose. She takes a good hard look at herself and says, Lorelei, you are dowdy. You have been dowdy for a long time. You have been dowdy forever.

She doesn't have much time. She tears off the dress, the bra, the girdle, the pantyhose. Now what? In quick succession, she tries on each piece she has brought home from the shop, deciding that the silver lace bra and thong would be the most appropriate.

For a visit from the plumber.

Is she losing her mind?

She slides the shoulder-padded dress over the silver lingerie, buttons up its prissy buttons, pins her hair back into its twist, and tells herself she's proper. Turning to the mirror, she presses a powder puff to her forehead, nose, chin. A light shade of lipstick, blot, and she's done. Well, maybe just a touch of mascara. Okay, a little eyeshadow, a swish of blush. She surveys the result. My, she does look more alive, doesn't she? The dark crepey circles beneath her eyes seem to have diminished, and the parentheses that frame her mouth appear to be softer. She really should wear makeup more often.

• • •

"So, what's the problem?" Juan turns the faucets of her sink, which respond with a gusty flow of water, not the *kazunk* sound she had claimed the pipes were making when she called. "It seems to be fine."

"It was making that sound it made just before the water stopped the first time," she lies. "I was afraid it was going to run dry again." She can't look him in the eye, not only because she's not a good liar, but because he looks so good standing there, T-shirt taut against his shoulders, hair shining silver in the morning light. His eyes seem to change from otter brown to panther gold, and he smells like the peel of a lemon.

"There's no good reason it would do that," he says. "The well's deep, the water pressure's strong, the quality is the best I've ever seen." He turns to face her, and she's forced to look right at him, right into the panther-like eyes she had feared, 3D-clear through the lenses of his glasses. "I don't see a problem," he says.

"You got new glasses," she says lamely. It's true. He has new glasses, steel-rimmed, the frames no longer taped together over the bridge with electrical tape.

And he's freshly shaved. And his jeans are new. And he smells like lemons.

The silver lingerie beneath her proper dress seems to burn right through it, searing through the linen as if it were on fire. Her hands fly to her breasts, attempting to conceal the tell-tale silver shadow she was sure was evident; her fingers then rise to cover her mouth and the giggle that escapes it—unexpected, uncharacteristic. She's weirdly light-headed, as if some airhead has inhabited her body and created a Lorelei she had never known.

She's school-girl giggly and she can't stop, caught in an interwoven net of feelings that threatens to unravel what's left of her composure. "It's like, it's like," she tries to explain, "when you go to the doctor and the pain disappears? Or your car runs perfectly when you take it to the mechanic? Or…"

"Are you okay?" Juan puts his hands on her shoulders and peers into her eyes. That's all she needs. He's so close, so close…

"You wearing makeup?" he asks.

"Uh…"

"I never saw you with makeup," he says.

"Well, I…" Her giggles decelerate into humiliation. "…I wear it at work. At my shop. Sometimes." Which she sometimes did, but never to this degree: Mascara. Blush. Eyeshadow, for God's sake.

"Well, that explains it then."

"Explains what?" She gathers her composure around her embarrassment; her lips draw into their usual purse, and she feels the old Lorelei returning.

"You looked different the last time I saw you, and today you look really different."

"Different how?"

"I dunno." He looks uncomfortable. "Like, not so…" He pauses. "…old?"

Old? She looks old? She's *mature*, not old. Proper. "Who are you calling old?" she demands. And then she remembers the silver lingerie.

"Is this the lingerie of an old person?" She yanks at the collar of her fine linen dress and bares the silver shimmer of one lacey bra strap. "VaVoom Bazooms is not designed for the elderly!"

Juan tears his vision from the surprising view to protest his innocence. "That's not what I meant," he begins, but Lorelei is on a roll.

"You said 'old.' Who are you to say 'old'? What are you? Eighty? Ninety?" She knew he wasn't, but this was war. "What's someone your age doing, wearing the same T-shirt every day like a kid who won't stop wearing the shirt of his favorite band?"

"I have a drawer full of these shirts," he says. "One for every day of the week."

"Well." She pauses to reload. "Look at you, with a ponytail!"

"Look at *you*."

She yanks the collar back into place. The bra strap vanishes from view.

"It's from my shop," she says. "I was just testing it out."

"Hey, I'm not complaining," he protests at its disappearance. "From what I can tell, it's nice. *Really* nice."

"Too nice for an old lady, apparently," she says, clutching her collar to her throat.

"Whoa, whoa. First of all, it's no crime to be old."

"It's a crime to be told you *look* old." Okay, so she's overly sensitive about the age thing. But still.

"Secondly, I'm not ninety," he says. "I'm seventy."

"Way older than me!" she says triumphantly.

"Thirdly, I meant it as a compliment."

"Some compliment," she says, somewhat mollified.

"Okay, I worded it badly." He gives her a half-smile which she returns with a frown. "All these years and I still haven't mastered the nuances of English. What I meant was, you look different. Younger. And I'm not saying younger is better, but that's what you look like to me. Maybe it's the makeup. But it's more. Attitude, maybe. I can't put my finger on it."

Neither can she. She has sensed a difference lately, not just in her face and body, but in her general state of being. It was so gradual that she barely noticed it until she became aware that some things, both physical and mental, seemed easier. Also, her emotions—usually under control—were unpredictable these days. Like today. Could it be that just having Juan in her life, even so peripherally, has caused this change? Could shifting her vision away from the minutiae of her life to thoughts of someone else create this difference?

Or could it be the other way around? Could it be that this strange shift in her appearance and attitude is what is catching Juan's attention?

It mystifies her. But she needs to hear more.

"So, what are you saying?" she prompts.

He shakes his head. "I think I've said too much already," he says, bending to pick up his tool box. "I've got to get going."

He can't go. She's not done. Lorelei can't just open the door and let him out of her life, not now, not when she senses there's more to this, she doesn't know what, but *more* somehow. It's been forever since she's felt something for someone. She can't even remember what that was like. But she thinks it may have felt like this.

"Wait," she says, and when he does, she gropes for a reason he should. "Um. Would you like a glass of water before you go?"

"Sure. That sounds better than my usual *cafecito*."

Relieved at not having to conjure up some excuse to keep him, if only for a few minutes, she retrieves the two Baccarat goblets and fills them from the sink. The water fractures the early morning light into a thousand rainbows as she carried the glasses to the table. "Sit," she says, and hands him one. They click their glasses together in a toast.

It's a familiar ritual, their drinking of the water, even though it's been practiced only a few times. But in this brief moment, it's as if they've shared it for a lifetime, this slice of morning, this clink of glasses, this waterborne reflection that spatters the walls of her quiet kitchen with clear shards of color.

"This is good," he says.

"It's the best. I've never had water this good."

"No. Not just the water. I mean it's good, sitting here. With you."

She nods. She doesn't want to agree too much, to seem too content. After all, just a few minutes ago, they were fighting. So she says, "I don't usually have someone over. Even for a glass of water."

"I don't get much company," he says. "Guess I'm kind of a loner."

"Me, too. I've always lived alone."

"Yeah. Who wants to share a bathroom?"

"Not me," she says.

"And who wants to share a TV?"

"Fighting over the remote. Who needs that?" How would he feel about Project Runway? Not good, probably.

"Sports. Women don't watch sports. You'd need two TVs." He stops to think about that. "I dated a woman who was a serious Dolphin fan, though. Wouldn't miss a game. I thought she was perfect until I realized that her liking the Dolphins was the only thing I liked about her."

"You can't have it all," she notes.

"She was a vegetarian. Beans, grains, weird green plants, I can't eat that stuff and nothing else. You can't be Cuban and be a vegetarian." He mulls that over a moment and adds, "Roast pig. *Ropa Viejo. Pollo* all kinds of ways. That's real food."

Lorelei is silent at that. Beans, grains, green plants, that's how she eats. But, "black beans and rice," she says, and he agrees. "That's different," he says. She doesn't ask why.

"It's not just food or TV or stuff like that," he says. "I guess I'm just meant to be alone. I like working, being physical. But solitary, that's me. Not good, but that's how it's been.

"I wasn't always like this. When I was a kid in Cuba, I was pretty wild: girls, drinking, fighting—crazy stuff you do when you're a kid. I wanted excitement, adventure. I wanted to be my father."

"Your father was an adventurer?"

He leans back and takes another drink of water. "I guess you could call him that. He fought with Castro in the attack on the Moncada Barracks, where the Revolution began. July 26th, 1953." He smiles ruefully. "I was born in '53. My mother never forgave him for not being there when she gave birth to me. She left my father and became a counter-revolutionary, a rebel. She went to prison when I was 14, and I never saw her again." He pauses, examining his glass as if he saw something there. "That was the same year Che Guevara was executed. I think the combination of my mother's imprisonment and Che's death did something to my father. He went a little crazy—questioning the whole Revolution, denouncing Castro—and was thrown into prison himself."

Lorelei silently listens, her mind tumbling with revelation. As long as she's lived in Miami, as many of her customers are Cuban, she's rarely accessed any of the emotions or experiences that they may have had. And now, sitting across from her, serenely relating his traumatic childhood, is Juan, whose losses loom large in comparison to what she had considered her own tragic youth.

"You were only 14? What did you do?" she asks.

"Went a little crazy myself," he says. "At first I became a revolutionary, trying to make up for my father's disgrace. My friends were excited by the promises of Communism, the romance of the fight. For us, it was an adrenalin-fueled fantasy, and nothing else mattered."

"What about school?"

"School? What was school to me? I quit and never went back. The mistake of my life."

"You seem educated to me," she says, and then lets slip what has bothered her since she first saw his flyer on her windshield.

39

"Except...you don't write very well for a smart person." She immediately regrets that comment when she sees his pained look.

"Yeah, I guess I speak better than I write." He shakes his head. "I'm pretty much self-taught. I read a lot, all kinds of things, so I guess my curiosity helps. But I never sat in a classroom and learned grammar, punctuation, spelling, all that stuff, especially English. I just picked up what I know from reading."

Juan seems to disappear into himself for a moment, then shakes his head. "Would you believe I wanted to be a scientist?"

Somehow, that doesn't surprise her. Juan seems methodical and dedicated to his work, qualities she assumes would have carried over into any profession he would have followed. "What happened?" she asks. "Why didn't you become one?"

"Long story, but when my father was executed by firing squad..."

"*What?*"

"Yeah. By then I was 17. Too late to go back to school, but not too late for me to get my own revenge. Like my mom, I became a counter-revolutionary, and was accused for somehow contributing to the failure of the sugar crop in 1970—just an excuse to get rid of me and the other rebels. Like my dad, I wound up in prison, but unlike him, I got out. I was allowed to leave during the Mariel boatlift in 1980. Which is how I wound up here."

Lorelei doesn't want to think about those ten years he spent in prison. Ten years. And, from what she's read and seen on TV, ten years spent in the most hellish of circumstances. With the spectre of the firing squad hanging over him each and every day. "What happened after you came to Miami?"

"I thought my problems would be over then, but they were just beginning." He sets his glass on the table and frowns in recollection. "I discovered if you came over on the boatlift, everyone thought you were trash because so many prisoners and crazies were released by Castro. The exile community here called me a traitor, even though I spent years in a Cuban prison as a dissident. All they remembered was that when the revolution was new, my father was a hero, one of Castro's Movement fighters who later fought for him at the Bay of Pigs. It didn't matter that he was later executed for treason. To the exiles, I was a pariah by association. The old exiles don't forgive, and they never forget."

"Have you forgiven yourself?" She needs to know that it's possible to do that.

"For what? Being young and stupid? For not being able to return to school because I had to struggle to make a living here? It's done. I can't live my life over again. I just want to enjoy what's left."

Enjoy what's left. What does that mean? Lorelei tries to remember the last time she enjoyed anything. Does her time in the bath count? How about when she tries on her new lingerie? Is that fun? That's pretty sad, when you don't even know what fun is.

She wants to have fun.

She's suddenly aware of the silver bra beneath her breasts, the silver thong between her thighs. Her lingerie burns into her skin, trapped beneath her proper linen dress, weighed down by her shoulder pads. She grips her water goblet with shaking hands, willing herself: Stop That! What's wrong with you? Stop that right now!

"Are you okay?" Juan asks.

Lorelei realizes she must look mildly crazed, gripping her glass as she conducts her inner reprimand. "I…just something came to mind. Nothing. Really. Nothing." She composes herself, her hand fluttering about the collar at her neck to reassure herself that she had not, indeed, ripped it away and bared her lace-clad breasts. The fiery feeling has subsided, at least enough for her to retreat into reality once more. But the feeling still lingers, a faint tingling beneath her bra as if to say, "Hey, we're here, and we're looking good."

This has really gone far enough, she thinks. If I sit here any longer with these crazy thoughts, I might do something I'll regret. I already have, flashing my bra strap at him. What was I thinking?

Lorelei rises from her chair and takes their empty glasses to the sink. "I have to get to work," she says. "I didn't realize how late it was getting."

Juan rises obediently. "Yeah, guess I'll be on my way. Didn't realize how late it was either. I wouldn't have had time to stop for my *cafecito*, so thanks for the water—it did the trick."

At the door, she hesitates. "Thanks for answering my call," she says. And then—perhaps in sympathy for his past, perhaps in empathy for their mutual mistakes, perhaps in a surge of sudden desire—she places her hand lightly on his arm.

He puts his hand over hers. "I should thank you."

"What for?"

"This." He touches the collar of her dress, moves it aside so just the silver strap shows. His eyes meet hers and she's sunk. She doesn't resist his kiss, not at all, not at all, because it's not at all what she remembers a kiss to be. It's soft, delicious, melting, a chocolate éclair of a kiss with a touch of forbidden fruit. It's the best thing she's ever tasted.

When his hand slides further to reveal more than just a wisp of lace, she stops him. "Not yet," she whispers. "This is too new. I need a little more time."

"However long it takes," he says. And kisses her once again.

•   •   •

She wants to be with him, get to know him, experience the kind of relationship she's never had before. She anticipates seeing him each morning on his way to work, to sit for a while in her kitchen and drink a glass or two of water. It's strangely satisfying, sipping from her Baccarat goblets, as if they were in some faraway place drinking champagne. She begins to notice things about him she finds endearing: a little nick covered by a tiny piece of tissue on his freshly-shaved face; the guava *pastelitos* he picks up at the Cuban bakery before he arrives; his repressed desire when he gives her a chaste goodbye kiss. Each time he leaves, she finds herself wishing he wouldn't.

On weekends, they venture out into the real world, often places she's never been, even though she's lived in Miami forever: Fairchild Garden, to wander lush paths beneath elephantine trees sculpted by time, showers of flowers and fairyland ferns amazing them along the way (why had she limited herself to skinny palms and melaleucas?); Key Biscayne, to walk the beach and feel the surf suck sand from beneath their toes (how had she forgotten this peculiar pleasure?); Coral Castle, to wonder why a tiny little man would spend a lifetime carving, in secret, all by himself, a thousand tons of pitted but impressive coral rock into a sculpture garden, all for his unrequited love.

"How did he do it? Why did he do it?" Lorelei asks.

"For love," Juan says. "Also, he was bonkers."

Little Havana was a frequent destination, one Juan knew intimately, having lived there since he arrived in 1980. Lorelei is surprised at the number of people Juan seems to know as they stroll Calle Ocho on a humid afternoon. "I thought you were a loner," she says as a group drinking *cafecitos* around a takeout window call out to him.

"I am," he says, waving to them in acknowledgement. "Except when I'm not."

That night, after indulging in *ropa vieja* and *fufu con masitas*, foods she would never have considered eating if she hadn't been lulled by the aroma of grilled meat while they waited for a table at Versailles, Juan suggests a way to work it all off: dancing. She feels the beat of the music before she sees a low white building with big green letters spaced above a striped awning: Ball & Chain. Above it flutters an American flag. As they enter, music pulsates like a racer's heartbeat, matching her own, energized by the crowd, the music, the refraction of light bouncing from the glow of neon to the bar's glittering pyramid of bottles. Laughter punctuates the music's rhythm, and voices—all Spanish—are raised to be heard. It's a sensory Cuisinart, blending sight and sound into a Latin froth.

They squeeze into the crowd at the bar, crushed between a curvaceous young woman in a barely-there crop top and a slight young man with an attempted goatee. Leaning close to Lorelei's ear, Juan asks, "What do you want to drink?"

She is baffled by this simple question. The last time she had a drink, it was the spiked grape punch she drank the night of the prom, and she knows how that turned out. She has no idea what she wants to drink, only that it's not going to be punch. "I don't know," she yells over the cacophony. "Just something that doesn't taste like alcohol."

"Got it." Juan signals the bartender. "Piña colada," he orders, "y uno mojito."

Sweet and icy, the piña colada fills her mouth with pineapple and coconut, reminding her of the Creamsicles of her childhood. She slurps it down like a milkshake, while Juan nurses his mojito and says, "Easy. It *is* alcohol, you know."

She knows, but it tastes so good that when the bartender asks if she'd like another, she nods her head, yes. She rations this one, taking sips, but soon it's gone. She does feel a little light-headed, not much, but the room is more lively, the music more syncopated, the crowd more jolly—a friendly crowd, a crowd she'd like to get to know, each one of them, and she gives her companions on either side, the buxom young woman and the slight young man, a great big grin. So nice! So friendly! So happy!

So when Juan asks if she'd like to dance, she hops off the barstool, even though she can't remember the last time she danced, maybe it was the prom, but that didn't count, a self-conscious box-step around the gym with Itzy, and then they left in his mother's Chevy wagon...

But that was then. And this is now. And she's dancing.

Sort of. Juan's snake hips slither in rhythm to the beat. Lorelei tries to mimic his moves, and he smiles at her affectionately in appreciation of her effort. The band plays on, a super-cool fedora-hatted group, intent on the music, focused on their playing, oblivious to the gyrating couples on the floor who expertly move it, shake it, and salsa to the max.

She doesn't know what she's doing, and she doesn't care. She's immersed in the moment—the lights, the music, the synergy of sensations that imbue her whole being. Her moves, however awkward, begin to align with Juan's, and she feels a surge of lust from his proximity—hot, rhythmic, sensual. She wants to meld her body with his until they are one.

Now she knows. Dancing isn't just exercise. It's a prelude to sex.

WATER, UNCONFINED

Awakening. Brightness sets its course; the water ascends toward the light, fights gravity, shatters into a colorless kaleidoscope when liquid meets air. Tumbling in ecstatic freedom, it mates with its new environment to create bubble offspring: a generation ephemeral as a rainbow.

Its effervescence soon subsides. The no-longer-virgin spring has been violated but not tamed. It rebels against the cold metal pipe that sucks it from its clear crystal depths into places both foreign and strange: the clear and hard containment of glass, the soft pink tunnel where it mingles with elements that transform its clarity to the color of too much sun. At last, it is expelled, a voyage that ends in rejection. Once exposed to the outside world, it can never return to its home.

But isn't this how it was meant to be? Was water's role to always be still, to hide from the world, to remain without function or purpose? Or was its role to play a role, to experience change, then evolve?

For water on earth is a friendly element, intent on mingling with others. When water meets salt, they show up in the most unlikely places—blood, sweat, tears, pee, amniotic fluid—testimony to the theory that life began in the saline depths of the sea. When it returns in its purest form as rain, water rushes to earth, eager to consort with foreign substances again.

Promiscuous yet shy, the spring is a contradiction, concealing, then revealing itself with the tease of a burlesque dancer. Always in flux, it flows ever onward, hiding and seeking forever.

SIX

It doesn't happen all at once. When you're a 60-year-old virgin, you take it a step at a time. Each step to Lorelei is a new revelation, for she has never gone this way before. Her explorations with Itzy were fumbles in the dark with lust as their only guide.

She discovers that sex is not a fast food experience; it's a gourmet menu, with each course offering new tastes and delights.

As an appetizer, Juan returns the next day and teaches her to kiss—really kiss. The few kisses she had shared in her previous brushes with lust were dry and dusty contacts, lips pursed in disapproval although her body felt hot and moist. With Juan, she learns that lips are meant to be soft and wet, the better to conduct the electricity they generate, sending shock waves that travel to parts of her she never knew could feel.

The next course follows soon thereafter. Still hungry for each other after their smoochfest, they spend a restless night apart until Juan appears early the next morning, hoping to see Lorelei before she leaves for work. She has no intention of leaving for work, and greets him at the door in the silken ivory robe (Natori #2345) she had plucked from the inventory at the shop before she left work last night, something she considered appropriate for a second date: not too revealing, very Lauren Bacall. Just right for the second course: heavy petting.

She learns that touch comes in many guises, and that it's not only placement but pressure that counts. She discovers that her body responds in surprising ways in surprising places, and that reciprocation is half the fun. She learns that when aroused, all of her senses come into play, and most of all, she learns how to play.

She's ready for the main course before the week is out. This calls for something spicy, hot, and chili-pepper red: VaVoom Bazooms' crimson silk teddy and matching thong. Its fragility is deceptive, the pure silk and fine construction having passed Lorelei's test for strength and endurance—qualities she knew would be necessary in the upcoming erotic encounter she has fantasized about all week.

Juan's appreciation of this fiery garment doesn't translate into tearing it off in his lust, like a hungry trucker would attack a Big Mac bag. He is an epicurean lover, preferring to slowly run his hands over the silky fabric before he explores beneath to savor what's there. He kisses her softly on each part he unveils, until she lies naked in the presence of a man for the first time in her life.

Sixty years she's waited for this moment, a moment she never imagined could be. It's less traumatic and more delightful than she had envisioned when, over the years, she had allowed herself to think of the possibility. Now that it's real, it seems unreal. At long last, she's no longer a virgin.

She's been starved for what she's missed all this time, and is surprised that her appetite is not appeased for long. She's greedy for more almost as soon as she's satisfied. She just can't get enough of him, so barely gives him time to rest before she's ready to go again.

Eventually, they are full. It's time for dessert, sweet and simple: he curls around her protectively, knees tucked into knees, until they both drift off into a shared dream. How long they lay this way, she doesn't know and doesn't care. She wants it to last forever.

But it does end, in a sleepy stretchy sprawl, and it's time to get up and return to the world.

And then she sees it: a small red spot on her sheet. He sees it, too, rubbing sleep from his eyes as if what is there isn't really there. He seems puzzled, confused. "You're not..." he begins.

She blushes bright pink.

"...a virgin?"

She nods. Yes, she is. Or was.

She can't decipher the look on his face. Shock? Disbelief? Or is it a look of delight?

"I deflowered a virgin," he says in awe. "I've never done that."

"Then I guess it's a first for both of us." She can't quite believe it herself—not only that she is no longer chaste, or that it was as good as it was, but that after all those dry and barren years, her body still has the ability to offer such proof. It almost surprises her that it's just a spot; it should be an exclamation mark.

"How...I mean why...I mean..."

"I know what you mean," she says, drawing the sheet around her. "Why is somebody my age still a virgin?"

"It's something to wonder about," he admits.

"I don't know. I guess there was a reason, and then other reasons got piled on top of that until I stopped wondering about it myself. It's just the way life was for me, and I assumed it would always be that way. Until..." She feels strange now confessing this, "I met you." She pauses. "Is this weird for you?"

"Well, yeah. In a way. I mean, if I knew this when I first met you, I wouldn't have been too surprised, I guess, because you seemed kind of...well, cold. Frigid, really. To tell you the truth, the way you seemed then, I really wasn't interested."

"Well, to tell you the truth, I wasn't either." Although she did have that crazy urge to touch him the first day he showed up.

"So, how did that change? I mean, one day you were Cruella deVille, and the next you were Cinderella."

"Cruella deVille?"

"Well, not really. But you sure acted like I was the last person you wanted around, until I got your water back." He reaches under the sheet and runs his hand over her breast. "Whatever the reason, I like the way you express your gratitude."

"Usually, I just say 'thank you.'"

Juan rises from the bed, then pauses. "'Turn on her water, turn on the woman.' That should be my new logo!"

"Only if you're planning on turning on more women."

"You're more than I can handle," he says with a sly grin.

"You're the first I've ever handled."

He laughs. "Was it worth the wait?"

"Well worth it," she says with a satisfied smile. "Very well worth it."

He sits back down on the bed and regards her with sudden seriousness. "You want to tell me what happened?"

"What do you mean?"

"Something happened, or you would have had a lover somewhere along the way. Is it that thing you wouldn't talk about when I told you about my own regrets? I'd like to know your story, but only if you're willing to tell me."

Her story. She had gone over it so many times in her mind, but she had never told anyone, aside from Sharleen––who was a part of it.

Sharleen was Lorelei's only friend in high school. She wasn't stupid, but played the dumb blonde role because she thought the kids would think she was, as she put it, cool. Her obvious efforts to be popular relegated her to the ranks of the uncool. As outcasts, Lorelei and Sharleen became friends by default. Lorelei worked hard in high school, and couldn't wait to get out. Sharleen said Lorelei plowed through as if she were on a mission, sitting up front in every class, waving her hand to answer before a question was finished. But how is that a flaw when you're sure you know the answer? She also said Lorelei should be more social, so she joined clubs: Opti-Miss, Atomic Energy, Future Teachers. She played xylophone in the band.

Her parents were oblivious to her academic dreams, too busy trying to keep their little grocery store alive when Food Fair opened nearby. They assumed after graduation Lorelei would work the cash register, but she was determined to go to college. She almost won the annual scholarship awarded by the alumni for Honor, Attendance and Effort. But then she had to get married.

Or rather, she *thought* she had to get married, because she missed her period after she let Itzy Morgenstern almost do It after the senior prom. "Almost" because she never removed her underwear, but Itzy was undeterred and proceeded despite the barrier. She hardly knew him although he was her chem lab partner, but Itzy and Lorelei were both dateless the week before the prom, and he blurted out the invitation along with a request to copy her homework. She figures she must have been desperate or crazy, but she said Yes, borrowed a dress from Sharleen and went. She doesn't know why she allowed him to even hold her hand, but she suspects someone spiked the punch and Itzy started looking good to her. Somehow they wound up making out in his mother's station wagon, and liberties were taken.

Itzy was as clueless as she was. Although she remained a virgin, he thought he was going to be a father. Terrified, they eloped, running off to Georgia the week before graduation. Thanks to Itzy's confessing to a friend the reason why he needed to borrow his car, they returned to a rumor that she was pregnant. Things were different in those days. The principal stood on principle. Lorelei would be denied the privilege of walking across the stage to accept her diploma. Her scholarship would be withdrawn, as well as any recommendations. So, after all that effort, there would be no college for her. She got her period the next month and the annulment the month after that. Itzy, who was allowed to cross the stage at graduation, went on to the University of Florida and a career in life insurance.

Alienated from the world she once knew, she drew closer to Sharleen, who comforted her with daily excursions to Dairy Queen and her antic impersonation of Charo. This never failed to make Lorelei laugh—a welcome break in the gloom that enveloped her whenever she considered her dismal situation.

She found herself confiding more and more in Sharleen, who listened with rapt attention, asking questions Lorelei couldn't answer at the time but which she pondered long afterward. *Why did you let Itzy touch you if you didn't really like him? What if you really had been pregnant?*

Her answers to Sharleen's questions would evolve over the years, solidifying into a rigid pragmatism from which she never diverged. Sex, she concluded, may feel good, but it leads only to trouble, and life is much simpler without it. As for being pregnant? There was a time she had thought she wanted children, but after observing from a distance what they can do to one's life, she hasn't regretted their absence.

After graduation, Lorelei and Sharleen bonded in the vacuum that now seemed to be their lives, sharing the uncertainty of what would follow. Despite her parents' insistence that she work in their store, Lorelei rebelled. Her dream of college had slipped from her grasp, and she could think of nothing that could take its place. Sharleen—as unmoored as Lorelei when it came to the future—suggested they both apply for jobs as salesgirls at Ladybug Lingerie. When the owner retired, their dedication to the shop inspired her to turn the operation over to them: the first step to their partnership in Ladybug Lingerie.

She had spent her youth burrowed so deep in the serious fluff of Ladybug Lingerie that the world had gone on without her. She let that one mistake—Itzy—lead to further consequences, and then let it control her life. And here she thought she had always been in control. Now she knows she never was. Where was she during the protest movements, the women's movement? Why wasn't she raising hell, smoking grass, making love? Didn't she know what she was missing?

And so she tells Juan her story. About Itzy, about the scholarship, about how she came to own a business that seems so incongruous with who she thought she was. About how her whole life had been a need to achieve dignity and respect, and how she had lost herself in the trying. Most important of all, she tells him what a miracle it is that she has found herself with him.

•　　•　　•

Sharleen is staring at Lorelei as she inspects the latest VaVoom delivery.

"What?" Lorelei says, exasperated that Sharleen seems more interested in what Lorelei is doing than in doing her own job, which is to straighten out the sale bras on the front table after a couple of teenagers pawed through them, totally scrambling the neat display. Well, at least they bought several, so young people are entering the shop, in large part due to the infusion of hipper styles Lorelei has ordered as of late. She has Sharleen to thank for that, she knows, but right now she's annoyed at Sharleen's stare.

"You're taking the best ones for yourself," Sharleen accuses.

"That is not true," Lorelei protests, feeling just a little guilty because she has selected a particularly sheer and delicate bra-and-panty set from the shipment and put it aside. "There are sets just like this in other sizes. Besides, you take your share of merchandise as well. I'm not taking any more than we agreed on long ago."

"Black. You've got the only black."

"So?" Lorelei tucks the sheer black set into some tissue, getting it away from Sharleen's accusing eyes. "We can always re-order."

"I've seen the other pieces you've taken before. What do you need such sexy lingerie for, anyway?" Her carefully-penciled eyebrows lift in curiosity. "You got a boyfriend or something?"

"Oh, Sharleen." Lorelei waves her hand dismissively. "Really!" But a rising pink blush gives her away.

Sharleen gives a little gasp. "You do," she says. "Oh my God. You've got a boyfriend." She stares bug-eyed at Lorelei as if she had grown another head. "I knew it! I knew there was some reason you look different. You're getting laid!"

"For God's sake, Sharleen," Lorelei snaps. "Control yourself." What she wants to say is, she's not *getting laid*. What she and Juan do is make love. But she's not about to tell Sharleen that. She's not about to tell Sharleen anything.

Lorelei sees that Sharleen's not about to let go, not now, not with Lorelei blushing like this, something she never has done until Juan brought it out in her. This is not the flush of menopause, which she's over and done with, but the blush of confession, the rise of blood to her cheeks that says 'yes' even as she says 'no.'

"Look at you," Sharleen fairly shrieks. "You're turning beet red! You *are* getting laid." She claps her hands as if applauding the feat. "Wow! It's about time. Who is he?"

"Get a grip, Sharleen. He's just a friend. Don't go jumping to conclusions."

"Yeah, like you'd wear something like that," she indicates Lorelei's newest lacey acquisition, "to impress a friend."

Lorelei busily arranges the new VaVoom pieces on a shelf, ignoring Sharleen. Inside, she is seething. What business is it of Sharleen's? Just because Sharleen has her own rogue's gallery of boyfriends on her iPhone on display for the viewing pleasure of anyone who comes into the shop, it doesn't mean that Lorelei needs to reveal her private life. This is different from Sharleen's multiple conquests. This is real.

Sharleen won't back off. "So that's what's with the makeup. Yeah, don't think I haven't noticed. I see you coming in with stuff on your face I never saw before, which, by the way, is long overdue. Trust me, you look *loads* better now. Younger. I didn't want to say anything before, but you were starting to look kinda peaked. Like, your age."

"Our age," Lorelei corrects. "We're the same age, remember?"

"Well, there's nothing *wrong* with looking your age," Sharleen amends, "but, come on now, it's not a crime to help Mother Nature a little bit."

Like *your* "little bit"? Lorelei is tempted to say. She's rarely commented on Sharleen's inappropriate mode of dress or her Jersey Shore makeup and hairdo. On the few occasions when she has, it's because Sharleen has gone over the top. Lorelei draws the line (especially the past few years) at muffin-top-revealing cropped sweaters, pants that show more than anyone needs to know, and skirts so short that Sharleen's rose-tattooed thong-slung butt cheeks are visible whenever she bends to put something in a drawer.

Those gaffes aside, Lorelei is aware that it is Sharleen's ebullient quirkiness and wacky wardrobe, in contrast with her own reserved personality and dress, that draws in the customers, particularly the younger, edgier crowd that has discovered the shop and its extensive VaVoom collection. Even the long-term conservative clientele has always been drawn to Sharleen, whose appeal may be that of an off-the-wall but fun cousin who can be depended upon to enliven Thanksgiving dinners.

Lorelei keeps her thoughts to herself, hoping that Sharleen will wind down. She's saved by the bell as its tinkle announces that some customers have entered the shop. She sweeps past Sharleen to greet them, and is relieved that it's two middle-aged women who have shopped here forever, Philharmonic board members looking for refined lingerie to wear beneath their gowns for the opening night festivities. This is familiar territory for Lorelei. Good. After the altercation with Sharleen, she's not in the mood right now to deal with some twit looking for crotchless panties. Especially since she took the last pair herself yesterday.

Thankfully, the Philharmonic ladies take up a lot of time, first with the preliminaries of chatting endlessly about the upcoming ball, then with what their grandchildren are up to, and then, finally, about their dresses and the particulars of what to wear underneath. They have brought them with them, hung from hangers encased in Neiman's dress bags which are lovingly unzipped as if to reveal precious treasures. Lorelei dutifully praises their exquisiteness—the chiffon, the beading, the elegant lines. And then she gets down to the business of what needs to be done: selecting appropriate underpinnings for such couture, a task that demands expertise as well as tact. Lorelei is a master of both.

She lays out her choices, items of silk, satin and lace, seemingly fragile fabrics overlaying the formidable construction beneath designed to mold, shape, and support sagging flesh. The ladies disappear into their respective dressing rooms, from which emanate discreet grunts and groans as they squeeze into the undergarments. When they are ready for Lorelei to hook up, adjust, or otherwise inspect the result, she enters their compartments and consults. The gowns are then lowered over this artfully constricted foundation, and Lorelei critiques the result. When the final decision is made, when both Philharmonic ladies approve of the other's appearance, only then can Lorelei rest.

The ladies leave, happily assured of an evening of well-supported elegance. Lorelei is satisfied as well, since such support does not come cheap. She has rung up a nice profit from the two ladies, and she is thankful for their patronage.

She has almost forgotten about Sharleen, until she is aware that she is perched on the stool next to the cash register. "Good sale?" Sharleen asks, as if she doesn't know.

Lorelei nods, not willing to engage Sharleen right now, especially since she's got that knowing smirk on her face, the same smirk she had before the Philharmonic ladies entered the shop.

"Then, let's celebrate!" Sharleen jumps off the stool and does a little boogie.

"It's a good sale, but it doesn't call for a celebration," Lorelei says. "It's hardly the first time we've had a good sale. And it won't be the last."

"I'm not talking about the sale. We've got to celebrate *you*." She gives a big Sarah Palin wink. "And whoever!"

Lorelei rolls her eyes. "Go away."

"That's what I had in mind!" Sharleen says. "Let's go away! Get your VaVoom booty off that chair, and take it to the Casino."

The only casino Lorelei knows of is way out in the Everglades: the Miccosukee Casino. The last place she'd go to celebrate, if she had anything to celebrate. Which she does. But not with Sharleen. "I don't gamble," she says dismissively.

"So you'll play the machines. Maybe lose a few bucks, so what. And there's Bingo! Have some drinks, watch a show, dance with some guys, have a little fun for a change!"

"That's hardly my idea of fun."

"Come on! Loosen up. Let's have a girls' night out." And there's that wink again.

"Stop winking at me," Lorelei says. "You look like Popeye."

"You *eat* like Popeye," Sharleen says. "One of these days you'll turn green with all that spinach you scarf up." She breaks into an arm-swinging jig, singing "I'm Popeye the sailor man" in a fake-gruff voice. The sight makes Lorelei laugh, as only Sharleen can make her laugh. Despite Sharleen's many annoyances, there are times like these that Lorelei is reminded that she does care deeply for this wacky little nutcase, and that, different as they are, her life has been made better by their friendship.

So: Girls' night out. Why not? Lorelei has surprised herself already in many ways. Who knows what other surprises could be in store?

WINONA

You'd think that after 500 years, I would have seen it all. But the tacky bottle blonde in the Dolly Parton getup is just one tacky blonde too many, the latest in a long line of bimbos who come here to the Miccosukee Casino convinced it's Vegas in the Everglades, their ticket to a big win, a big spender, a big happily ever after. Maybe my job as casino manager is starting to get to me—the busloads of bug-eyed tourists, the topsy-turvy world of sunshine nights and blackout days—but when I see how this particular nut case has trashed the Bingo Hall, I guess that's when I lose it.

Okay, here's the scene: I hear the crash all the way from the Bingo Hall to my office down the corridor. I run to check it out—not easy in spike-heel boots. The Bingo computer is down again, so we have to temporarily revert to manual Bingo, balls and all, until the computer is up and running again. Susie Billie, the caller, is wrestling the Bingo cage away from this berserk blonde person, who has ripped the ball-filled cage right out of its holder. The players throw themselves across their Bingo cards to protect the week's worth of grocery money they've invested, thinking that all those carefully marked numbers may now be worthless since Blondie has invalidated them in her mindless frenzy. Bingo balls fly through the air like numerical hail, bouncing, rolling, skittering down aisles and between chairs, while Susie yells Miccosukee curses at anything that moves.

"What's the problem here?" I ask Susie in English, Miccosukee not being my native tongue although I do understand it, particularly when it's not being yelled. I've spoken all the ancient Indian dialects—Tequesta, Timucua, Calusa—but I'm good at picking up whatever the language is of the time and place in which I'm living. More importantly, it's not just the language, but the slang, the catch-words, the *attitude* of the times that I've perfected. TV and movies were my teachers in the twentieth century; the Internet, with its barrage of words, music, videos and snarky comments, has been an astounding resource in the twenty-first. Compared with some of the other changes I've had to adapt to through the centuries, communicating with contemporaries is a piece of cake. Language begins in the spirit, and words are just one way of talking. As I travel through the ages, I adopt the outward manners of the times in which I live, yet I am who I am to the core.

But back to Susie, who is too angry to extricate her tangled tongue, so I turn to Blondie herself. "What's going on?" I ask, expecting the usual capitulation and apology. I rarely have to call security because I can handle trouble myself. If the intonation of my voice doesn't stop people in their tracks, the fact that I'm six-four in my heels does. Intimidation is one of my assets—it must be the Indian queen in me. But this Blondie is a feisty little beer-breath broad. She crooks her head back, looks me straight in the eye, and tells me she's been cheated out of her winnings and she's calling the cops.

I have to laugh. *Calling the cops.* Where does she think she is—Miami? This is Native American territory; the casino is on sovereign Miccosukee land. The state has about as much authority here as a school crossing guard. The only court around here is the tribal council. "Tell it to the chief," I say. That usually shuts them up. But...

"I'm not leaving without my hundred bucks," Blondie announces. "I won it fair and square. N-32:BINGO! That's the number, my winning number. Bingo!" she barks at Susie Billie. "Bingo, bingo, bingo!"

"It was N-22," Susie says. "Twenty-two, you...you tourist." Susie's eyes and mouth compress into that horizontal look she gets when she's fighting to control herself, a problem she's had since she was demoted from Poker to Bingo.

"See? See?" Blondie points wildly at Susie. "See that look? That's the look she gave me when I called Bingo, like I made it up or something." She swings around, puts her hands on her hips, glares at me. "And I'm not a tourist. I'm a native."

Native. Now there's the wrong word to throw at me. But I let it go. What, I'm going to define the meaning of "native" for this nitwit? Instead, I say, "I think you should leave now."

"No problem," she says. "Gimme my hundred bucks and I'm outta here."

I'm ready to pick up this dustball and toss her out on her fat little ass, but there's something about her defiance I like, something that reminds me of myself when I was younger, oh, maybe three or four hundred years ago. I was always looking for action then, stir things up a little, keep those juices flowing. One thing about being perpetually youthful is that you're more or less always in heat. A few centuries of that can make you nuts, so you have to look for ways to sublimate that drive. I do it by distracting myself with work or hobbies—I must have macrame'd a hundred hanging plant holders in the 1970's—but I find that people are the best diversion, a never-ending source of entertainment. So, to fend off the boredom of what up to now has been a slow night, I think it might be fun to keep this feisty little blonde around just to see what she'll do next.

"I can't give you a hundred dollars," I tell her, "because you didn't win it. What I will do is give you another chance to play. But first you've got to pick up all those Bingo balls, and then you've got to behave yourself."

At this, Susie Billie explodes. "What? Another chance?" she screams, her arms flapping like a frustrated penguin's. The players, stunned until now into silence, join her lament, a hubbub of whining protest. "See?" says Susie, acknowledging the crowd with a grandiose sweep of one dimpled arm. "Nobody wants her here."

Blondie takes this as a challenge. "Yeah?" she says with a sneer. "Then guess who's staying?" She plunks herself back into her vacated seat and busily lines up her cards.

"I quit," announces Susie, who has quit before, numerous times actually, only to return again and again, sometimes within minutes, because she knows full well that calling numbers is the easiest job she could ever get, requiring little in the way of exertion, either physical or mental. *Whoo-ee,* she's been known to say, *don't take much of a brain to do that, does it?* And she's grateful for the opportunity even though she still sulks about the demotion from Poker.

"Good," observes Blondie, "so quit," which just riles Susie Billie even more. Face set into horizontal, she advances, slipping and sliding in a spastic ballet over the scattered balls until she trips and falls headlong into Blondie's lap. Enraged, Blondie shoves her away, then pounces, taking the table and cards and markers with her. Tangled together, they wrestle—shrieking, pulling hair, the whole cat-fight bit—atop the rolling balls in the aisle. It's a pretty even match, their being somewhat the same build: short, pigeon-breasted, a little roly-poly in the nether areas. The crowd, as they say, goes wild.

Entertaining as the spectacle is, I still have a job to do. "Okay, Blondie, time to go home." I pick her up around the waist until her feet are dancing above the floor. She's wiggling like a worm on a hook but she's an easy tote, lots easier than some of the heftier customers I've had to eject. I just load those guys under one arm like a sack of flour and off we go.

But Blondie is a battler. She won't give up. She thrashes about wildly, and as I'm attempting to feed her through the door, she bangs her head and goes limp. Uh oh. She's bleeding. Not that I have to worry about being sued here on Indian land, but it's not my intent to physically damage the occasional crazy who frequents the casino. My demeanor may be war-like when called for, but I come in peace.

Back I go to my office, lugging Blondie piggyback down the hallway. She starts to come to as I lay her out on the couch, and gives me a cross-eyed look. "Wha hoppen?" she asks. I'm on the phone to get the house doctor up to take a look, when Blondie gives a whoop that my ancestors would be proud of. "Blood!" she yells, jerking upright. "I'm bleeding!" She's staring at her hand, which she's just used to wipe at the cut on her forehead. She plops back on the couch with a fuzzy look on her face.

Doc gives her a look-see, then reaches into his pocket and extracts what's left of the sub he had been eating when he got the call. "No big deal," he says around the ham and cheese mush in his mouth. "She'll be okay, maybe a headache and a hangover." He waves his hand in front of Blondie's face. "Hey, Cookie, you got somebody here to drive you home?"

Blondie lifts herself up on one elbow. "Home? Who's going home? I'm on a roll," she slurs. She scrambles to her feet, wobbles to the door, blanches white and sags like a wet paper towel. I rush over and drag her back to the couch. "Okay," I say, "who'd you come with, and where is he?"

"No He," she mumbles. "She's in the bathroom. Barfing."

Great. Now I've got to deal with not one, but two drunks. "What's her name?" I ask. "I'll get her and call a cab for the two of you."

"Lorelei. Barfing." And then she giggles.

I find this Lorelei staring at her watery-eyed post-barf face in the mirror in the ladies room. "Lorelei?" I ask, knowing it's her from Blondie's sketchy description ("dark hair, flat-chested, wearing some droopy knit purple thing I told her made her look her age but did she listen?").

"Your friend had a little accident," I tell her when she turns her gaze to me. Her eyes pop open and instantly deglaze. "Sharleen? Sharleen had an accident?"

So Blondie's name is Sharleen. It fits. "She's fine," I assure her. "Just a little bump on the head. But I think she'd better get home. I'll call a cab for both of you. You don't look in any condition to drive, either."

"I had a little wine," she says.

"Whatever. You're not driving."

"Chardonnay," she says. "One glass. Well, two. Coulda been three. Sharleen said it would loosen me up."

"Well, it worked. You're very loose."

"I don't usually drink. Water. I drink water." She teeters a bit when I help her to the door, but seems to regain some degree of poise as we make our way to my office. "I'm really quite all right now," she says, but I can tell that she's not really quite all right because the words come out as if she has practiced them first.

"I'm sure you are," I lie, "but I'm either calling a cab or calling someone to pick you up. You can get your car tomorrow, when you're feeling up to it."

When she sees Sharleen, she folds her arms like some schoolteacher and shakes her head. Not a good move, it turns out because it makes her dizzy and she plunks down next to Sharleen on the couch.

"I'm calling a cab," I say. "Neither one of you is leaving behind the wheel of a car."

"No cab. It'll cost a gazillion dollars from here," Sharleen says. "Is there a bus or something?"

"Oh, please." Lorelei's disdain for that mode of transportation is manifested in an unsuccessful attempt to rise from the couch. "I would rather walk." Which she clearly is not up to at the moment, because she plunks right back down.

"I know," Sharleen says, perking up with a new idea. "Let's call your boyfriend."

"Oh no." Lorelei shakes her head repeatedly. "No no no. We're not calling Juan."

"Juan!" Sharleen squeals. "Juan! You got a Latin lover!"

Lorelei gives her a look that would kill if it weren't somewhat cross-eyed from booze.

"Give him a call," I say.

She shakes her head. "No no no. Absotutely not."

"Then I'm calling a cab. I hope you've got a bunch of cash on you." I begin to dial, a process that ends abruptly when Lorelei snatches the phone from my hand. The lady is quick for a drunk.

"All right all right. Forget the cab. I'll call Juan." And so she does.

* * *

Both ladies are asleep, totally zonked out, by the time Juan arrives. He seems puzzled as he peers into my office, but when he spots the ladies sprawled out on my couch, he nods and says, "Are they okay?"

"They will be," I say. He's built pretty well for someone his age, but I dismiss that thought because I'm not looking for trouble. I scrape Sharleen off the couch and lug her out to his truck. It's hardly a chariot for these two ditzy babes, with its hand-lettered sign on its rear:

WATER WATER EVERYWHERE, INC.

Need a well? Call "JUAN" at (305)555-WATR (305-555-9287)

Typical. I load Sharleen into the front seat, fortunately big enough for three, because here comes Juan with Lorelei stumbling beside him.

Lorelei has sobered up enough to walk, steadied by Juan's arm around her waist. He seems oddly amused by this excursion, and looks up long enough to say to me, "This is so not like her, you have no idea."

Our eyes meet for just a second. In that second, I feel a shock. Where have I seen eyes that color before, eyes the color of amber? He must feel it, too, because he pauses and asks, "Do I know you?"

"I don't think so," I say. But...why did I get that shock of recognition? Uh oh, bad sign, forgetting like this. Next thing you know, I'll be lining up for the Early Bird dinner. "Have you been to the casino before?" I ask.

He shakes his head. "I'm not a gambling man," he says. "And Bingo's not my game."

"Bingo," Lorelei mumbles.

"Yep," he says, smiling down at her. "We're going home."

As he helps Lorelei into his truck, I'm compelled to do something so foreign to myself, I feel like someone has borrowed my brain: With the tip of one finger, I touch the water drop design on the back of his T-shirt.

It's as if I touched lightening. Suddenly, I'm whirling back into time's matrix, a shadow web woven from dream and memory, remembered in the language of my origin.

● ● ●

Cushioned by the pelt of a white panther, shaded by a canopy of boughs, I sit high on a litter above my entourage. Four strong men carry me on their shoulders to the tribal house of the Timucua chief, Cacique Athore, where I will become his principal queen, ranking above his other wives—even his sister, whose child by him, according to our laws of lineage, will be his successor. I, too, am descended from royalty, chosen as the tallest and most beautiful of all the women in the tribe. Once my friends, now my followers, those women now walk behind me bearing bowls of perfect fruit.

Trumpeters announce my arrival on horns of bark from which hang tinkling bells of silver and gold. My chief awaits, dressed in a soft deerskin cloak painted azure, red and black, his hair entwined in grasses atop his head. My hair hangs long and loose to my waist. It brushes painfully against my freshly-carved tattoos which, like those of the chief, are symbols of our rank, only mine are fewer and newer. Our lips are painted blue and our nails are long, filed with a shell until they are sharp as knives. I wear a loincloth woven from the silkiest moss, a crown of feathers plucked from rare birds. My arms and neck are weighted with ropes of gold and pearls.

Before the ceremony, we must drink from the ritual spring which has sustained the lives of the royal family since time began. The spring is deep within the forest, and so we travel side-by-side, each on our own litter, each with our own entourage. The Chief— the Cacique—is descended from the sun itself. He was born 6,000 moons ago, long before the time I was born. He claimed me as his future principal queen when, as a young woman, I was given to the Timuqua as a peace offering from the Tequestas, prized for the unusual color of my eyes: clearest blue, not the deep brown of others from my tribe.

The day has come for our consummation, which will follow the ceremony of the spring. We descend from our litters and kneel before its clear waters. The jungle rises in a flowered canopy above our heads, and the spring mirrors our faces. We break its stillness with our cups, and drink.

My cup is carved from a perfect conch shell, its interior an iridescent pink that glows like morning sunrise. The pale ivory exterior is etched with two mourning doves, perfect to my eyes, but not perfect enough for the Chief, for whom the cup was originally made. He saw fault in the etching of the doves, and deemed it unworthy for drinking Cassina, the ritual Black Drink consumed during ceremonial purifications. So it became mine, which I will drink from ever after.

Upon our return from the spring, my litter comes to a sudden halt. With a simple motion of his hand, the Chief has ordered the bearers to stop. Standing in our path is a Spaniard, whose ship we have seen off our coast. With sign language and a few words in our language, he says his name is Ponce, and indicates he wants to trade trinkets and beads for, not just gold, but water from the spring he had heard existed here. The Chief receives him with polite disdain, then dismisses him, professing ignorance of such a spring.

But the Spaniard blocks our way, as rooted to the pine-needle path as a stump. He stands his ground, erect and stubborn. His mantle of silver hair, flattened from the helmet that he now carries beneath one arm, and the crackle of lines that map his face are signs that his youth is behind him. He claims he knows there is such a spring, having surreptitiously observed our ceremony where we drank from it, and now requests permission to draw water from the spring for himself. Enraged, the Chief signals his bodyguards who draw their bows in unison, a forest of arrows aimed right at Ponce's head. Ponce's soldiers reach for their weapons, but stop at his order. Not only would their assault result in his immediate death, but theirs as well, for they are greatly outnumbered. I see nothing but blood in our future, and, without thinking, I cry out, breaking the silence expected of me.

"Do not begin our life together with death," I plead. "Send them on their way in peace, with the promise they won't return." The Chief's shock at my audacity is clear, but I know that what first attracted him to me was just that trait. He considers me for a long moment, then nods to his bodyguards. "Take their weapons, and escort them to their boat. They must leave this place and never return."

Ponce gives a curt nod, acceding to the power of our arrows, then bows to me. I regard him as the queen I will be, my head high and still and regal. As he is led from the forest by the Chief's bodyguards, he turns for one last look. My eyes slide beneath my lowered lids, then lock onto his. Eyes the color of amber, the eyes of a panther.

Our locked eyes do not go unnoticed.

Despite the warning, Ponce returns the next day. Desperate to recapture his youth, Ponce and his soldiers have crept back to steal water from the spring, barely escaping with barrels of it in a hail of arrows. Within days, the spring becomes a trickle, then is gone, and so am I. The Chief has accused me of causing its disappearance. He had caught the look I exchanged with the Spaniard who is his enemy, and ends our marriage before it begins. I am devastated, for I truly love my Chief, and try to make him understand that I defended the Spaniard, not because he captured my heart, but because I feared that bloodshed on our sacred day would taint us both forever.

My pleas are to no avail. I am banished from the Timuqua tribe, my bridal tattoos still fresh, my only possession my conch shell cup carried in a deerskin pouch from my belt. I am left to wander the jungle alone. Desperate and angry, I am determined, not only to survive, but to find the elusive spring and keep the secret to myself.

I discover it in a grotto much later, escaping the fate of the Timuqua, who, devoid of the spring's magic, will age and die, as people do. This grotto is to the South and to the West, in the land of the Calusa, a tribe even more fierce than the Timuqua. The spring is mine. The Calusa have not discovered it, or me, so I have enjoyed its benefits for many moons. It is a lonely life, but I stay in hiding, knowing that if I were to be discovered, I would either be sacrificed or made a slave to the Chief of the Calusa.

One day I hear a horrific commotion on the beach. I creep to the edge of the jungle to see what is happening. A ferocious battle is being fought between the Calusa and a group of soldiers from the ship anchored just offshore—men in the battle dress of the men I had seen when my entourage encountered them on the Timucuan trail. And there, in their midst, is the Spaniard himself, his sword useless against Calusan arrows. Defeated, the surviving soldiers are retreating to their ship when Ponce falls, a poison arrow through his thigh, just a few steps from where I watch from the jungle's edge. Once again, time stops, and I stare into those panther eyes for what seems like an eternity. Something makes me crawl to where he lies and hand him the pouch with my shell cup that still contains a little water from the spring. He drains the cup before his men drag him into the water and onto the ship, their escape accompanied by the terrifying howls of the Calusa. Much to my dismay, my cup goes with him.

Before long, cupping my hands to drink from the spring becomes futile as it begins to disappear, its last traces just puddles in the mud. Desperate, I put my heart to the earth and sense the path it is taking, and find it once more before it moves on again. In this way, I follow the spring through the ages, losing, then finding it again in places I never knew existed. My journey has evolved into an eternal search that continues to this day, for I have lost it once again.

● ● ●

I'm suddenly pulled back through time's tangled web, back to the present and an amber-eyed guy with a water-drop symbol on a black T-shirt. Touching that symbol may have whirled me into the past and back again, but the tingle still remains.

I haven't felt that tingle for decades, the *zzzzt* that shoots from my toes to my nose as if I had stepped on a live wire. I've been zapped enough over the centuries to recognize the signal emitted by some unwitting person who'll be my next guide to the spring. Could this guy be the one? I hope so, because it's about time. My hoard of water is running out, and I'm noticing little signs of age. When I can't remember the names of people I only met a couple of hundred years ago, I know I have to replenish.

The spring has been on the move for some time, which means I'll have to follow. I've been on its trail over the centuries, and I'm on that trail again.

Every time I lose the spring, I find it again, and create a new life for myself in each new place. When I lost it in the 1980s, I found it somewhere up in Okeechobee. I had hitched a ride on a hired-hand's truck and, as we lay together in his bunk, I was zapped by that old familiar sizzle. The next day I put my heart to the earth, felt the spring's ripple deep within the rock, and traced it to where it emerged, cupped in a secluded, shadow-laced pool. That cowboy never knew the real reason I stayed—not just for him and his rough-handed loving, but for the promise of eternity flowing through the rock beneath his bed. Years later, when it was time for me to go, he never knew the real reason I left: the spring had moved on.

I found it again when I met a sun-leathered guy who wrestled alligators, and knew I hit paydirt when, snuggled in his hammock, I felt that long-awaited zap. I discovered the spring nearby, deep in the Everglades, guarded by a panther. Sensing my power, it slunk away from the spot where the spring burbled up from the muck. Luckily, the Miccosukee casino, not far from there, needed a new manager, and I fit the bill perfectly: Native American (they didn't care what tribe), smart, formidable, and damn good looking. It was a snap to nab the job, almost custom-made for this six-foot-tall Indian maiden. I had found a place in the world that suited my needs—the most important of which was proximity to the spring.

Although my gator-wrestling lover has moved on to a safer occupation due to an unfortunate event, I have remained close to my source, which has served me well until now. Little by little, my spring diminished, then vanished, and my saved water supply is almost gone. Once again, I'm on the hunt, looking for a sign.

It may have just appeared.

After all this time, I've been zapped again, this time by an amber-eyed silver-haired well-digger. Whoever Juan is, he's my guide to the spring. And wherever he's going, that's where it will be.

I watch as he piles Lorelei next to Sharleen in the front seat of his truck, buckles up both of those ditzy drunks and drives off. I jump into my Jeep and follow, headlights off, distancing myself from the red taillights of his truck, secure in the knowledge that at this time of night with light traffic on this Everglades road, there's little chance of losing him. He's probably so spaced out from the whole night's experience that he's not aware I'm behind him, but I don't want to arouse his suspicions.

Oh, no. He's headed toward the city. Miami: horrific memories. I don't like cities to begin with: noisy, crowded, concrete-and-asphalt abominations. I never go to Miami if I can help it. Centuries later, I still can't forget what happened to me in my village, and while losing your virginity is no big deal—I've done it many times—still, the very first time should be more special than in a ritual ceremony in front of the entire Tequesta tribe.

The last time I had to go into the city, I passed what I realized could have been the site, just off the expressway at the mouth of the river: the Tequesta village where I was born—and where my virginity was first taken before I was offered to the Timucua. I would never have recognized the place, not after all those centuries. When it was uncovered by bulldozers after an old building was demolished to build a new condo, the contractor didn't know what he had discovered.

The site was just a bulldozed stretch of dirt and rocks. But I remember an entire village, houses set up high on poles, an impressive ceremonial arena, long canoes resting against the riverbank. Now all that remains are animal-shaped holes cut in a circle into the limestone rock of the ground. The archeologists argued about the meaning of the turtle, shark, manatee, and dolphin shapes. I could have told them, but why would I do that? The developer insisted they were just meaningless holes in the ground, since he wanted to cover them all with steel-and-glass towers and a three-story parking garage, which would have been just fine with me. But the Circle was saved, commemorated by a plaque, and the developer got to build his building anyway.

Several stories of glass and steel don't erase the memory I've got of the place, of being naked and spread-eagled on a ritual rock carved in the shape of an eye, of being watched by the full moon overhead and a thousand Tequesta eyes as the chief drove himself far inside me and pounded away to the sound of drums. This was no way to initiate a 12-year-old into womanhood. It was so traumatic that it left me sterile, for I was unable to conceive despite the chief's constant efforts, and almost ruined sex for me altogether. Soon after that, I was given to the Timucua as a peace offering (unknown to them, a damaged gift, since I was not only not a virgin any more, but sterile). When I was chosen to marry Cacique Athore, the Timucuan chief, to become his principal queen, I began to understood the allure of sex. In the vernacular from this era that expresses it best: he was hot. As only a young girl can be in the presence of a god-like man, I was in love.

Oops. My mind is wandering. Can't lose Juan in the increasing traffic.

Juan is turning off the main road. Where are we? There's a sign: Melaleuca Lakes. Melaleuca? Give me a break. Where do they come up with these names? They're all alike, these developments, like mushrooms taking over the earth. They should just number them: Fungus I, Fungus II. This used to be piney woods in the heretofore. Deer, panthers, heron, osprey. Bugs. Serious bugs. Bugs are all that's left here from those woodsy days.

I follow him to a house where he turns into the driveway. I circle the block to avoid suspicion, then park discreetly down the street and watch.

First out is Sharleen. Juan extricates her from the truck and tries to get her to walk. No go. She's hammered. He picks her up like a sack of cement and struggles up the porch stairs, only to realize he doesn't have a key. He stands there, Sharleen slung over his shoulder, and seems to ponder what his next step will be, which is to lower her onto a porch chair while he goes to get Lorelei from the truck. Sharleen slumps into the chair, sliding little by little until she's sitting on the floor. She doesn't seem to mind.

And here comes Lorelei. At least she's walking. Sort of. She leans on Juan, staring glassily up at him with a goofy smile on her face. He asks her something, and she hands him her purse in which he fishes around to extract her key. He opens the door and manages to get her inside. He reappears after a minute or two to wrestle Sharleen off the porch floor, and the door shuts behind them.

Now what? Do I sit here all night? I'm getting low-level zaps, tiny *bzzzts* up and down my spine. I get out of the car, run and look in the window but the bougainvillea protecting the house fights me back, their nasty briars hidden swords in their flaming pink petticoats. I can't see anything anyway—the blinds are down. Between the bougainvillea and the blinds, I figure this lady is paranoid.

I creep noiselessly around the side of the house. The *zzzts* are getting stronger now. I drop to the ground, slide with my heart to the earth, feel a faint ripple grow stronger and stronger. I see the pump of a well, sense the thrum and pulse of water, beating, beating, beating.

I feel electrified. Zapped. The same sensation I've had many times before.

I know what it means.

I have found the spring.

SEVEN

God, her head hurts.

Everything hurts: her head, her stomach, her feet from those stupid shoes Sharleen lent her to offset the drabness of the dress she wore last night (Sharleen's opinion).

Lorelei has a blurry memory of smoke-filled rooms, carnival lights, the incessant bing-bong from machines fed by glaze-eyed automatons. A vague recollection of trying to walk, leaning on someone. Juan. She thinks.

What she does remember is a very large woman. Indian. With tattoos. Tall, so tall she had to look up to see her face, a face that looked softly carved—not from stone, but from butter.

It's coming back to her. The Indian woman. The bathroom. The unseemly barfing event. Was she drunk? She was drunk. Two glasses of wine—or was it four?—and she was gone. She never drank that much before in her life, aside from the two pina coladas with Juan at Ball and Chain, which made her happy, not drunk. She had been led down this path by Sharleen, and willingly. What had come over her?

True, she has become more...well, relaxed. She smiles through her misery when she thinks of Juan. His arm around her, his smiling down at her with that crooked funny smile. He was there for her. But how did he get there? She has a dim recollection of being somehow threatened by that Indian person, not wanting to call him but having to.

She will never have another glass of wine. Water. That's all she'll drink. Wine doesn't do it for her, doesn't do a thing except make her feel bad.

Water. Now water, that's a different story. Water makes her feel—what is it?—high? No, not high. High was how she first felt when the wine hit her, a nice feeling at first, a floating feeling where everything looked and sounded bright and happy, the blinkety blink of neon, the maniacal music of the gaming machines, all swirling together in a cartoon world that slipped and slid around her until it all went bad.

Water—her water—gives her a mellow glow with a pulsing heart of sunshine.

The water. Could it fix her hangover? Why not give it a try?

She pours herself a tall glass from the faucet, and another for Sharleen, who is moaning on the bed in the guest room, an ice pack on her head. Although Sharleen's car is here—left when Lorelei offered to drive to the casino last night—Sharleen isn't in any shape this morning to drive Lorelei back to the casino to get her car. She doesn't want to ask Juan to take off work, not after he drove out there and rescued them last night.

Lorelei downs her glass of water, and before long, starts to feel better, at least well enough to drive to the casino and back without a disaster. When she convinces Sharleen to sit up long enough to drink her entire glass down, she remains sitting, to Lorelei's surprise. Not fully recovered, but decidedly improved. Her eyes are actually open, something she barely accomplished since last night's adventure.

"How'd we get home last night?" Sharleen asks.

Lorelei hesitates, not wanting to bring up Juan, but Sharleen does. "That guy. What's his name?"

"Juan." She tries to sound casual, but Sharleen pounces.

"Your boyfriend!" Sharleen perks up substantially at the memory. "Cute!" she pronounces. "Didn't he have a ponytail? Something hairy...a beard?"

Lorelei shrugs, at once embarrassed and proud. "No beard. Ponytail." And yes, he is cute. But she's not about to wax poetic about Juan's attributes with Sharleen right now, because, knowing Sharleen and her nosy nature, the questions would never end.

Like this one: "Is he good in..."

"Drop it, Sharleen."

After another glass of water and a bag of M&Ms from her purse, Sharleen is ready to roll. Lorelei drives Sharleen's Kia, not confident yet in Sharleen's ability to steer straight, but optimistic enough to believe that by the time they reach the casino, Sharleen's driving ability will be restored enough to get her home safely once they have retrieved Lorelei's Prius.

The drive to the casino is long and desultory, its soundtrack the intermittent sputter of poor reception from Y-100 radio (Sharleen's choice since it's her car) underscored by the whir of wheels on asphalt. The road stretches flat, shimmering with heat, in a straight shot through the Everglades, the only relief dismal strip malls, housing developments, billboards, gas stations, gun shops, parched palm trees, flattened possums and ramshackle shacks of unknown purpose. Unfortunately, for what will be their second round trip in the past 24 hours, they have to return via the same grim route.

They had filled two thermoses with water for the trip, which prompts a little conversation.

"What's in this anyway?" Sharleen asks, waving her bottle around. "Caffeine? Cocaine?"

"It's just water," Lorelei says.

"I think there's something in it." Sharleen leans over and studies Lorelei's profile, silhouetted against the glare of sun coming through the windshield. "You're not as wrinkly as you used to be."

Lorelei doesn't know whether to be flattered, insulted or baffled. She had thought her skin had improved, but sex can do that, she had heard. She also gave those sweaty tangled nights with Juan credit for other things that seemed to be happening: the limberness, the looseness, the overall tightening of everything head to toe. Strangely, sex also seemed to have affected her hair as well: she hasn't needed an Eternal Ebony touchup for months, a fact sullenly commented upon by Clarissa the colorist when she went to her salon for a haircut recently. "You're going to someone else for your color," Clarissa had accused, shaking her head in disbelief when Lorelei denied it. She credited the effect to an increase in her intake of black beans, but even she didn't believe that. It was a mystery.

"You mind giving me some of your water to take home?" Sharleen is asking. "Maybe you could bring an extra bottle to the shop."

"I'm not dragging another big bottle to the shop," Lorelei says. "You want some, come and get it. You're welcome to it. Besides," she adds, "it's just water."

But she suspects this isn't really true. The water from her well isn't like any bottled water she's ever drunk, which covers every brand that promised to upgrade her organs in any way. She has vigorously sampled, not just water, but a vast array of foodstuffs, vitamins, minerals and herbal products that make claims for ailments she never thought she might have until she discovered that there was a natural remedy for them. She had even tried a colonic once, but that was too much even for her. Nevertheless, the proprietor of EarthFood was always overjoyed when she walked in the door.

But in her never-ending quest for the perfect drink, nothing had even begun to compare with the water that came from her tap. It not only tasted ethereal, it had other effects she was only beginning to acknowledge. It made her feel almost—otherworldly.

She once won ten yoga lessons when a customer sold her a raffle ticket for some charity. She didn't plan to use them until the customer, a recent divorcee trying to find herself, talked her into going with her to the class. Lorelei wasn't into yoga, all that twisting and stretching and balancing and ommmm-ing, but what kept her going, the carrot on the stick, was the quiet meditation at the end of class when they just lay there, splayed out like road kill. For those ten minutes, she felt totally relaxed. And it was there, in the very last class of the ten-session series, that she didn't just relax. She felt spirited away.

Her body was there, but her mind was gone. Off it went into a realm of light, a place without thought. It was like nothing she had ever felt before: not nothing, but not something either. She didn't have a word for it.

When she drank the water from her well, the feeling she got from it was the same wordless feeling she had experienced in meditation: an inexplicable state of being there and yet not there, mellowness with clarity, an awareness surrounded by light. She didn't know what was happening to her; only that something had. She was seeing the world through a strange new prism, but she sensed that the refraction had been turned on her as well. She knew she looked different. Her mirror reflected subtle changes day by day—changes noticed by both Sharleen and Juan.

But it was more than that. She no longer felt invisible to the world.

How did that happen? It was more than just the makeup she now applied, more than the fact that she had ditched some of her more dowdy outfits in favor of a few new pieces that flattered her. She had been noticing more of a bounce in her walk, and—was she acting differently, too? She hadn't thought much of it until a customer said to her, "Well, aren't we in a good mood today," bringing her to the startling realization that she must have appeared to be a dour old biddy before her recent evolution.

Now, watching Sharleen pout, Lorelei feels stingy. How can she deny that pleasure to Sharleen—Sharleen, her best (and only) friend from high school, who has stuck with her throughout her (she now realizes) crabby moments and helped build Ladybug Lingerie into a successful business? She experiences a surge of love for her little buddy Sharleen, her friend for all these years.

"Sharleen?" she says in a softer tone. Sharleen sinks further down in her seat, ignoring her. "Hey, Sharleen. I was just kidding," she says. "I'll bring an extra bottle to the shop for you to take home. But," she warns, "I'm not promising anything. After all, it's just water."

"I know," Sharleen concedes. "But you do look good."

"It's sex," Lorelei says, and like they did when they were kids, they burst out in uncontrollable giggles.

•   •   •

They both make it safely back to their respective homes in their respective cars, and by Monday, they are back at the shop as if nothing had happened. Lorelei, true to her word, has filled an empty five-gallon Crystal Creek bottle with water from her well for Sharleen to take home. Sharleen greedily stashes it in her car for safekeeping, then proceeds to drink great quantities from the bottle in the shop, creating multiple moments where she has to run and pee. Lorelei's annoyance at her frequent disappearances into the bathroom is exacerbated by Sharleen's constant checking herself in the mirror for any sign of change, which as far as Lorelei can tell, hasn't happened.

"Well, I do feel peppier," Sharleen asserts, although she admits she's disappointed that her appearance hasn't suddenly blossomed into what she had hoped would be a replay of her 20-year-old self. Sharleen's apparent surge of peppiness has a definite upside, in that her energy spike has resulted in the unexpected sale of some items that would ordinarily have been ignored (neon orange thong, seamed 40's-style nylons, a glittery tiara that somehow found its way into the last VaVoom delivery). So, all in all, despite Sharleen's periodic absences for purposes of peeing and personal inspection, it's been a good day.

So good, in fact, that the next day Sharleen has exciting news to report. "I don't know if it was all that water I drank or what, but I slept like a rock last night," she says as she folds a stack of bikini panties at a speed Lorelei had never observed before. "I mean, I could barely make it through *Dancing with the Stars* and you know how much I like *Dancing with the Stars*. It would take a hammer to knock me out like that."

Lorelei can relate. But last night, her sleep was interrupted. In that half-dream state upon waking she thought she heard something. Well, not exactly heard. Felt. She couldn't explain it.

"So," Sharleen continues, "what I'm thinking is, I don't know if it's the water, I'm not saying it is, but I'd like to just kind of drink *lots* of it for, you know, a few weeks, like an experiment, because I'm thinking that if it makes me feel this good after just one day, then imagine what weeks of that would do." She pauses. "I'd like a few more bottles."

"What are you planning to do? Water your lawn with it?"

"I want to do what you do. Drink it, maybe soak in it. It's made a difference for you and you know it."

"If there's anything different, it's because I watch what I eat. It's not magic."

"Yeah, you've been eating like an anorexic rabbit since I've known you, and what good did that do you? Same old Lorelei until now."

"Excuse me?"

"So what I'm thinking is I'd like to have a regular supply because I can see how I felt after drinking it yesterday."

"I gave you five gallons to take home. Since you can drink all you want from the shop's supply, that should last a couple of weeks." Lorelei opens a box from the new VaVoom shipment and holds a fragile lace teddy to the light. "I don't know if I like this color so much. It looks like grape Koolaid."

"Maybe you just want to keep the water all for yourself," Sharleen accuses.

"Okay, this is ridiculous," Lorelei says, exasperated. "It's just water. Maybe it does have some beneficial qualities—vitamins, minerals, whatever. But I will tell you this: it's not magic."

Sharleen is silent for a long moment. Then she asks, "What if it is?"

•　•　•

That night, sleeping alone, Lorelei lies awake with Sharleen's question repeating in a loop as she tosses and turns. Skeptical Lorelei battles with Gullible Lorelei ("Nonsense, fairy tale, magical thinking" vs. "What explains all the signs of youth, then?") until Skeptical Lorelei wins and she falls into a restless sleep.

Later, deep into the night, she senses something on the periphery of consciousness: not a sound, but, as she had felt the night before, a sensation as if there were a presence nearby. She swims up from a dream involving Wolf Blitzer, an ice cream truck, and a pair of Mickey Mouse ears. But it's not the dream that awakens her. It's something outside. She leaves her bed and peers through the blinds of her window.

Bougainvillea scratches against the wall outside like a dog wanting to come in. Moonlight casts long shadows from the melaleuca trees, fingers of darkness that reach across her lawn. She can see the moon, so fat and full she feels she can touch it. She opens the window and humidity pours into her room, carrying with it the scent of her neighbor's jasmine, a whiff of barbeque, and the bark of a far-off dog.

"Who's there?" she asks, not expecting an answer, but hoping that who-or-whatever that presence is would take her question as a threat. She slams the window shut and locks it, then creeps through the moonlight-striped living room to peer through the blinds once more. The twin palm trees flanking her porch shimmy a breeze-driven hula, but nothing else is moving.

Just a dream, she tells herself, and climbs back into bed. She wishes Juan were here.

• • •

Juan is staying over tonight. She had told him of the strange feeling she had experienced the night before, of an awareness—some sixth sense—that there was a presence outside, yet she heard and saw nothing. To satisfy her lingering uneasiness, Juan checks outside, until, finding nothing, assures her that yes, it must have been just her imagination.

She's relieved he's here. His visits are becoming more and more frequent, but their overnights haven't evolved into everynights. She stays at his house now and then, but it's a process, getting used to sleeping somewhere other than her own bed. After so many years of sleeping alone, Lorelei has an ingrained need for solitude, privacy, and her own inner life. When she feels that need arise, she'll suggest to Juan that perhaps his fish miss him. He does need to tend to them, which he does on schedule, so they take a breather every few days, allowing each other that space. So far, it's worked for them.

Juan dozes off before Lorelei does. She snuggles, half awake, in his arms, cozy and satisfied. His breathing descends into a soft snore as he falls deeper into sleep. Lorelei has just dropped off when she is startled awake by a cry from Juan. *"¡Corra!"* he yells. *"¡Tomalo y corra!"* His feet thrash and twist the sheet in what seems a panic to escape from…what?

"Wake up! Wake up!" Lorelei shakes him until he opens his eyes and stares at her as if she's a stranger. "You're having a bad dream," she says, and holds him until he's fully awake. "It's okay. You're here. With me."

Juan falls back onto his pillow. "That was...I don't know what that was." His forehead is wet with sweat. "What did I say?"

"It was in Spanish. *'Tomalo y corra!'* I think it was."

"Take it and run." He puts a hand to his forehead in puzzlement. "What was that?"

"Do you remember anything?"

"It's just...it's crazy." Juan closes his eyes. "I'm running, stumbling, tangled in a jungle somewhere. It's dark. Night. I'm carrying...I don't know, some kind of barrel on my back. Weighing me down. Hard to run. There's shouting, screaming. Savages of some kind shooting arrows at us. Some of my guys are hit but we don't stop, we're just running away, that's all we can do." He shudders. "It seemed so real." He pauses. "Real, like it was happening to me, but not me. Another me. In another time."

"Maybe it was the fish."

"The fish?"

"That fish you ordered for dinner tonight. I told you it didn't look good, snapper should be pink, not green, but you ate it anyway."

"It was snapper with green sauce. It was supposed to be green." He pauses. "It wasn't the fish."

"Well, if it's not the fish, then I guess it's just one of those crazy dreams that comes out of nowhere." He shakes his head, as if to shake off the dream.

But his thoughts, she could tell, were still stuck in that nowhere: a place dark, tangled, and very, very scary.

•　•　•　•

Before two weeks have passed, Sharleen has finished her five-gallon water supply and wants more. Not only has she drunk up her allotment, she also has defied Lorelei's mandate to control herself around the shop's water bottle, which she drained within days.

Lorelei is disgusted. "I told you to ration yourself. If you think I'm lugging in another bottle for you, you're crazy. These things are heavy! You're binging on water. It can't be good for you."

"You're the one who always says 'hydrate, hydrate,' like it's some kind of mantra. So now I'm hydrating, and you're bitching about it." Sharleen's reflection in the shop's full-length mirror doubles her righteous anger. "Not only that, but you haven't even noticed that there's something different about me."

Different? What's different? Lorelei appraises Sharleen's reflection. "Well, you may have lost some water weight. You probably peed it right out of you."

"You don't pee off 10 pounds in two weeks," Sharleen says, and lifts up her shirt to prove it. "Look! Muffin top: gone!"

Not really, Lorelei is tempted to say, but doesn't, because while it's not really gone, the previously plentious muffin top has receded to a soft blip around Sharleen's middle. And now that she's studying Sharleen, Lorelei also notices that Sharleen has been smoothed out all around, like someone had taken a rolling pin and flattened out her skin. It's not something so drastic that Lorelei would have noticed it before—not that she was looking. The effect was more subtle, as if something was different but she wasn't quite sure what.

Clearly, Sharleen not only had noticed the difference, but she was positive she knew the reason. "It's the water! It's not all your beans and greens and grains and whatnot; it's the water that changed you. And now me," she adds with a triumphal grin.

The water. Suddenly, the question that Lorelei has suppressed since it kept her up at night escapes into the full light of reality. What if the water *is* somehow…magical? What if her newfound youthfulness can't be attributed to her healthy lifestyle, the food she ate, the miles she walked on the treadmill she hated, and all those expensive vitamins, herbs and minerals she ingested each morning and night? She had adhered to that regimen her entire adult life, but until she began to drink the water, none of those things had stopped the inevitable decline the years had brought. And certainly none of them had sparked the sensuality that lay buried so long within her.

Sharleen's eyes go wide with sudden revelation. "You know what? We could sell it over the Internet! No store, no rent—it's almost all profit! People make millions like that. We could go on Home Shopping Network!"

Warning bells are clanging in Lorelei's head. She has to stop this now, or Sharleen is heading down a slippery slope that can only end in disaster.

"The only thing we're selling is lingerie, so just calm yourself down," Lorelei says. "You're blowing this all out of proportion. Okay, so you lost some weight. You're looking good. You should be happy about that. But we are not selling water. If you think it's helping you, then be my guest. Come and take a bottle now and then. I don't care. But I don't deliver."

Mollified but unrepentant, Sharleen acquiesces with a sigh. "Okay. So, can I come and get a couple bottles after work?"

"A couple of bottles? How much are you drinking, anyway?"

"I don't just drink it. I stick my face in it, too."

"Your face?"

"I figure fifteen minutes for a good soak. I use a snorkel. I'd stick my whole body in it, too, if I had enough water. I mean, if you could swim in it, imagine how that would be."

"Okay, two bottles," Lorelei agrees, feeling somewhat guilty since she has unlimited access to the water at home, available for drinking and soaking in her bath whenever she wants.

"Make it three, and we've got a deal."

•   •   •

"Do you notice anything unusual about the water from my well?" Lorelei asks Juan as they share a sleepy breakfast.

"Unusual? How unusual?" Juan stirs berries into his oatmeal and ventures a bite. "If I eat this stuff, will you please not comment about the source of pork when I order a Cuban sandwich?"

"Oatmeal is better for you than pork."

"You were saying about the water?"

"Do you notice anything different about me since I've been drinking it?"

Juan has the look on his face of a man trapped by the question, *Does this dress make me look fatter?* "How do you mean?" he hedges.

"Do I act any different?" she asks, knowing very well that she does.

"You're more...sexy," he ventures.

"Okay. What else?"

"I don't know." He takes two more bites of dreaded oatmeal, allowing himself time to think about where this is going. "You dress different?" She nods. Emboldened, he continues. "Hair is different? Walk is different? Talk more? Laugh more?"

"Better, right?"

"You were fine before," he says. "Just fine."

"But?" She tips her head quizzically.

"Okay." He pushes the oatmeal away. "What's going on here?"

Lorelei gets up and pours herself a glass of water from the tap. "Look at this," she says, holding it up so the sun infuses it, transforming its clarity into crystal shards of light. "This doesn't look or taste like any water I've ever had."

"Thank you very much," he says. "I will take complete credit for this discovery."

"I'm serious. I didn't really give it much thought before, but I think I've changed since we've had this water. And, in all modesty, I think it's for the better."

"You've always been for the better."

"Very diplomatic. But I didn't really make the connection until Sharleen did."

"Sharleen? The crazy queen?" Juan goes to the pantry and rummages around. "I'm still hungry. You got any Pop-tarts?"

"You'll find a pig before you find Pop-tarts in there." She reaches in and extracts a box of granola bars. "Here. Eat. Be happy."

As he munches, she continues. "Sharleen is convinced that the water has improved me, and she insisted that I let her have what she calls 'an experiment.' She's been drinking gallons of the stuff for a couple of weeks now. And I have to say, she's looking better."

"You mean she's cut her hair, bought some skirts that cover her crotch, and is wearing shoes she can actually walk in?" He smiles a big granola smile.

"She lost ten pounds in two weeks. But that's not what's unusual. She's kind of— smoothed out all over. Like everything's shifted. It's not drastic. I didn't really notice it much, but then I see her every day and don't really look at her, I have to say."

"What else?"

"Her face has changed. It's lost some of its, I guess you'd say— poochiness. Not so wrinkly." Lorelei pauses. "She said she soaks her face in the water. She uses a snorkel."

"She uses what?"

"I know. But what's weird is that I'm starting to think, well, maybe that's what happened to me. I drank the water, and, yes, I've seen changes."

"So what are you saying? That it's got some magical thing going for it?"

"Magic is pretty strong a word. But what could account for it?"

Juan chews thoughtfully for a moment. "It's the purest water I've ever come across," he says. "But having some kind of power to improve someone, not just physically but psychologically? That would be as nutty as..." he holds up what's left of the granola bar, "...this."

"But...I do see a difference in her. And in myself, too." She pauses. "I know you only drink it while you're here, but have you seen any difference in yourself?"

"Yeah. I have x-ray vision. And I didn't want to tell you this, but I can fly." He nods. "It's the cape. I don't like to wear it in public."

"Really. I'm asking you."

"And I'm asking you. Do you consider Sharleen a reliable source?" He shakes his head. "She really uses a snorkel?"

Lorelei takes Juan's bowl to the sink and scrapes the oatmeal down the disposal. She watches as the last remnants disappear in a clattering whirl. "She thinks we should sell it."

"She thinks you should *what?*"

"Sell it. Another brilliant Sharleen thought."

Juan makes a crazy-face. "She is definitely certifiable."

"Certifiable," Lorelei agrees.

• • • •

It was Ruby Braithewaite who started it. Ruby Braithewaite, old-line Coral Gables matron, long-time customer of Ladybug Lingerie, faithful purchaser of shapewear (Maidenform Ultimate Slimmer #12657) that reined in her formidable figure, and multiple recipient of the services of Dr. Rollie Wellington, plastic surgeon, whose talents she regularly employed until the face she presents today in the shop barely resembles the one she walked in with thirty years ago.

Ruby, having studied her own face in the mirror for a lifetime, noticing any flaws that needed correcting by the notable Dr. Rollie, was also a student of the faces of others. She had, in the recent past, commented on the improvement that Lorelei had undergone, comments Lorelei had brushed aside with her usual homilies about nutrition and exercise. But today it is not Lorelei who is the object of Ruby's observation, but Sharleen.

"You've been up to something," Ruby says to Sharleen, her lips forming a Juvederm-plumped smile. "Spa? Juice diet? Dr. Rollie?"

Sharleen preens, flattered by what passes as a compliment from Ruby, who is known to be hyper-critical of the appearance of others. "Well, I have lost a little weight," she admits.

"A little?" Ruby says. "Looks like someone's done more than just diet. Looks like someone's been undergoing renovation." She studies Sharleen with a practiced eye and pronounces, "Total makeover!"

"Not really," Sharleen says. "I've been..." She stops when she sees Lorelei give her a warning look. "Well, it's a secret."

"What kind of secret?" Ruby persists, clearly on track now to discover any new path to youth and beauty that she hasn't already trod.

Lorelei puts on her gracious shop-owner face and inserts herself between Ruby and Sharleen, for she knows that this customer in particular spreads news faster than Twitter. "The secret is in our new line of shapewear," she says with a smile. "Show her our Spanx," she says to Sharleen, turning to shoot her another warning look.

"Spanx isn't new," Sharleen says. "We've carried it since..."

"Our *new* Spanx," Lorelei says through gritted teeth.

"Oh. Okay." Sharleen hustles off to gather up the appropriate pieces of squishwear, then guides Ruby into one of the fitting rooms. Ruby pulls Sharleen in after her, unaware that Lorelei is just outside, nonchalantly arranging robes on a rack, a pretense to eavesdrop on their conversation and peer through an opening in the curtain.

"This isn't the secret, is it?" Ruby hisses, shaking a pair of Spanx high-rise panties in Sharleen's face. "You're hiding something."

"No I'm not."

"I can tell. I understand. Sometimes we don't want to share our beauty secrets. Lorelei—she's a sly one. Never could get her to talk about what's she's obviously had done. I've tried, God knows I've tried."

That, Lorelei knows, is true.

"But," Ruby says to Sharleen, going for the gold of flattery, "you look *fabulous*. Slimmer. Toned. Your face—I remember that face! Thirty years I've been watching it slide down your neck, wondering when you were going to do something about it, and...you have!"

"Well, not really..."

"You can't fool an expert," Ruby says. "It's clear you've had work done. It's subtle, very nicely executed, but still: done. And so fast—just in the past few weeks! I don't recognize it as Dr. Rollie's work, though. Who did it?"

"Nobody. I'm telling you. Nobody. It just...happened."

Ruby attempts to purse her lips—a difficult task—and settles for a blank Botox stare. "Nothing just *happens* in the world of plastic surgery. Somebody does it. Somebody sticks needles into you, somebody carves out your fat belly, somebody slices and dices and makes you into the object of beauty you were meant to be!" Ruby cries. "Who is it? Tell me!"

Terrified, flattered, and congenitally unable to keep a secret, Sharleen blurts, "It's the water."

"Water?" Ruby's face goes even blanker. "Where?" She brightens. "The Spa at the Biltmore? The pool? The whirlpool? The volcanic mud wrap?" All of which Ruby has done with little to show for it. "What water are you talking about?"

Sharleen parts the fitting room curtain and indicates the bottle atop the water cooler at the rear of the shop before she notices Lorelei, who gives her a warning glare.

"*That* water?" Ruby asks, pointing with a poison-green-enameled nail. "I get bottled water at home, and if it made any difference, Dr. Rollie would be off my payroll."

Lorelei forces a laugh. "Oh, Sharleen, you are such a kidder." She turns to Ruby with a shake of her head. "You know Sharleen. She just loves a tall tale now and then. Don't you, Sharleen?"

Sharleen catches the menace in Lorelei's voice and nods obediently. "Ha ha. I'm such a kidder," she parrots.

Ruby's eyes ping-pong between Lorelei and Sharleen. She pauses to study each one, looking them both up and down. "What the hell," she pronounces, and heads for the water bottle. She yanks a paper cup from the dispenser, fills it with water and gulps it down. "Tastes different. Good, actually." She shoots them a defiant look, and refills the cup once, twice, and once again. "There," she pronounces. "Let's just see what happens now."

"It doesn't happen that fast..." Sharleen begins.

"Well, keep me posted!" Lorelei interrupts. "Maybe Sharleen knows something I don't know."

"If she does," Ruby says, "then it'll be news to all of us." She burps discreetly. "If it works, I'll be back for more." And with that, she's out the door.

•   •   •

Two days later, Ruby is back. This time she's brought a gallon jug with her. "Fill 'er up. If I like it, I'll order more."

"It's not for sale," Lorelei protests. "It's just for the shop, for our customers."

Sharleen scurries up. "What happened?" she asks with the look of someone who knows the reason and wants it verified.

"Well," Ruby says. "I'll tell you this: it'll never put Dr. Rollie out of business. Didn't do a thing for me in that department. But it's hard to put my finger on it—something was different. I felt lighter. My bones moved a little better. I skipped my Paxil and nothing bad happened." She thrusts the jar at Lorelei. "How much is it? I want to give it another try, see if it does anything else before I put in an order. What company is it?"

Lorelei and Sharleen exchange a look. "It's...just Crystal Creek," Lorelei lies.

"Crystal Creek?" Ruby gives her a skeptical look. "I get Crystal Creek. Doesn't taste like this." She marches to the cooler, studies the water within the bottle. "Doesn't look like this, either. This has—I don't know—some kind of sparkle to it. Or something."

"It's the light," Lorelei says. But Ruby is undeterred. She begins to fill her jug from the cooler. "Put it on my charge," she says. "Whatever it costs."

"$50," says Sharleen. "To fill your gallon jug."

Lorelei stares at her. "Where did you get that from?"

Sharleen stands her ground. "$50. That's our price."

Lorelei strides to the cooler and shuts it off. "Sorry, Ruby, but our water's not for sale. I'm happy you think it made you feel good, but I'd feel we were cheating you if we sold you something that's just plain old water."

"Just let me..."

"No fill-ups," Lorelei insists. "Help yourself to a cup, that's what it's here for, but I'm not selling anything other than lingerie here."

Ruby gulps down the small amount she was able to get into her jug, then refills a paper cup twice before Lorelei stops her. "Ruby, let's just call it a day, okay? Maybe you should go home and rest. You seem a little anxious."

"I've never felt better in my life!" Ruby attempts another pass at the cooler. Lorelei cuts her off, crumples the cup and tosses it in the trash.

"I'll be back," Ruby says, clutching her empty jug.

"Great!" Lorelei says. "We have a new Spanx shipment due any day. You'll love it."

Ruby is hardly out the door before Sharleen is all over Lorelei. "See? I told you we could sell the water! She woulda paid $50 for just a *gallon*! That's $250 for a five gallon bottle! With Ruby spreading the word—and you know she would—we'd have a real surge of customers. What's wrong with you?"

"What's wrong is that we'd be running a scam," Lorelei says. "Selling water? For $250 a bottle? Why don't you pitch a little snake oil while you're at it?"

Sharleen grabs Lorelei by the shoulders and steers her to the mirror. "Okay. Look at yourself. You tell me what happened. When did you go from Maggie Smith to Catherine Zeta-Jones?"

She stares into the mirror and sees what she may have seen so many years ago: loose tumble of pitch-black hair, blue eyes wide and clear, skin smooth and taut, and a once-angular figure now firm and shapely as that of...Catherine Zeta-Jones.

"Catherine Zeta-Jones?" she repeats.

"Well...that's stretching it," Sharleen admits. "But close enough. And definitely an improvement over before." She eyes Lorelei warily. "It's the water. For whatever reason, it works. For all we know, it could be the fountain of youth."

The words take Lorelei's breath away. "That's ridiculous," she manages to say.

"Maybe. But who cares? All I know is, we're crazy not to take advantage of it."

Sharleen whips out her cellphone. "Look. I'm Googling 'Fountain of Youth.' Watch and see how many places call themselves that."

Scrolling and clicking, Sharleen's nimble finger travels from site to site, all Florida attractions with claims to Fountain fame: the sludgy water of a nondescript drinking fountain in Punta Gorda, a trickle emerging beneath a marker in St. Petersburg, a sulphurous spring-fed lake in Warm Mineral Springs, and the biggest, kitchy-est claimant of all—the Fountain of Youth Park in St. Augustine.

Lorelei has a sudden flash of horror at how this could escalate into the terminal tackiness of the Fountain of Youth Park. "I'm not selling water. Just forget about it."

Sharleen looks thoughtful for a moment, rare for Sharleen. "Well, then, let's give it away. Make it an attraction, something that would bring customers into the shop."

"We *do* give it away. It's here for anybody who wants it."

"Yeah, in a paper cup! How classy is that?"

Lorelei is offended. All these years she has striven for elegance – aside from her concession to Sharleen's insistence on the VaVoom line, which, she has to admit, has brought in a new, if not-so-classy, generation of customers.

Sharleen reminds her of that. "VaVoom! You didn't want VaVoom, and look—we can't keep it in stock." She picks up a handful of brightly-colored thongs and tosses them at Lorelei, where they land at her feet like deflated balloons. "I do come up with a good idea now and then, but you just can't give me credit, can you?"

"I've given you credit." Lorelei stoops to rescue the thongs from the floor. "Yes. It was a good move. Thank you."

"Well, here's another good move," Sharleen says. "Wine glasses."

"I'm not serving wine," Lorelei says, neatly folding the thongs. "We're not a bar."

"I'm not talking about wine. I'm talking about water. Our water! Served in wine glasses! How classy is that?"

"What's your point?" Lorelei asks.

"Presentation! That's the secret. It could bring in a slew of customers who have never been here. We serve them water that may or," she concedes, "may *not* do anything for them, but if it's served in a classy way, well, they may *think* it's doing something."

"That's not something I'd promote."

"You don't have to. Ruby is a one-woman P.R. firm, and once she gets the ball rolling, it'll just keep on rolling. We'll have business we never had before."

Well, Sharleen may have something there. Business has increased, but so has their rent. "Okay, you're in charge of this

TIME IN A BOTTLE

little venture," she concedes. "Pick up a pack of plastic wine glasses at Wal-Mart…"

"Plastic! Wal-Mart!" Sharleen is appalled. "If we're going to do this, let's do it right." She thinks for a moment. "Crystal. Nieman-Marcus."

"Are you out of your mind?"

"Okay, then. Macy's."

"Are you going to wash all those glasses? It's Wal-Mart and plastic."

Sharleen shakes her head in resigned disgust. "Okay. But you just don't know classy."

• • •

By the third week, Sharleen has to make repeated Wal-Mart runs to supply enough glasses for the customers who swarm the shop. Ruby has indeed spread the word, and by the third week, the word has spread far beyond Ruby's domain. Matrons migrate to Coral Gables from South Miami, Miami Beach, Aventura—even as far south as Homestead and as far north as Fort Lauderdale—just to see what all the fuss is about. *Is it true?* they wonder. Has this shop kept its secret from Victoria's Secret?

Sharleen busily fills glasses while Lorelei fills orders. These women of a certain age have never, until now, considered looking at, much less trying on, a line as naughty as VaVoom. Whether it's the water, or their perception of the water, doesn't matter. They try on lacy bits they never would have tried before, and they tell each other they look *fabulous.*

Lorelei, with Sharleen's help, fills increasing numbers of five-gallon bottles at home each day, lugging them to the shop early in the morning before the first customers appear at the door. It's exhausting. So exhausting that Lorelei finally, against her better judgment, has to go to Juan for help.

96

"What?" he asks when she tells him about the new direction the shop has taken. "Don't tell me Sharleen has taken your brain and exchanged it for hers."

"I know it sounds crazy, but Sharleen was right. We've got more customers now than we can handle. They're buying lingerie, but they also want to buy water—in five-gallon bottles. For $250 a bottle, Sharleen insists, but I say No. I can't sell lingerie and water, too. It's easier to just give it away." She paces the kitchen, pausing to give the soup bubbling on the stove a furious stir. "I'm overwhelmed. I'm stressed. I can't keep doing this."

"So stop." He gets up to taste the soup. "Needs more cumin."

She scoops a spoonful of the spice and throws it into the pot. "Whoa," he says. "Calm down."

"I need your help," she pleads. "Could you just put a load of bottles into your truck and take them to the shop for me? Sharleen and I can fill them here, but they're too heavy for me to take to my car and then into the shop."

"Is this a one-time deal? Or am I going to have to plan my days around this?" When she doesn't answer, he guides her to a chair and sits her down. "Listen. Do you want to sell underwear, or do you want to sell a gimmick? The water is the toy in the Happy Meal. They may think they're getting something magical, but when it breaks, when they discover it's a fraud, they may not want the Happy Meal again."

Lorelei is quiet a moment. Then, "It's not a fraud," she says.

"What makes you so sure?"

"It's not just that I see a difference in myself. Or that Sharleen's looking better and better. I see some of those women who come in every day—yes, some do come in every day—and, well, something's going on with them, too. I'm not imagining it." She takes a deep breath and says it: "Sharleen thinks you might have tapped into the fountain of youth."

"Sharleen." He sighs and shakes his head.

Juan goes to the sink and pours himself a glass of water. Instead of drinking it, he holds it up to the light. It glimmers faintly, as if it were lit from within by a firefly.

"I'm not discounting that there may be some benefit to the water," he says. "But I think there's a scientific reason for everything. So I've done a little research myself." He takes a long drink of water. "There was an article in one of my scientific journals about a U.S. Geological survey. It said that radium shows up in about 3 to 4 percent of water. What interested me was that it turns up in places with certain rock formations, like Florida's limestone. Florida's one of the three most likely places to find radium-laced water."

"Yikes. You mean my water could be radioactive?"

"It does have radium, but they've tested the water here and what they've found is so low in picoCuries of radium that it's harmless—way below the limit of 5 picoCuries, so no problem. But," he adds, "what's also interesting is that some of the aquifer water tested is also high in magnesium."

"What does that do?"

"Epsom salt is really magnesium sulfate. Ever soaked in an epsom salt bath?"

"Yes, when I felt really sore and achy after work. It made me feel better. But actually," she adds, "I haven't needed to do that for a long time."

"You'd think it would be the other way around. The older you get, the less your body absorbs magnesium, and the better the chance you've got a magnesium deficiency. So, by that logic, you'd need more, not fewer, epsom salt baths, right?"

"What are you saying here? That my water has radium and magnesium?" She shudders. "Am I being poisoned?"

"No, no, no," Juan reassures her. "I'm just doing my science project thing, looking for logical explanations for supposedly magical happenings." He takes another swallow and grins. "See? Nothing happened." Then, to Lorelei's alarm, his eyes pop wide.

He gives one loud croak, then another: "Ribbet! *Ribbet!*" He hops once, then three times. "I think...I'm turning into a *frog*." He hops madly across the kitchen. "Kiss me! I want to be the prince again!"

"Oh stop it," Lorelei says. "I thought you were convulsing or something."

"Kiss me anyway."

"First tell me that it's safe to drink this water. I don't want to glow in the dark."

"It's safe, but if it makes you feel better, I'll have it tested. Even if there is some indication of radium, it's not going to be enough to hurt anyone."

Lorelei gives him his promised kiss, then leans back with another question: "If it does have radium and magnesium, could that explain all this weirdness?"

"There's a scientific explanation for everything," Juan repeats, and then, almost to himself, adds, "Almost everything, anyway."

WATER, WHEN IT SEEKS A NEW LEVEL

Water is nature's Michelangelo. A patient artist, it sculpts mountains and carves canyons grain by miniscule grain. Gravity is water's muse. A creative force, it lures liquid through rock, seeks a path to the heart of the earth. It defies man's attempts to reverse water's course, but man's perseverance too often prevails, defeating gravity's seduction.

Time is closing in. As more of itself disappears, the spring feels life wane in increments. It shrinks within the shelter of rock. While the weight of water is still on its side, it must carve a new pathway or die.

The spring settles into its smooth solid base, finds a soft spot of porous rock. There, day by day, week by week, it focuses its power, infinitesimally displacing the weakened rock to create a finger that points the way to escape. The finger becomes a channel, the channel becomes a stream, the stream becomes a river that will lead to its new home.

In time, the spring will be safe again. But time is running out.

EIGHT

Sharleen has sold a five-gallon bottle of water. To Ruby. "She made me an offer I couldn't refuse," Sharleen says, backing away from Lorelei's fury. "$300! And another $500 worth of lingerie! How could I say no to that?" She puts the table with the VaVoom teddies between herself and Lorelei, then grabs a lacy black number for emphasis. "She bought six of these, in every color! She said she looks great in them now, and you know what? She does! For Ruby, anyway."

"I don't care if she looks like Beyoncé," Lorelei hisses. Several women have paused in their perusal of items, gripping a stemmed plastic glass in one hand and lingerie in the other, to listen. Lorelei motions toward the back office. "I need to talk to you. Now."

Lorelei leads the way, and, once inside the office, lays into Sharleen. "Now you've set a precedent. I told you we weren't selling water, and what do you do? You sell it, not just to anyone, but to Ruby, the mouth of the south."

"That's $800 in one sale. How can you argue with that?" Sharleen counters. "Remember when we didn't make $800 in one week? How worried we used to be that we might not even make the rent some months?" She stalks to the pyramid of bottles stacked in a corner, awaiting their turn atop the cooler visible through the glass door where a line of women waits to refill their glasses.

"That's beside the point. We're selling lingerie, not water," she insists, but she knows it's too late. The word is out, thanks to Ruby. The genie is out of the bottle.

•   •   •

A clot of customers is waiting for Lorelei outside the shop door the next morning. As usual, the behemoth city garbage truck is blocking the alleyway entrance to the store, and she's forced to go in the front door. "We're not open yet," she says, but she knows what they're there for, and it's not just lingerie. She edges by them, trying to be cordial, but she's in no mood to deal with them now.

She had a sleepless night last night. Every time she would drift off, she'd awake with a start, sure there was someone outside. But when she crept around the rooms, listening through open windows, there was nothing but the scrabble of some possum scurrying beneath the hibiscus, its tail a ratty whip just visible in the darkness. Or the whisk of a palm against a blackboard sky chalked with scurrying clouds. Night sounds. Normal sounds. Sounds she'd find almost soothing if she had someone to share them with.

It wasn't what she heard that makes her skin prickle with awareness. It was another sense, the sense of a Presence, that had compelled her to creep about, seeking its source. She finally fell asleep just before dawn when the rising sun awakened her. Its hot dry rays poked through the blinds, nudging her until she crawled out of bed in a crabby mood that she carried with her to the shop.

Now she hurriedly fumbles to open the door, ignoring the clamoring crowd of middle-aged matrons who reach out to her as if she were Elvis at the Las Vegas Hilton. "Not open yet," she repeats with a fixed smile, then shuts the door before they swarm inside.

Where is Sharleen? She should be here by now. Lorelei straightens the merchandise, patting thongs, bras, and teddies into place even though they are already perfectly aligned. The merchandise had never been so tossed about before Ruby spread the word about the water—a mixed blessing, since sales have never been higher. VaVoom's sales rep is ecstatic, and has put in a rush order to fill in the unexpected depletion of favorites.

Oh, there she is. Lorelei sees Sharleen at the door, and rushes to open it before Sharleen does, for she knows Sharleen will let in, not just herself, but the eager masses of frantic women who are shoving and pushing behind her. "Not open yet," she calls to them as Sharleen squeezes through the small opening in the doorway Lorelei allows her.

Sharleen looks rumpled, as if she had slept in the clothes she's wearing, and then Lorelei realizes that she probably *has* slept in the clothes she's wearing because it's the same outfit she wore to work yesterday. Judging from Sharleen's makeup-smeared face and uncombed hair, the clothes were probably off for a good deal of the time before she arrived this morning, but they received a pretty good pummeling before that occurred. Lorelei doesn't even want to know how Sharleen came to be in this frazzled state, but Sharleen is all too happy to inform her anyway, after a perfunctory apology for her lateness.

"What a night," Sharleen begins. "I'm chatting it up with this guy in line at Publix, very very cute guy I figure about 30 or whatever, he notices the sub sandwich I've got and says 'Is that your dinner?' And I say 'Yeah,' and he says 'Why don't you ditch that and come with me to South Beach, I'm meeting some friends, we're gonna grab a bite somewhere and then head on down to Treehouse, you like to dance?' And I say, 'Yeah,' because why not? and then we're outta there, over the causeway, and we eat some pizza and walk on Ocean Drive and go up to his friend's place and smoke a joint…"

"You *what?*" Lorelei sees the restless crowd pressing against the door and gives them a little wave to mollify them. It doesn't. Recognition of their presence only energizes them, and some begin to rap on the glass and demand that she open up.

"Yeah, and then we hang out until it's time to go to this amazing club called Treehouse, and you can't believe how *fun* the place is, all flashing colored lights and this weird loud music and everybody jammed up dancing, I've never seen any place like this, you and me, we've missed a *lot*, and then he gives me this pill which makes everything even more fun, and we're dancing and dancing and then I'm back at his place or his friend's place, I don't know where I was, and let me tell you I think I had the best sex of my life, except I can't remember most of it but what I remember was *fantastic*."

"Spare me the details," Lorelei says. "Where's your car?"

"I took an Uber to Publix where I left it when I went with Alex, or Alan, or whatever his name is, and then I drove it here."

"Well, now you can drive it home," Lorelei says, trying to remain calm. "Go home, take a shower, change your clothes, get your head on straight and come back ASAP. I can't handle this crowd alone, but I don't want you here in this condition."

"What's wrong with..." Sharleen begins.

"Go home!" Lorelei can't listen to one more word from Sharleen. "Just...go home. And get back here when you're clean and sober."

"I *am* sober," Sharleen says, offended. "I only had a few drinks."

"And pot. And pills. And who knows what else." Lorelei can't repress her next accusation: "You come in here looking like hell, smelling like weed, bragging about random sex with some randy kid, and you think that's OK? Have you lost your mind?"

Lorelei doesn't wait for an answer. She steers Sharleen to the door, squeezes her out again, and reassures the crowd that the shop will open in ten minutes. Some boo this time frame, something she didn't anticipate.

Lorelei takes several deep yoga breaths, gives the merchandise one last adjustment, then, to fortify herself, goes to the cooler and pours herself a nice big glass of water. Ah. That's better. She opens the door.

•   •   •

Sharleen doesn't come in until mid-afternoon. All traces of the night before have been erased. She's cleaned up, and her outfit is subdued for Sharleen. Her skirt hits her at a modest mid-thigh, and she's wearing a sweater whose buttons are actually buttoned. Although Lorelei could use some help with the crowd that has grown in size as the day has gone on, she isn't in any rush for Sharleen to pitch in. She's wary that Sharleen's seeming stability is just temporary, that she could revert to wacky mode at any moment, triggering her obsession about selling the water. Several women approach Lorelei with an offer to buy five-gallon bottles of the elixir, an offer Lorelei dismisses with a shake of the head and a smile which she hopes deflates the whole idea. Nevertheless, the water disappears from the cooler at a record pace. Customers, chattering excitedly in English, Spanish, and Spanglish, are buying lingerie in multiples. They are also drinking, and Lorelei has replaced the bottle more times than she can count.

Now Sharleen is here and ready for business. Her relatively conservative attire is a sobering effect that gives Lorelei pause. Sharleen is up to something. But what?

Sharleen is happy to tell her. "I was going to just go home and sleep it off," she says, "but then I said to myself, 'Sharleen, what you need is total immersion.'

"So what I did was take those three big bottles of water I had, drank some, then dumped the rest in my tub, and just soaked my whole self in that for about an hour. Face down, snorkel up. I'll tell you, it's better than a month at a spa.

"And here's the best part." She points at her head, hair freshly poufed into a blonde froth. "It's my brain—it's working overtime. I have a plan."

"We're not selling the water," Lorelei interrupts, "if that's where you're going."

To make her point, she does not refill the empty bottle, but tapes to the cooler the "out of order" sign she has hastily scrawled on the lid of an empty VaVoom box. Sharleen glares at Lorelei, but says nothing. Several disappointed women exit the shop with their purchases but not the hoped-for water.

Sharleen steers Lorelei into the office and lets loose. "We're equal partners, remember? If you had your way, we'd be stuck in the 1950s, all bullet bras and girdles of steel. Don't forget who pushed you into ordering VaVoom, and aren't you glad I did? So give me a little credit here for having good ideas. I know, you're the brains and I'm the bubble-head, but there's more than bubbles inside this head."

"I never said…"

"It's not that soaking my head in the water made me a genius or anything, but it maybe melted away some of the stupid."

"Well, given your condition when you walked in here this morning, I'd say there was a lot to melt away."

"I'm going to ignore that," Sharleen says with an eye-roll, "because I want you to hear me out. I've got a really really great idea."

Lorelei, feeling responsible for Sharleen's purported low self-esteem in the brains department, accedes with what she hopes is a willing-to-listen expression. "All right. Let's hear it."

Sharleen goes into presentation mode, head high, back straight. "We're a business!" she pronounces. "We can't keep giving the water away, any more than we'd give away our merchandise. Let's operate like a business and go professional with this. Get organized with the bottling process. Slap on a fancy label, and five-gallon bottles will sell for $300. Ka-ching!"

"$300? Who—besides Ruby—is going to pay $300 for a bottle of water?"

"Some of these women will spend $1000 for eight ounces of LaMer crème; for them, $300 for five gallons of our water will be a bargain."

Lorelei can't deny the water's mysterious properties: first Lorelei, then Sharleen, now Ruby and the milling masses of women who are crowding her shop, pleading for bulk sales of the water they've been getting for free. From the obviously well-off to the secretaries here on their lunch break, they seem eager to shell out whatever it takes to stave off the signs of age. Still, Lorelei has to ask, "What makes you so sure?"

"Because they see the difference in you and me, and they're seeing the difference in themselves."

Assuming it's true, what's she going to do with that?

Lorelei likes her world the way it is. There's security in the expected, knowing that each day will be like the day before, and that her days to come will follow the same comfortable pattern. She has worked too long and too hard to disrupt a life that has finally settled into what she takes to be happiness. She has a successful business, and now, much to her surprise, she has a lover. What more could she ask, especially at her age? Which, she concedes, is an age she no longer looks. And that brings her back to the source of it all: the water.

It's not that she wants to keep it all to herself, as Sharleen had accused. She *has* been willing to share, first with Sharleen, and then with her customers. But she sees trouble ahead if Sharleen has her way: trouble she can't yet define, but the kind of trouble that comes with money, with publicity, and most of all, with the spectre of disbelief and ridicule that inevitably accompanies claims of any kind of mysterious happening. Especially such an outlandish claim as finding the fountain of youth.

And then there's the question of proof.

Juan has sent the water for testing. That would be the final proof. Lorelei finds herself hoping that there's nothing out of the ordinary about the water, except perhaps that it has healthy properties which would explain the sense of well-being it brings when imbibed. Yes, that would be good. Then Sharleen would abandon her crazy scheme, the women would come to enjoy a free glass or two, and sales would continue to rise.

But what could explain what she sees in the mirror, the changes she's experienced both inside and out? There's no question she's not the same Lorelei whom Juan first met the day her well ran dry. She sees those same changes in Sharleen, and, to a lesser degree, in the women who come to buy lingerie and drink from a bottle of water some seem to revere as a sacred chalice. The more often they come to the shop, the better they look: a little weight loss here, a little jowl-smoothing there—incremental, but enough so that they keep coming back for more.

Suppose there is some evidence that this water's magic is founded in science? That kind of proof would produce a deluge of unwanted scrutiny as well as fame—something she's never considered within her realm of reality. She would lose her anonymity. And her quiet life would be changed forever.

WINONA

I come to Lorelei's at night to meditate on this problem, creeping along the ground, heart to the earth, listening for the distant music of the water beneath me. My body is electric with knowing, but my brain can't devise a solution.

I know where the spring is now. Lorelei's well taps into it, only there's no outside access. The spigot for a hose must be inside the garage—locked, as I know since I tried it. At night I prowl around, looking for a solution. This is a dilemma I've never encountered in all my centuries of seeking and finding the spring. I've always discovered it in nature, bubbling up between rocks, hidden in a grotto, trickling among dense ferns. Here it's imprisoned in steel, pumped up from the depths into an interior space where it's accessed solely by the turn of a handle on a faucet. That's not as nature intended.

Daytime excursions to Lorelei's don't work. I'm too visible—one neighbor walking her dog spotted me, thanks to her ratty little off-leash chihuahua whose staccato yipping gave me away as I was checking out Lorelei's back yard. I made up some lame excuse, something about looking for my cat, and scrambled out of there pronto. I can still see her standing there, mouth agape, as I strode to my Jeep and drove off. I don't exactly blend into the background.

Meanwhile, the signs of aging are becoming more evident, wearing on me, bit by bit, as each day seems to bring a new ache or pain. Before now, I've found the spring before any deterioration was noticeable, although once there was a brief, humiliating necessity for bifocals, followed by a series of hot flashes, a time which I'd rather forget altogether. But those intermittent detours into the aging process were quickly cured by my re-discovery of the spring, which, I have to say, was met with more than mere relief each time. I was uncharacteristically jubilant, a joy some of my contemporaries attributed to some uptick in my sex life, a part of me I never concealed. Whatever boyfriend I had at the time was thrilled at my enthusiastic response to his efforts, assuming it was due to his own talents in that arena, which were often quite exceptional to begin with because I choose my partners well.

First rule of selection: don't look for love. It brings you nothing but heartbreak.

It's hard to remember how it felt to be loved, but I remember how it felt *to* love. I loved my Chief, Cacique Athore, if love when you're young means admiration for his strength, adoration for his majesty, and hunger for his touch. That hunger was never satisfied, for our marriage ended before it began, when my Chief unjustly blamed my plea to spare Ponce's life for the disappearance of the spring.

I knew Chief Athore could be consumed with jealousy, and I knew he could be unforgiving. After all, he had ordered the execution of one of his entourage for the crime of smiling at his sister, who was his first wife and mother of his heir. But I never would have dreamed of betraying him in any way, and thought he loved me as much as I loved him. Hadn't he chosen me to be his principal queen above all the women he could have had? Hadn't he caressed me with his eyes as I stood naked and proud for his approval? Hadn't he shared the sacred water from the spring with me as a testament to his love?

I suppose I was lucky. He could have had me executed, rather than exiled. Maybe my avowal of love had some effect; maybe he did love me after all. But none of it matters now. That was the beginning of my search for the spring, and the end of my ability to love.

And so I learned. Love is ephemeral, and can be snatched away in a moment. But life can be infinite. As long as I have the spring.

Which is why I'm demeaning my dignity, groveling about Lorelei's yard in my search, impeded by this recent lack of agility. Creeping along the ground isn't the problem; it's the getting up that's getting to me. I grab hold of a tree trunk to pull myself up, and discover that melaleuca trees are not made for grabbing. They peel like a bad sunburn, smell like turpentine, and make me sneeze—not a good idea when the slightest sound brings Lorelei to the window. I see her peeking out of the blinds and freeze in place, but stillness and silence—traits imbued in me since I was a child—become almost impossible when I feel a sneeze coming on. I stifle it, but even so, it ripples the air around me. For centuries, I've never sneezed, I've never coughed, I've never had the most minor ailments. Until now. Aches, pains, sneezes: my immune system must be collapsing. If I don't find the spring soon, trouble will surely find me.

NINE

The fountain of youth. Lorelei wishes she could have washed those words right out of Sharleen's mouth. They went straight from Sharleen's lips to Lorelei's brain. She can't stop thinking about it.

Neither can Sharleen, who is so wound up in her grandiose plans that she can't wait until the next day. Lorelei is soaking in her nightly bath when she hears pounding on her door. Terrified that the Presence she has only sensed has now materialized into some creature demanding entry, she leaps from the tub, hastily wraps herself in a towel, and tiptoes to the door to peer through the peep hole. There, to her combined relief and chagrin, is Sharleen.

"Aha," Sharleen says when she sees Lorelei's soggy self, still dripping from her bath. "Yeah, bath time, sure, you can soak in the water whenever you want, but how about the rest of us? That's pretty greedy, don't you think?"

"What is wrong with you?" Lorelei grips the towel around herself. Her wet hair hangs in licorice strips around her shoulders. "It's late! What are you doing here?"

"We need to talk."

"We've talked. Now I want to go to sleep."

Sharleen is already inside. She deftly steps around Lorelei and plants herself on the couch. Snagging some nuts from the bowl on the coffee table, she munches as she speaks. "So here's what I'm thinking. We go into mass production ASAP. We've got a market base already with our customers, but once the word gets out, there's no telling where this could go."

Market base? Mass production? Since when did Sharleen go to business school? She's got the jargon, but not the fact-based knowledge. Lorelei can't deal with this version of Sharleen right now. The lovely feeling she normally enjoys after her bath has dissipated, thank you Sharleen. "Go home," she says. "We can talk about this tomorrow," although she doesn't want to talk about it tomorrow. Or ever.

"Okay, here's what I'm thinking," Sharleen persists. "Where can we buy those bottles wholesale? We just can't keep re-using Crystal Creek bottles. And we need to design labels, something that speaks to the customer, something that reflects what we're all about."

Lorelei is stunned, not just by Sharleen's new vocabulary, but by her intensity, something that Sharleen has failed to exhibit in the past about anything not fun-or-sex- related, preferably in combination. "Are you on something?" Lorelei asks, remembering some kind of purple pill she had once spied in Sharleen's medicine cabinet. "Or did you have too much wine with dinner?"

"No, no wine. I drank about a quart of our water, though, which reminds me, I need another couple of bottles, maybe three." She pops another nut into her mouth and adds, "Wouldn't mind a glass of it right now. These make me really thirsty." She gets up and heads for the kitchen. "I'll help myself, no need to bother," and she does, filling a big glass from the faucet.

"'*Our* water'?" Lorelei feels suddenly very proprietary of what is, essentially, hers. "Hold it right there. This isn't community property. It comes from *my* well on *my* property. I'm happy to share, but it's not yours to turn into whatever kind of business you have in mind."

Sharleen takes a big gulp. "Okay. Here's the deal. I was going over the books..."

Lorelei blinks in disbelief. Although Sharleen is her equal partner, she's never been that interested in the details of their finances, just the bottom line. Whenever Lorelei has sat her down to explain that what comes in, must go out, she can tell when Sharleen's eyes glaze over that not much is sinking in. Sharleen's talents lie in other directions, but math is not one of them. The news that she has actually cracked open the books on her own is a revelation that Lorelei needs a moment to digest.

"So," Sharleen is saying, "we're doing much better now, I'd say maybe a third more sales than…before." She pauses meaningfully. "That's totally great. But I see our expenses are up, too. Did you know our rent has increased?"

"Did *I* know our rent has increased?" Lorelei is incredulous. Every time she's shared that information with her, Sharleen has tuned out, as she does when Lorelei tells her about the inexorable escalation of their taxes, insurance and utility bills. "Where have you been all these years? Of *course* our expenses have skyrocketed. We're in Coral Gables, not Kissimmee. It's not going to get any cheaper."

"My point exactly." At that, Sharleen whips out several sheets of notebook paper with indecipherable scribbles. "I've been working on a plan, and I got so excited I couldn't wait till tomorrow to get it in shape so it's a little rough. See?" She gives the pages a good shake. "Here's the answer! Sell the water! Problem solved."

Lorelei can't handle this right now. "It's almost midnight. I'm not willing to listen to anything at this hour." She takes Sharleen's glass away before she can refill it. "Go home. I'm going to bed."

"Business plan, ready ASAP," Sharleen says as Lorelei shuts the door. "You'll love it."

Lorelei lies awake long after Sharleen is gone, her mind a swirl of questions. What if the water *does* have some kind of magic? Is Sharleen's startling evolution even more proof that there's something to it? Would it make sense to go commercial and insure their financial future, or would that simply create problems she can't foresee?

Lorelei is just drifting off to sleep when she hears a scruffling sound outside. "Sharleen! Go home!" She peers out the blinds, hoping it is Sharleen. This time she gets a glimpse of the source of the scruffling. It's the Presence. And it throws a shadow.

• • •

The following day, Juan has the results of the water test but dinner's ready and Lorelei doesn't like food to get cold. She doles it out onto their plates: *pallomilla* steak, because she has acceded to Juan's wishes for some "real meat," *papas asadas* as a manly potato accompaniment, and kale salad, because she, too, has a voice in what they eat.

"There was someone outside last night," she says, stabbing at an elusive kale leaf. "This time, I'm sure it was a person."

"What did it look like?"

"I don't know. A shadow. It disappeared before I could get a good look. It sounded like it had a run-in in the bushes with a raccoon or possum, like it was surprised, but then there was silence. I didn't see it again."

"Maybe it *was* just a raccoon or possum. What makes you think it was a person?"

"It wasn't an animal," she says. "It was tall, and had a human shape. It went by in a flash. And then it was gone."

"Well, I'm glad you didn't go outside to check it out. Maybe we should call the police."

"Maybe." She prods the meat with her fork. "It's a little after the fact. If it happens again, I will."

"I'll stay over tonight. That is," he says with a grin, "if you don't mind."

Lorelei doesn't mind, not at all. The nights he goes home, she finds more and more that she misses him terribly. Sometimes she doesn't want him to go home again, ever. "I have dessert," she says.

"Fruit again?" he sighs. "Nothing decadent?"

"Just me," she says, rising to clear the table. "Oh. And flan."

He stands up to help her, and surprises her with a kiss. "Decadent," he murmurs into her neck as she balances plates in both hands, happily helpless when he cups his hands over her breasts.

"Later," she promises. "After dessert."

"You're the dessert," he says, but greedily digs into the flan she puts before him. He scrapes the last trace of it from his dish, takes a sip of espresso, sighs and says, "You've mastered the best part of any meal."

Lorelei is pleased. At last, she has perfected her flan after many trials and errors, and has discovered Café Bustelo.

Before they pursue their passion, Juan reaches into his jeans pocket for the paper crammed into it, and smooths out its wrinkles. "Ready for the test results?"

She slides her chair closer to see what is written there.

"Okay, here we go," he says. "The results show 46 ppm of magnesium, which is the same as other mineral waters. But this is usually removed from bottled waters through reverse osmosis. And city water counteracts magnesium when fluoride is added, so you're not going to see a high magnesium count there."

Lorelei has forgotten most of her high school science. "So, that means the magnesium is still in the water from my well?"

"Right. And—this is interesting—there are 14.4 picoCuries of radium per liter, plus or minus 6.4."

"Is that a lot?"

"It is high, but well within the range of safety. Still, that's unusual."

She doesn't know how to phrase her next question, but decides it has to be asked. "Would...would all this have anything to do with...the, uh, change in my appearance?" She puts her hand on her throat, now tight and smooth where it was once loose and wrinkly. "Radium and magnesium might be why all this looks better?"

He takes her hand and kisses its palm. "You know," he says, "I don't really notice those things. All I see is who you are."

"That's a lovely thing to say." She reaches over and ruffles his hair affectionately, surreptitiously looking to check its color. Juan's infrequent exposure to the water hasn't saturated him to the degree that Lorelei has been steeped in it, but there has been a faint smoothing of his sun-induced wrinkles, and strands of ebony have appeared here and there in his silver hair. Never having spent much time before a mirror, Juan hasn't been aware of these slight changes, but his virility has escalated to the point where they are falling asleep later and later these nights.

"I do think the water has changed us both," she says. "It's like we've come to a pause—even a reversal—in aging."

"Listen. I don't know what radium and magnesium might do, but who knows? Maybe they counteract the aging process in some way, but there are a million concoctions on the market that claim to do the same thing. This may be different, or it may not. There's a lot we don't know, and maybe will never know."

"So. It's not dangerous, in other words." She hesitates. "Like if the women in our shop drink it, it's okay?"

"My guess is if it works, for whatever reason, and can't hurt, why not? You're fine. Sharleen is fine. The ladies are fine." He taps the paper lightly. "It's safe to drink, as far as these test results show. I don't think you're liable, if that's what you're worried about. But," he adds, "I'm not a lawyer. I'm just a well-digger."

Lorelei stands to finish clearing the dishes, and Juan joins her at the sink. He's become quite the little helper, vigorously rinsing the dishes until they're almost spotless before putting them into the dishwasher. "You don't have to scour them before they're washed," Lorelei reminds him. He does look cute at the sink, busily splashing away; she finds something oddly appealing about a guy who takes domesticity so seriously. But in his enthusiasm, he creates a mess that she needs to mop up, and the sudden thought occurs to her that the water he's sloshed on the counters and floor can be measured in dollars and cents.

"Sharleen thinks we should sell the water," she says.

"I know. You told me. I thought you had dropped that idea."

"Well, I did. But something has happened to Sharleen," she says, omitting the mention of Sharleen's total immersion experience. "It's like she's switched to this new persona. She's laser-focused on this idea, so much so that she showed up at my door late last night insisting we talk about a business plan. It was like she was on a mission."

She takes a towel and absently wipes the countertop. "What scares me is that I'm starting to think she might have something there. Maybe I should at least listen to her. If there really is something positive going on with the water and it's not harmful, perhaps we should consider doing something more than just give it away."

"All of a sudden you're hopping on the Sharleen train. Is she that convincing?"

"You know, business has gotten better, but our expenses keep going up. Plus, I wouldn't mind making a little extra money to put aside for retirement," Lorelei says. "It couldn't hurt to at least consider the possibilities."

"It's your business," Juan says. "It's your water." He frowns, scrubbing a pot with even more vigor than usual. "I haven't even thought about retirement. I can't afford it, and besides, what would I do? Play golf? Play Bingo?" He laughs. "Oh, I forgot. That's Sharleen's department."

Lorelei goes into the living room and flops onto the couch. "I don't know. There's a lot to absorb. If the water really does have some kind of weird properties, and if they're good, not bad properties, and if it can't hurt you, then why not share its benefits?"

Juan pours two glasses of water and brings them into the room. He hands one to Lorelei and holds the other up to the light. "Let's say, for the sake of argument, that this is water from the mythical fountain of youth. I don't believe in magic, but I do believe in science. It could be that whatever elements contained in this water do have some beneficial properties, and that this water could be sold, and that there are people who are either gullible enough or smart enough to buy—even invest—in such a so-called miracle."

"And that's a bad thing?" Lorelei takes a good swig from her glass and leans back into the cushion. "Is it any different from someone selling vitamins or sunscreen or...kale? If there's something that improves your well-being in some way, and it costs money to get it, what's wrong with that?"

"Promoting something supposedly miraculous isn't the same thing. There'll be all kinds of testing, not to mention the FDA. How would you handle mass production? Then there's marketing, promotion, sales, plus all the crazy internet noise, pro and con, that you would have to defend or justify or prove. Is it worth it to you?"

With Juan defining what this could entail, she wonders what she was thinking. They would be stepping into a pit of commercialism, negativity, looney-tunes from all walks of life, and allegations that it was just a giant fraud.

"So maybe we should just keep it all to ourselves, then," she says. "You're right. Why create problems?"

"Don't put it on me," Juan says. "This is your decision to make. If you want to sell something you think is too good not to share, maybe even make some money on it, that's your right. But my feeling is, this could be an invitation to trouble. I hope you'll examine all sides of this venture, and not let Sharleen's Amazing Conversion sway you in a direction you may regret in the end."

Later, after a deep soak in the tub, after playful love among the bubbles, after they stagger to her bed and dissolve into each other, Lorelei is drifting off to sleep in Juan's arms when she is jolted awake by Juan's harsh whisper, "There's something outside." She clutches the sheet around her while Juan peers through the blinds.

"I see it," he says. "I see its shadow." He scrambles out of bed.

"Don't go," she pleads. "Call the police."

"I want to see what's up first," he says. "It's probably nothing."

"I'll go with you."

"No. Stay here. Lock the door." He pulls on his jeans, grabs his flashlight and one of his sneakers, and strides through the house. She hears the front door open and shut.

Then, silence.

WINONA

Juan is staying at Lorelei's tonight. I caught glimpses of him through the kitchen window. He was looking pretty intense, so I scooted up beneath the window to have a listen—not as easy as it was before, when my hearing was so sharp I could hear the slither of a snake at 50 yards. Now I have to strain to hear voices on the other side of a wall, when once they'd be clear as wind chimes in a storm. But, I am happy to report, my hearing isn't completely shot. When I press my ear to the ground I can still hear the flow of the spring deep in the earth, attuned to the beat of my heart, as if my blood and the spring are one.

Juan and Lorelei are having some sort of disagreement. I hear words that strike fear and anger in me: "sell the water." It's repeated in variation several times, along with other references to "business plan," and, even more frightening, "Sharleen." This Sharleen must the Blondie who passed out in the casino that night. If I have to deal with that wackadoo as well, it's double trouble.

The light goes out in the kitchen, and they go into the living room, where their conversation is lost to me. Soon they head into the bedroom, but that damn bougainvillea beneath the window keeps me from getting close enough to hear what they're saying, much less doing. I'm sure it's something I haven't done since my last boyfriend lost a heap in the casino and went back to Minnesota. Just as well. I haven't been in the mood.

No sense in hanging around here. They're in for the night, and this is all too depressing. Besides, there's a possum giving me the evil eye, and I'm not up to grabbing him and tossing him over the hedge. Nasty oversized rat. I scramble away, carelessly in the open, where the moon throws my shadow on the lawn.

I hear the door slam. It's Juan, striding toward me, barefoot, bare-chested, clutching a flashlight in one hand and some big object he's wielding in a threatening manner in the other. As he gets closer, I see it's a shoe.

I could outrun him, even now, but I stop, curious. There's something about his stride that reminds me of someone, a memory that flickers on the edge of consciousness. I hold my ground until he's right in front of me, waving the shoe, blinding me with the brightness of his flashlight.

I have to laugh. "Don't shoe!" I call, raising my hands.

He slides the light up and down, sees I'm a woman and seems to relax. "I'm not shooting anyone. It's a sneaker." Regretting that confession, he adds, "Someone inside is calling the police." I know he's bluffing, and can't resist another chuckle. He raises the flashlight again and stares at me in shock. "What the hell? The casino manager! What are you doing here?"

I figure the lost cat story won't fly, so I just shrug. There's no way I'm telling him the truth.

"Did you follow us?" he demands. I can see Juan's face in the moonlight; his amber eyes lock on mine. There's that tingle again, and I sense that he feels it, too. "What do you want?" His voice is hushed now. "Why are you here?"

I know why I'm here, but something else is drawing me.

It's Juan. And not just because I'm sure I could seduce him, as I did all the others, giving me access to the water. It's something else.

Those eyes. That walk. I've seen them before. Or have I? These days, given my recent water deprivation, I don't trust my own memory.

And then, as if on cue, the well pump kicks on with a loud humming sound, and we both turn in its direction. "You have well water," I say, hoping to distract him from the fact that I'm trespassing on private property. But I stupidly don't leave it at that, and add, "It's the best water there is."

Juan turns and looks at me with narrowed eyes. "So," he says. "*That's* why you're here."

"What?" I'm trapped. He knows. But how could he? There's no way he could figure out who I am, or why I'd be looking for the spring.

"Yeah. You shop at Ladybug Lingerie, right?"

"What?"

"Don't play innocent with me. *Ladybug.* Where you buy your fancy underwear. It's not enough to drink it free from the bottle in the shop. You want to buy it, they won't sell it, so you try and steal it from the source." He points to the pump. "And how did you figure you're going to do that? Break into the house?"

My thoughts—at least in passing—exactly. But I still have no idea what he's talking about. "I don't shop for underwear," I say, not adding that I don't *wear* underwear, fancy or not. What's he talking about—a bottle? Of water? *My* water, from the well? I need clarification. "This water is in an underwear store?"

"Like you don't know." He frowns and shines the flashlight right in my eyes again. "You tell your pals who shop at Ladybug to stay the hell away from here. And if I ever see you here again, you'll be in the slammer before you can say Bingo."

"I never say 'Bingo.'" I raise myself to my full six feet, minus the boots that I ditched earlier, the better to prowl around. "I'm the manager." I snatch the flashlight from his hand and shine it in his face. He throws an arm up to block the light. I lower it, but his face is clear in the moonlight. His eyes shine like panther eyes, luminescent in the night. I lean closer and something happens between us, as if we shared a bolt of lightning.

The back yard, with its rat-tailed possum, peeling melaleuca, stunted palm trees, tipped-over garbage cans, and humming pump, disappears, and I am peering out of a tangled jungle on the edge of a beach, watching as a Spaniard crawls through the sand, wounded in a hail of arrows. I creep toward him with my shell cup. He drinks. And then he's gone, dragged back to his ship by his men. Taking my shell cup with him.

The vision vanishes, and I am once again in the yard, with the possum, the palms, the humming pump—and Juan. I see him differently now. Not just as a possible conquest to lead me to the water. There's more to him than that. Somehow I sense that he has traveled through time—in spirit, if not in the flesh.

"I know you," I say.

Juan shakes his head. "Just stay away," he orders. He turns abruptly and strides back to the house.

I know that stride. I know those eyes. Now I know who Juan is.

TEN

"What was that all about?" Lorelei asks when Juan returns. His face is pale and he seems distracted. "Who were you talking to?"

"You won't believe this, but—remember the casino manager? That Indian woman who called me to come get you and Sharleen during your drunken girls' night out?" He throws his sneaker in the direction of its mate.

"I was not drunk," Lorelei protests, although her recollection of the night's events is fuzzy. "I was just a little tipsy."

"Whatever." He steps out of his jeans and gets into bed. "Anyway, it was the casino manager. Who, apparently, shops in your store."

"What makes you say that?" Lorelei tries to reconstruct what the woman looked like. She has a vague recollection of someone tall, strong, and bossy.

"How else would she know about your water? That's what I think she was doing here, snooping around your well."

"I'm calling the police." She reaches for the phone, but Juan waves her off.

"She's gone. I think she took my warning seriously not to come back." He leans against the pillow and stares at the ceiling. "I knew Sharleen's crazy ideas about selling the water would come to no good. Now we have a water stalker."

Lorelei doesn't remember the woman, but wonders if she's a customer who Sharleen helped and, big mouth that she is, shared the secret of the water with. She snuggles down under the covers and plays back the scenario that led to this intrusion. Maybe selling the water is a bad idea. But then, it might help. Could Sharleen be on to something? Or would it just be asking for more trouble, like the stalker? She drifts off, still arguing to herself, lulled to sleep by Juan's soft snore, a reassuring confirmation that he'll be there for her, whatever her decision.

• • •

¡Corral! ¡Corral!

She is startled awake by Juan's yell, and shakes him to wake him up. He rolls over, wide-eyed. "You're doing it again," she tells him. "Another nightmare."

Juan seems dazed. He flails his arms over his head, then reaches down and grabs his thigh.

"What is it? What's wrong?" Lorelei reaches out and is roughly pushed aside. Juan looks around wildly, then fixates on Lorelei's shocked face.

"Who are you?" He grabs her shoulders and glares at her.

Terrified, Lorelei tears herself away and jumps out of bed. "What's wrong with you?" she says, backing away from him. "You're scaring me."

Juan shakes his head, then rubs his hands through his hair. It sticks out in wild patches like a punk rocker's hairdo, wet with sweat. "Ay ay ay," he mutters. "What a dream." He looks up and shakes his head again. "I'm sorry."

"You should be. You were acting like a wild man." Juan looks so contrite that she takes his hand and strokes it. "What was that all about?"

"Give me a minute." He takes several deep breaths.

"Was it that same dream you had before?" she asks.

He nods. "Only this was different. Worse." He closes his eyes to replay the dream. "I'm running. Through sand. Hard to run. Savages chasing me. Shooting arrows." He shudders. "I'm hit. In the thigh." He looks down at his leg, seemingly surprised that it's whole. "I fall, trying to run, but I can't. I'm crawling in the sand, trying to reach...I don't know. A ship. Offshore."

"Maybe you've seen too many Pirates of the Caribbean movies."

He doesn't laugh. "I'm crawling, terrible pain, struggling through that damn sand. And then I see..." He pauses, blinking. "I see..."

"What? What is it?"

"Beyond the sand, in the jungle...a woman, looking at me. She comes to where I am. Gives me water from...from a shell." He closes his eyes, struggling to re-create the image. "It's like...I've seen her before."

"Her?" Lorelei feels the jagged edge of jealousy and pulls away. "What Her?"

Juan shakes his head, dispelling the image. He draws her to him and smiles for the first time. "It's just a dream. She's my dream girl."

Lorelei puts her arms around him. He's hot and sweaty, and she doesn't mind that. His tense body stirs something in her that goes beyond sympathy. "I thought I was your dream girl," she murmurs, running her hand across his chest, damp as a teddy bear left out in the rain. She nestles deeper into his arms, but he extricates himself before things get too involved.

"I need a shower," he says. "Don't go anywhere."

Lorelei has dozed off by the time Juan returns, but he looks serious, not romantic, when he awakens her.

"I don't know if it was the dream," he says, "or if the dream somehow brought back what we were talking about the other day." He pauses. "You know, about the water being from the fountain of youth."

127

"You mean, the water you just showered in," she says, teasing.

"Well, yeah. But whatever the reason, it triggered the memory of this half-forgotten story I heard when I was a kid."

Lorelei, half-asleep, looks at him quizzically. "What?" she says with a yawn.

He lies down next to her and crosses his hands behind his head. "You know those stories that get handed down from generation to generation until they've become some kind of legend and you don't know if they're true or not but they're probably not?"

Lorelei knows about family stories. She's got some of her own.

"Well, my family's got this crazy story that's been handed down for a long time."

"How long?"

"Like...500 years." He shrugs his shoulders at her skeptical look. "I know, I know. I never really believed my dad when he told me—he was always making up stuff—so I kind of laughed it off and forgot about it."

"What's the story?"

Juan rubs his temples as if he's squeezing his brain for memories. "My father's name was Juan, too. He was named after his father, who was named after his father, and pretty much all the way back to the First Juan."

"Who's that?"

He hesitates. "Juan Ponce de Leon."

"You're kidding."

"I'm just telling you what I was told."

Lorelei raises her eyebrows. "Sure," she says with a little smile. "Do go on."

"Anyway, the story goes that Ponce heard that in the New World there was a spring that bubbled out from a limestone cave. All around it were trees hung with golden fruit harvested by beautiful maidens, and the waters restored life."

"Oranges," Lorelei surmises, adding, "and beautiful maidens. Can't forget the beautiful maidens."

"Right," Juan says with a quick grin. "So here's a 53-year-old guy going through a major mid-life crisis. He hears about this spring that can give him everything he wants: youth, gold, maidens. He becomes obsessed. He has to find that spring. He talks the King of Spain into giving him three ships, that there's gold to be found in the New World and heathens to be converted. He sails from Puerto Rico in 1513 and hits land that he names La Florida for all the flowers he sees."

"Good thing he didn't see the huge roaches first."

Juan nods in agreement. "But flowers and roaches are all that he sees—no gold, no fountain, not even a maiden. This is Timucuan territory. He seeks out the Chief, and on a path, sees the Chief's entourage. He blocks their way and asks if he and his men could drink from this magical spring. Stupid question, of course. This enrages the Chief, who becomes livid, and orders his bodyguards to kill him."

"And did they?" Lorelei asks, trying to remember the story of Ponce de Leon from her high school history class.

"No. He escaped somehow. But he still believed there was a fountain of youth. He went back years later, this time to the west coast of Florida, where he was shot with a poisoned arrow, courtesy of the Calusa tribe, and died after his ship reached Cuba."

"So...what does that have to do with your family?"

"Supposedly, after he escaped from the Timucuans, he returned to his family in Puerto Rico, and he and his wife had another kid. A son, Luis. Who was the ancestor of all the other Juans—right down to me."

"So, Luis was a blip in the Juan line, then."

"Yeah. I guess Luis named his own son Juan, and then it was all Juan from then on."

He suddenly becomes silent. He closes his eyes and seems to go somewhere else.

"What is it?"

"That woman," Juan says. "Her eyes. A strange color, barely blue. The color of water."

"You mean the woman in your dream?"

"Yes. But also..." He pauses. "No. It can't be."

"What can't be?" Juan's dazed look frightens her.

He waves away whatever it is. "Nothing. Just a figment of my wild imagination."

"Oh," Lorelei says, because anything else would seem jealous. And how could she be jealous of someone in a dream?

"Dreams. Stories. All made up," he says reassuringly.

"Does anyone else in your family know the story?"

"I don't have family here; I left a few behind in Cuba, but they've all died. I do have relatives in Puerto Rico who might know. They claim to be descended from Ponce de Leon." He pauses in thought. "Maybe I should contact them. If nothing else, it would be a good thing to get in touch with them. Maybe they know something I don't know."

"Like maybe who your dream girl is?"

Juan reaches out and folds her into his arms. He smells like fresh-cut pinewood after a rain; his shower-damp hair brushes her face like soft tinsel, and she wraps herself tightly around him as if to smother his thoughts, vanquish his dreams, dispel any desire for a mysterious woman with eyes the color of water.

ELEVEN

"Well, now that you've had time to think about it, whaddaya think?" Sharleen is actually wearing a suit today—a suit that plunges deeply enough to display the latest VaVoom confection (pushup #3247, midnight black), indicating that Sharleen's attempts at business propriety would inevitably be trumped by her inner tramp. She opens a shiny-new leather briefcase and retrieves a clutch of papers. "Coach," she announces at Lorelei's raised-eyebrow reaction to the briefcase. "Gotta stay classy."

Lorelei is more amazed by the array of papers that Sharleen is spreading out on the table than she is by the classy briefcase. The papers actually look organized, something Sharleen is not. "When did you learn to type?" she asks Sharleen.

"Manager at Staples helped me," Sharleen says with a wink, and Lorelei guesses that it wasn't out of the goodness of his heart. "We had a kinda after-hours confab," she says. "I talked, he typed. I gave him ideas—great ideas, I will say—and he organized them into this business plan. Then he did this whole chart thing, to show how it can grow." She extracts it from the pile and admires it. "In color, too. No extra charge." She winks again.

"And what do you propose to do with all this?" Lorelei waves her hand over the array of papers. "And who is this Staples guy, anyway? What did you tell him, and what's he going to do with all this information?" Lorelei is surprised at her own reaction to the exposure of what has been until now undercover. "Suppose he tells everyone?"

"Nah. He's not saying anything. I made him promise, and he swore The Secret Oath of Staples."

"The what?"

"The Secret Oath of Staples. They call it the S.O.S. It's the oath all the people who work there have to take once they're hired. Because they handle very personal stuff, private business deals, like that. So they have to swear they'll never divulge anything they learn."

"That's bullshit."

"Oooo. Listen to you!" Sharleen brings her hands to her cheeks in mock horror.

Lorelei shuffles through the papers and plucks out what appears to be a business plan of sorts. "So," she says, scanning it briefly, "what you want to do is separate the lingerie sales from the sale of the water. Like it's two different entities." She focuses on one section and adds, "But they're both sold within the shop itself." She looks up. "What this means is that the water could dominate sales and the lingerie will go by the wayside."

"No, no," Sharleen protests. "If it really gets that big, and we're really raking it in from the water, well then, we can..." Her face puckers in thought. "...open a water bar! Next door!" She grins, obviously pleased at her own creativity. "I need to put that in the plan." She grabs the paper away from Lorelei to scribble something in the margin. "Have to have him re-type that." She finishes with a flourish. "Brilliant!"

This is getting out of hand. "No. Bad idea," Lorelei says. "Remember the casino manager? The one who practically had you arrested when you went bonkers in Bingo?"

Sharleen looks baffled. "Casino manager?"

"Yes. Tall, pushy, made me call Juan to take us home. The Indian woman."

"Oh yeah. I don't remember much about her. I was a little…indisposed."

"Well, Juan caught her sneaking around my house last night. Looking for my well. For the water." Lorelei pauses before exploding, "She's a customer! Of the shop! Who wanted to figure out how to get our water from the source!" She points an accusing finger at Sharleen. "She's your customer, isn't she? And you told her about the water, and where it was." Lorelei surprises herself with her sudden fury. "We've opened up a can of worms!"

Sharleen's face goes blank. "What are you talking about?"

"Your customer! Tall. Six feet maybe." Lorelei tries to remember details. "Dark hair. Boots. Very strong."

"What?" Sharleen backs away. "Don't you think I'd remember an Indian customer who's six feet tall?"

Lorelei goes and gets herself a cup of water from the bottle. "Then who is she? What was she doing in my yard?" She sips the water, lost in thought.

Relieved that the accusation has ended, Sharleen leaps back into sales mode. "So let's talk about the logistics of this. We need to find a bottler. Even if we cornered the market on empty Crystal Creek bottles, Juan can't lug enough bottles to the store to keep up with demand…"

"Okay," Lorelei interrupts, "this is not happening." She disregards Sharleen's look of dismay, and continues. "This is Ladybug *Lingerie*. If…*if* we decide to distribute the water, it will be as a side perk, not as the main attraction. This has to be low-key, not blown up to the mammoth operation you would like to see."

"But…"

"Bear in mind," Lorelei says, hoisting her cup, "this is *my* water from *my* well and if I so choose, I can stop delivery tomorrow. And," she adds deliberately, "keep it all to myself."

"I knew it." Sharleen begins cramming the papers back into the briefcase. "Okay. You win. I give up. You're the boss, you own the well, I'm just a lowly peeyan."

"Peon," Lorelei corrects her.

Sharleen glares at her. "You are such a control freak. I come in here with some pretty damn good ideas and because they're not yours, you just squash me like a bug." She shuts the briefcase with a click, and gathers it to her bosom. "I'm your partner, not your sidekick."

She exits the shop in a huff, pushing her way past the lineup of women who have been waiting for the door to open. Lorelei can see them through the door; some have brought their workout water bottles with them, apparently in the faint hope they can cajole her into letting them take water home. They are a persistent bunch.

She flashes ten fingers at the group and mouths "ten minutes." She needs more than ten minutes to sort out her feelings. Maybe Sharleen is right. Lorelei *had* thought of her as more of a sidekick than a partner: Ethel to her Lucy, Shirley to her Laverne. This new persona of Sharleen's is disorienting.

The crowd is getting impatient. A woman raps on the glass with turquoise fingernails. Lorelei sighs. Let the games begin.

She heads for the door and stops short when she sees a stray paper from Sharleen's presentation lying on the floor. She bends over to pick it up, ignoring the persistent tapping of fingernails on glass. It's a computer rendering of what looks like a label: ocean blue background, with "Spring Chicken" in a bright yellow cartoon-y typeface. Beneath it, a chicken. A saucy chicken who wears a feathered hat, a fancy bra, and funky sandals on her tiny chicken feet.

Spring Chicken.

Not bad.

Maybe Sharleen is on to something after all.

•   •   •

"Where did you get the chicken from?" Lorelei asks, handing Sharleen the chicken label she had found on the shop's floor. They are sitting on the rumpled couch in Sharleen's living room after clearing away the explosion of fashion magazines, Cheetos bags, bra thrown off during some previous evening's activities, and the remains of joints in an ashtray. Lorelei is here after an exhausting day at the shop where she worked alone after Sharleen walked out.

"It's a stock photo." Sharleen's in the waning stage of sulking, miffed but coming around after Lorelei apologized. "We just dressed her up on the computer at Staples."

"I like it," Lorelei says, not mentioning that she would dress the chicken a little less trashy, but that's a matter of taste. She shuffles through the pile of papers Sharleen has spread out on the coffee table and plucks out Sharleen's version of a business plan. "You've given this a lot of thought." She smooths out the paper, wrinkled from being angrily crammed into Sharleen's briefcase as she stormed out of the shop. "You do make a case for sharing something that's clearly beneficial. Both for us and for our customers."

Sharleen breaks out into her first smile of the day.

"However." Sharleen's smile dims at the word. "We want our primary purpose to be selling lingerie, not water," Lorelei says. "So let's talk about how we can share the water with our good customers, and have it benefit our sales. I think there's a way to do that."

Sharleen focuses on excavating some Cheetos bits embedded in the couch upholstery. "What?" she says, not looking at Lorelei. She flicks at the bright orange nuggets with an equally orange fingernail.

"If we give away a bottle with each $300 worth of merchandise—which they don't have to buy all at once—then that would rightly put the focus on our merchandise, and not the water."

"Why give it away?" Sharleen protests. "They'll pay for it! Ruby paid without blinking."

"Ruby's an idiot. Besides, it's not fair to the customers who can't afford to do that."

"Who says it has to be fair? Youth and beauty are commodities! They're bought and sold all the time."

"There are too many negatives and complications," Lorelei says, silently taken aback at Sharleen's expanded vocabulary. "This way, if we just give it as a gift as a sales promotion like cosmetic companies do, with no magical promises, then it's up to the customer to take advantage of it or not."

"We're giving it *away*." Sharleen silently picks away at her Cheetos project, adding bits to a little pile she's accumulating on the coffee table. Several minutes pass. Lorelei wonders what's going on in her head, and, for lack of anything to do, straightens up the coffee table, lines up magazines, folds the empty Cheetos bag into a crinkly square.

Sharleen breaks the silence in a small voice. "Well, can we keep my Spring Chicken label? Put it on the bottles we give away?"

"Of course," Lorelei says, relieved. "It's a great label. It's a creative, terrific label and a great great name for the water." She smiles at Sharleen—not a smile of triumph, but a smile of compromise. Isn't it nice when partners can agree?

· · · ·

"Why *not* put an ad in the paper?" Sharleen demands. "What good is a promotion if you can't promote it?" She snaps a paper with the proposed ad she and Staples guy have designed. "It's tiny! Three columns, 5 inches, only $1200. Worth every penny!"

"It's not just the money," Lorelei says, placing the latest box of arrivals from VaVoom on a countertop. "I've told you—we need to keep it low-key, for our present customers only. A discreet little sign near the cash register, that's it."

"I'm not even asking that it be in color," Sharleen says, although the ad design she's waving in the air has the chicken, festively dressed in a multi-colored outfit, "Spring Chicken" in neon yellow on a bright blue background along with the ad copy. Sharleen reads it out loud, as if hearing it will convince Lorelei that the ad would be indeed compelling to *Miami Herald* readers.

"SPECIAL PROMOTION!!! LADYBUG LINGERIE!!! Special water for our special customers (our loyal customers know what we're talking about!) For every $300 you spend on our exquisite sexy lingerie, you can take home a five-gallon bottle of our own Spring Chicken water. FREE!!! Surprise your guy – he'll love how you look in Ladybug!"

Lorelei is not impressed.

"I won't even go into how tacky that is," she says. "A simple little sign that tells about the promotion will be sufficient. Just word of mouth has brought in too many women who are here because they think it's some kind of Lourdes. I truly would prefer a customer who appreciates our merchandise for what it is, even if they only buy a $35 bra. I don't want to encourage $300 purchases so they can lug home a bottle of water that could very well be just that: a bottle of water."

"If those women hadn't seen some kind of difference, they wouldn't be pounding on our door at 8 a.m."

"We are not advertising something that has no proven effect."

"I'm proof! You're proof! They want what we've got!"

"End of discussion." Lorelei turns her attention to the VaVoom box and slices it open to reveal a flurry of lace teddies in sherbet shades: tangerine, strawberry, banana, cherry. She no longer craves the cream of the crop of each new shipment, having more than her closet will hold. But this new arrival has whetted her appetite, and she plucks a strawberry bit of fluff from the assortment for herself. She knows Juan will appreciate her choice when she sees him tonight.

•   •   •

Juan is feeding the fish when she arrives at his place. They split their time between houses, but now she feels more at home at Juan's than at her own. She likes being with him in his world. Peaceful and cozy, Juan's house is a haven of soft lights, cushy furniture and burbling aquariums. Her décor is more practical than aesthetic, neat and tidy as a dollhouse. Her energy goes into the shop, which she updates periodically and keeps in tiptop shape. Her house is not a home.

She bought it when Melaleuca Lakes was a new subdivision, a straight shot to her shop over what was then an empty highway unencumbered by traffic, strip malls, and high-rise condos. Inertia has kept her there, despite the surrounding area's evolution into urban chaos. She considers it just fine for her purposes: affordable, convenient, a roof over her head, a no-brainer in upkeep. She barely noticed as Melaleuca Lakes slid downhill, never recovering from the recession as other neighborhoods had. Her solution for the deterioration of the house next door and its perpetual "For Sale" sign was to plant fast-growing bushes that concealed the sight of it. The Sale sign had been up so long it had become part of the scenery, almost decorative as vines wrapped around it like a gift from the jungle.

"Dinner!" she calls, hefting the carton that contains the bean soup she made at home, a steak for the grill—and a Ladybug bag with the strawberry teddy. She sets it on the counter and waves the Ladybug bag in Juan's direction. "I have a surprise for dessert," she says, shaking the bag provocatively.

"Great." Juan seems distracted, tossing fish food into the tanks with less care than he usually takes with his little jewels, who zip among the flakes in piscatorial pursuit. "There's room in the fridge."

"It's not a cold dessert," Lorelei says. "Actually, it's pretty hot." She pulls the teddy out by one lacy shoulder strap and holds it up to her body.

Juan looks up and smiles in appreciation. It's hardly the enthusiastic response she was hoping for. She tosses the teddy onto the couch and goes about the task of getting dinner ready. First she's got to clear the dining table of all those papers, unusual for

Juan, whose idea of a messy house is shoes left on the floor or a couple of days-worth of newspapers left on the counter.

She's organizing the papers into a pile when she realizes they are printouts of articles. Curious, she begins to read one from the *New York Times*: "In Andalusia, On the Trail of Inherited Memories." She stops short at a passage:

"There are scientific studies exploring whether the history of our ancestors is somehow a part of us, inherited in unexpected ways through a vast chemical network in our cells that controls genes, switching them on and off. At the heart of the field, known as epigenetics, is the notion that genes have memory and that the lives of our grandparents—what they breathed, saw and ate—can directly affect us decades later."

Another article catches her eye, this one from Earthpages.org: "Deep DNA Memory Theories: Can We Remember Our Ancestors' Lives?" She skims down until she sees:

"... is it possible that the DNA helix holds some of the important memories of our ancestors? Theories that suggest that we can tap into the deep nature of DNA to uncover ancient memories are not new. In the 1960s, some psychological researchers claimed that there may be keys that unlock our DNA, revealing experiences of generations of our relatives who lived long before our present time."

She takes the stack to the couch and begins leafing through the various articles. There are references to the film, "The Matrix" and the TV series "Russian Doll"; experiments with rats at Emory University; a video game, "Assassin's Creed"; Jung's theory of the collective unconscious; past life regression.

"I meant to clean that up before you got here." Juan's voice startles her. He reaches over to grab the stack of articles. "I'll take those," he says, but she won't give them up.

"What is all this?" she asks. "When did you get so interested in DNA and memory?"

"I guess I'm curious." He reaches down and scoops up a *Discover* magazine that has escaped and fallen on the floor. Turning to an article he had marked with a Post-it, he reads the title to her: "Grandma's Experiences Leave a Mark on Your Genes."

Lorelei wonders if the reason she takes her temperature when she isn't sick is a genetic remnant of the time her grandmother almost died from the 1918 flu pandemic.

"It's an intriguing theory," he says, "but there's no hard evidence that genetic information can carry memories. Still, a part of me believes there's a world we don't know or understand—at least yet." He shrugs. "What can I say? I'm a frustrated scientist."

She eyes him skeptically. "I think it's more than just your curiosity. This sudden interest in genetic memory is really connected to that family legend you told me about the other night, isn't it?"

He taps the articles into a neat stack and places them on the table. "I've been giving this a lot of thought, so I decided to do some research. I can't explain it, but I felt that the dream I had— you know, that dream, where I was wounded and escaping from Indians—was in some way connected to the crazy story my father told me."

"So you think it has something to do with those family Juans that go back to..." She's suddenly fearful of saying the name "Ponce," as if it would crystallize fantasy into reality, take them into a scary new realm she's not willing to explore.

Juan gets up and peers into an aquarium, adjusts a filter, fiddles with something else. Then, as if speaking to the fish rather than her, says, "There's something else."

The fish tanks burble away, the sound of a kid blowing bubbles in his soda through a straw.

"That Indian woman from the casino?" he begins. "The one creeping around your house the other night?"

"You shooed her away." Lorelei's heart is beating fast. "She won't be back, right?"

He turns to face her. He looks perplexed, as if he's stumbled into an unfamiliar place. "I don't know."

"Should we call the police?" Lorelei gropes for a solution to this trespassing problem, something solid, logical, do-able. "Set up a camera?"

"No, no. It's not that." Juan rubs his eyes with the heels of his hands, as if to erase something. "She's the woman in my dream."

"She's *what?*"

He hesitates. "When I caught her in your yard, I suddenly had this weird, almost déjà vu feeling when she stared at me. And then later, during my dream, the woman who gave me a drink from her shell was Indian. With the same color eyes as the woman in your yard."

"How could you tell in the dark?"

"It was hard, even with the flashlight. But when I shined the light on her face, her eyes kind of glowed. Blue-ish. Like water."

"You looked into her eyes?" He can't look into another woman's eyes, just hers, no one else's, his amber eyes are meant for Lorelei's only. And right now she feels like poking them out.

"What were you doing out there anyway? Seducing the casino lady?"

"Oh come on. You know better than that."

If she were standing, she'd stomp her foot like some petulant kid. She knows she's behaving like a jealous girlfriend, but that's what she is: a jealous girlfriend. "What am I supposed to think? You tell me you're dreaming about this person, and now you tell me you've been looking into her eyes, and since when are you waxing so poetic about eyes that aren't even mine?" Where is this coming from? She sounds like an idiot. But she can't help it. This jealousy thing is all new to her.

"I don't understand any of this," he says. "These images from my dreams keep coming to me, more and more lately. It all started the night I came to the casino to take you and Sharleen home."

Lorelei doesn't remember much of that event, but one thing surfaces: the way Juan looked at the Indian woman as they were leaving the casino. It was just a flash, but there must have been something about that instant that registered in Lorelei's brain.

"I had the same weird feeling then..."

"I know," Lorelei interrupts. "When you looked into her eyes."

Juan's quick intake of breath confirms it. "It was nothing. I was so involved with getting you two into my truck that I didn't think about it. It was only later that it crossed my mind, but I dismissed it as just one of many crazy moments in a very crazy night." He shakes his head in recollection. "I really forgot about it. And then...the night I caught her in your yard, it happened again."

"You didn't tell me."

"I didn't tell you because I didn't realize it myself," he says. "Not until I had that dream later. Even then, I didn't connect the two things. It's like a chemistry experiment, when you have something in one beaker, and something else in another, and then you pour them together and there's some kind of catalyst thing going on and boom, you've created something altogether new."

Oh, now he's getting all scientific on her. But she only says, "An 'aha' moment."

"Right. Like, Aha, this woman in your yard is the same one in my dream. And...what's that all about?"

That's what Lorelei would like to know.

WINONA

There are places where my appearance attracts no more than a brief sideways glance, if that. Lincoln Road on Miami Beach is one of them, and this is where I shop, when I shop. A fountain-studded, palm-tree shaded pedestrian mall that dead-ends at the public beach, it's several blocks of assorted shops and outdoor bars and restaurants crammed with sunburned tourists, real-and-semi celebrities, and fresh young poseurs who hope, not just to see and be seen, but to be discovered. Here, I'm just another tattooed six-foot-tall woman (six-four in my boots, don't forget)—possibly a wanna-be model, possibly a glamorous transvestite—looking for something tastefully sequined at Forever 21 for my nights in the casino, trying on those great fringed boots in the window at Steve Madden, then taking a break at an outdoor cafe with a frosty root beer—the only beverage I drink besides water.

The first time I tasted root beer was, oh, around 1850 or so, in the kitchen of the burly farmer who boiled sassafras into what he called a "tea" and successfully seduced me, unaware that it was not so much the drink he concocted as the little waterfall behind his house that worked for me. But he was a charmer, so I drink an A&W toast to him as I sit beneath an umbrella and watch the parade go by. No one gives me a glance.

Being gawked at doesn't bother me, although I prefer to avoid staid suburbia where women my height and, shall we say, formidable appearance do tend to attract attention. I put Miracle Mile, the main street of Coral Gables, in the Suburbia category, even though it's not your usual cookie-cutter shopping mall. Neither a miracle nor a mile—it's only a half-mile long—it was given its hyperbolic name in the '40s, and is lined with businesses from upscale shops that have been there for generations, to downscale chain restaurants. It caters to a wide demographic, from Latina socialites to soccer moms, most of whom would give me not just a second glance, but a wide-eyed stare.

Today I brace myself for my excursion to Miracle Mile, home of Ladybug Lingerie. I dress my most conservative self—a difficult endeavor, but there's no need to attract even more attention than I already do. I'll tell you, of all the things I've done in my quest for the spring, wearing a pantsuit and flats is one of the most humiliating. That, and pulling my hair into a ponytail so it doesn't look so wild and Cher-ish. I've often been compared to her in appearance ("Oh look, Wilbur, isn't that Cher over there?"), but, unlike Cher, I've maintained the same youthfulness throughout the years without any surgical help. And I intend to stay that way. Which is why I'm here at Ladybug Lingerie, the object of startled looks as I open the door.

What is wrong with these people? Haven't they seen a tall woman before? It's not like I'm dressed inappropriately for this place. Most of the women here have on pants, and, not to be judgmental or anything, some of them look pretty shabby compared to me, with their jeans and yoga pants and flip-flops. It wasn't easy finding this pantsuit in my size, but it's amazing what Goodwill has on their racks.

There is one thing that does make me stand out from this crowd. I'm Native American. Not many of us do our shopping in Coral Gables.

Hey, there's that little blonde firecracker I encountered at the casino, so drunk I had to carry her from Bingo to my office. What was her name? Sharleen. Lorelei's friend—is that why she's in her shop? Wonder if she remembers being bonked on the head as we went through the door. Probably doesn't recall anything, although the look on her face now is registering recognition.

So she does remember me, despite my mundane attire. She's making agitated faces at Lorelei, who is busy with a customer and hasn't noticed me. Until now.

Lorelei's mouth drops, and she stands so motionless that I think she's gone catatonic. Sharleen, however, quick on those spike-heeled feet, is by my side before Lorelei makes a move. Sharleen seems to have recovered from her initial shock, and, to my surprise, asks if she can help me. Apparently, she works here.

"Just looking," I say. What I don't say is I'm looking for the bottle of water that Juan mentioned the night he caught me prowling.

"Um," Sharleen begins, "this is embarrassing, but—do you remember me?"

Choosing to feign ignorance—no need to complicate matters, although the look I see on Lorelei's face means complications soon to ensue—I say, "No. But you do look familiar."

Sharleen seems relieved at that, and goes into full-speed saleslady. "Just look around, but I will tell you we have some fabulous new pieces that just arrived." She eyes my boob area—unconfined as usual, but firm enough to pass as bra-encased—and guesses: "36-D?" I wouldn't know, since I've never had the need to find out. To avoid any further discussion, I agree. "But," I add, "I'm not looking for a bra. I'm...just looking."

She won't give up. "I know. You want something suitable for lounging. Something silky," she whips an ivory caftan off a nearby hanger, "for those quiet evenings at home."

I have never had a quiet evening at home, and if I did, I wouldn't be wearing anything like that. Or anything at all. I do prefer my native dress, which is undress.

"Just looking," I repeat, and attempt to make my way around her, which is easy, given my size and her lack of same. I sense

145

confrontation in the immediate future, and sure enough, here comes Lorelei.

This lady is cool. Poised. Clearly conscious of customers' attention that is focused on the two of us. But there is blind fury beneath that façade, betrayed by the narrowing of her eyes which are staring so hard into mine that I feel she is boring a hole in my brain.

"If you don't mind," she says, indicating the way with a pointed finger, "I'd like to have a word with you in my office." I'd prefer not to have a word with anyone, but I follow her to the back of the shop, lured by a glimpse of an object of interest next to the doorway: a bottle of water atop a dispenser. Even more interesting are the numerous full bottles lined up along the hall to her office. A treasure trove. Soon to be mine, if all goes well.

"Mind if I have a glass?" I ask as we pass the dispenser. "It's hot outside and I'm really thirsty."

What's she going to say: "No"? She's too much the lady for that, so we pause in our journey while I select a lovely plastic glass from the stack on the adjoining table and pour myself as much as it will hold.

I know at once this is my water. Crystal clear, sweet and smooth, it goes down like liquid silk. "My, that is delicious," I say, and before she can object, I pour myself another glass. After all, most of the women wandering the shop are carrying their own glasses of water, so how could she deny me my own?

I already sense the water's magic as a small but familiar tingle spreads from my belly to my brain. This is why I'm here. To verify what I've suspected. Now I have proof, which calls for a next step, unknown as yet.

Lorelei watches me closely as I drink, staring into my eyes as if she were a lover. "Why don't you bring that into my office?" she says, each word as frosty as a snowman. "We can talk in there."

Without asking, I fill my glass one last time, greedy for as much as I can get. Once inside, she shuts the door. "Now," she says. "What's going on?"

"I don't know what you mean."

"You know what I mean." Her eyes haven't left mine. "Who are you? Why were you sneaking around my yard?" She takes a deep breath. "What's your connection to Juan?"

I couldn't tell her that, even if I were willing. The Juan I encountered the other night was the Juan I glimpsed so many centuries ago. And yet he wasn't. The eyes that met mine were—and weren't—the eyes I met on the path and on the beach. She wants to know who I am. What I want to know is, who is Juan?

So I try to answer her first question: Why was I sneaking around her yard? That's a tough one to answer honestly, so I don't. Instead, I remember what Juan's assumption was when he caught me: that I was looking to steal the water I had heard about at the shop. "I heard you wouldn't sell it," I say as an excuse, "and I guess I'm going through some kind of…" What would she identify with? "…menopausal nuttiness." When I see a flash of recognition, I elaborate. "I just get desperate sometimes. You know. Hot flashes. Can't sleep." What else have I read about, not having fully experienced it myself? "Emotional ups and downs."

Lorelei is unmoved. "And you think stealing my water is your answer?" she accuses. "What makes you think it's a cure-all? It's not magic. It's just got…certain properties that improve your health."

We both know she's lying. Improve your health, my ass. She's looking much younger than she did the night at the casino, although given the circumstances of that night and her inebriated condition, anything would be an improvement.

Then she says something that makes me realize that, felonious as sneaking around someone's yard to steal their water may be, what really seems to be upsetting her is her next accusation. "What are you doing in Juan's dreams?"

"I'm in Juan's dreams?" I don't know what she's talking about.

Apparently, neither does she. She becomes flustered and waves her hand as if she could erase what she said. "Never mind, never mind," she says, shaking her head. "It's just...never mind."

"Listen," I say. "I really came here to see if you would sell me the water I've been hearing about. My symptoms have been giving me so much grief that I'm desperate," I do my best to look pathetic, not easy for me, "so I'll pay anything."

"Sorry, no. It's store policy." She says it in such a way that if I put a gun to her head, I think she'd say the same thing.

I finish up the last of my glass. A drop in the bucket, so to speak, of what I ultimately came for. I need to figure out some other way to get enough to tide me over until I can make a plan about how to get to, if not the source, at least a temporary solution. And then, right on cue, it walks through the office door.

Sharleen. "Hi, guys," she says brightly. "What's going on?"

"I was just leaving," I say. "I was hoping to buy some water, but apparently it's not for sale."

Sharleen blocks the door, ignoring Lorelei's furious head-shake. "Wait! We have a special offer for our customers."

"No we don't," Lorelei says. If looks were knives, Sharleen would be sushi.

"Sure we do." Sharleen's got a message, and she's going to deliver it. "Did you see our sign at the front register?" she asks, not waiting for an answer. "With every $300 worth of merchandise, you get a free bottle of water."

"Sounds like a deal," I say. "Show me the merchandise."

"The special offer is over," Lorelei says, but Sharleen is out the door and I'm right behind her.

Lorelei doesn't want to make a scene in front of all those other customers, so she remains, arms folded, face creased into a frown, in the office doorway. "One bottle. *One*," she calls after us, before she slams the door shut. Exit Lorelei.

I roam the store, tossing negligees, bras, teddies, panties, whatever comes within arms' reach, into Sharleen's waiting hands. She makes several trips to the counter with my bounty, piling everything into a rainbow of fluff. "Let me know when I hit $1200," I tell her. She runs to the cash register and starts totaling up what I've grabbed so far.

"$935.46," she calls. Customers have stopped their strolling to stare. I grab a couple of caftans and add them to the pile. "$1252.35," she says with a giddy grin.

"Four bottles?" I say to confirm this transaction. "I have four bottles' worth of merchandise, right?"

"Right!" Sharleen is ecstatic. Lorelei is not. She has opened the door to her office to see what the commotion is about. She looks apoplectic.

Sharleen can't bag my goodies fast enough, folding each item professionally but quickly, clearly pleased with this sale. I can't wait to get out of here and home safely with my four bottles. For all I care, I could give this fluff stuff to Goodwill. It's only the water that matters.

"I'll drive my car to your back entrance," I say, handing her my credit card. "I'll load everything there."

"Thank you, Miss..." She looks at my card. "Ibi? Winona Ibi?"

"That's me," I say. I never needed a last name until the last century or so, so I picked the Timucuan word for water: ibi. It has a nice ring to it—short, easy to spell, and a palindrome for good measure. I sign with a flourish, and run to my car. I want to collect my booty before Lorelei does something to stop me. But what can she do? It's all legal.

What she does do is stand in the back doorway and fume while I load up my Jeep with, first, four bottles of water—they've called it "Spring Chicken"—and, almost as an afterthought, my bags of lingerie. I have to wonder why the chicken on the label is wearing clothes, but, whatever. As I drive away, I see two figures in my rear view mirror: Sharleen, waving happily. And Lorelei, rigid with fury.

Four bottles. Fine for now. But what will I do forever?

TWELVE

The UPS guy looks so exhausted that Lorelei gets him a cup of water before she signs for the third delivery today. Each delivery has increased the number of boxes he has to carry from his truck, and she tells him to just stack them where he can find room. The earlier shipment, boxes of panties hastily opened, leave puddles of Kool-aid colors spilling across the countertop like the aftermath of kindergarten snack time. Still unfolded and unshelved from the morning's delivery, they are snatched by eager hands—young and flawless, old and mottled—eager, not just for the garments themselves, but for what will accompany their $300 purchases: a five-gallon bottle of water with a chicken on its label. There was no need to advertise; word of mouth has spread the news far and wide.

Sharleen is energized, seeming to gain, rather than lose strength with each heavy bottle she lugs to the back door in order to load up customers' cars with their booty. They wait impatiently in the alleyway for their turn, a parade of Lexuses, BMWs, Mercedes and the occasional Ford or Prius, their owners as anxious for their bottles as a hungry baby would be for his.

"We're gonna run out," Sharleen whispers to Lorelei as she waddles past the office, hugging a bottle. "Call Juan to get that new truckload over pronto. He was supposed to be here by now."

"He's on his way, but he's stuck in traffic."

"If he doesn't get here soon, we'll have a riot on our hands. Look at that," Sharleen says, indicating several restless women with armloads of lingerie waiting in line at the cash register counter. "I have enough for the next six in line, but the rest—I've told them the water will be here any minute, but if it's not, they may just dump their stuff and leave."

"We'll have to give them vouchers if they can't wait for Juan to get here." Lorelei rummages through a drawer. "We can use these gift certificates and write 'Water voucher' at the top. Tell them we'll give them their water when they can come back." Having miscalculated the number of bottles they'd need today, they had left half of those that they had filled last night for Juan to bring later, when they had more room. Lorelei sees another long night ahead, filling bottles, loading up Juan's truck. Who knew this would get so out of hand?

Apparently the word has traveled beyond Coral Gables to the affluent denizens of Miami Beach and points north, judging from the condo parking decals on their cars. Several license plates are from Broward and Palm Beach Counties. A few times in the past week, Lorelei had been on the verge of announcing they're shutting the entire water operation down, but then she had a reality check. Sales have gone through the roof, along with their income from the shop. They can easily cover rent and expenses as well as invest in their retirement—which, given their ages, isn't that far into the future. At one point, before all this happened, the future was a gnawing concern that they rarely discussed. The subject was too scary, their income too little, their hopes for the shop too limited. Now, for the first time since they started the business, they're able to stop worrying.

But Lorelei hasn't stopped worrying about that woman, Winona, and whatever was going on with her and Juan. Despite the ongoing chaos of the shop, her mind would take unexpected detours into moments of obsession: Why did Juan dream about

Winona? Would she be back, and what would Lorelei say to her if she showed up again? What could she do to make her disappear? Could she have her arrested for stalking? And who was this Winona, anyway?

"We're out." Sharleen's panicky announcement interrupts Lorelei's brief foray into Winona-land. "We're out, and there's a long line of pissed-off customers with gold credit cards and $300 worth of merchandise, waiting for their water, and they don't want vouchers. Now what?"

Here's what. It comes in the form of a short skinny woman with a big fat purse, slung messenger-style from one shoulder to the opposite hip. She is dressed in fashion-mag hip, long black tunic top over tight black tights that disappear into what looks like combat boots, if Gucci made purple suede combat boots. Her Easter-basket hair—grass-green, chunky-chopped—allows glimpses of pink scalp through its celluloid transparency. She slides glasses, their frames as thick and black as licorice sticks, down a sliding-board nose punctuated by a diamond in one nostril, and peers around the shop with steely eyes the size and color of dimes. One hand, heavily laden with multiple rings, dives into the purse and withdraws the tools of her trade: notebook, pen, cellphone to record her findings.

She is Maya. Just Maya. Fashion editor, taste arbiter, society-maker-or-breaker, undisputed star of the *Herald*'s Lifestyle section. Maya herself is here, in Ladybug Lingerie, surveying the scene with double-dime eyes. Maya, Lorelei knows, is capable of creating either triumph or trouble, and from the curl of her lip as she scans the chaos of the shop, Trouble could well be what Maya has in mind.

Several women in line recognize Maya; others don't, but they sense her fearsome aura, the glow of power emanating from a skinny green-haired woman armed with a notebook, a pen and a phone.

She clips the phone on a band on her wrist, clicks the pen and scribbles something in her notebook. She moves on, taking notes as she walks, lifting a nightie here, a bra there, dangling a thong from two fingers as if it were alive. The women stare, transfigured, their restless maneuvering in line stilled by the movements of this skeletal sharp-eyed sleuth.

Maya surveys the line of women, then selects a rather beefy but well-dressed customer with an armload of satin-y gowns. "Could you tell me what you ladies are waiting for?" Maya asks in a voice resembling the cracking of nutshells. "Is there some...special offer, perhaps?"

The woman, who apparently recognizes the often-photographed Maya, is only too happy to respond. "We're supposed to get water with our $300 order, but it looks to me like they just promised something we're not getting."

Lorelei has elbowed her way past the teeming crowd of women, oblivious to the raised eyebrows and pursed lips that follow her. "May I help you?" she asks. Although Lorelei is taller than Maya, able to look down upon the choppy green mass of hair to where the gray roots are embedded in her pink scalp, she nonetheless has to shake off the intimidation she feels.

Maya removes the phone from her wrist, shoves it under Lorelei's nose and asks, "So what is this water you're offering for free in exchange for the purchase of your merchandise?"

"Water?" Lorelei stalls. "It's just water...like Vitaminwater." Out of the corner of her eye, she sees Sharleen edging her way through the crowd.

And here's Sharleen, welcoming Maya as if she were the Queen of England. "Pretty exciting!" Sharleen enthuses, waving her fingers in the direction of the jostling women laden with silk and satin goods.

Maya smiles a vulture smile and transfers the phone to a more favorable location beneath Sharleen's snub little nose. "So," she begins, "tell me about this water. What's so special about it? Vitamins? Minerals?" Her metallic eyes blink rapidly. "Chemicals of some kind?"

Sharleen shoots a glance toward Lorelei, who glares stony-faced at her. "No, no chemicals!" she says. "It's all natural, straight out of the ground."

"Ah," Maya says. "Straight out of the ground."

"From a well," Sharleen adds helpfully.

If Lorelei could, she would throttle Sharleen on the spot. Maya closes in like a prosecutor in a bad TV movie. "And what would be the origin of the water from this well?" She doesn't wait for an answer. "Would you say it could be from the...fountain of youth?"

"What?" Lorelei is stunned. Just hearing the words makes her ears ring. "That's ridiculous," she sputters. "Where did you get that from?"

"My source tells me that this water is miraculous. My source says..."

"Source?" Lorelei demands. "What source?"

And then she knows. Laden with an armload of lingerie, Ruby Braithwaite is waving a big hello to Maya from her place in line. Maya responds with a thumbs-up.

"Your source is delusional," Lorelei says with a nod towards Ruby. "We never made any such claims about the water."

The line is growing longer. The ladies are increasingly agitated. Rumbles and mumbles have escalated to a chorus of dissatisfaction. "The water is on its way," Sharleen cheerfully reassures them, her optimism belied by the panic in her eyes.

"False advertising," accuses a lady through Juvaderm'd lips, joined by another who warbles, "I drove all the way from Boca." At this, various locations ("Aventura!" "Weston!" "Bal Harbour!") are shouted by others equally disenchanted that their journey has been for naught. Maya observes the escalating chaos with a look of satisfaction. She has her story.

• • •

On the front page of the *Herald's* Living section the following day:

MAYA'S MUSINGS
H2O: UH, OH

There must be something in the water, or why was this anonymous little shop swarming yesterday with frenzied customers battling for any bits of lingerie they could get their hands on, as long as it added up to $300?

$300? Why $300? Because that's the promotional gimmick offered by Ladybug Lingerie, a fading decades-old shop in Coral Gables that until recently catered strictly to the girdle-and-flannel-nightie crowd, to prime the pump of sales: Buy $300 worth of merchandise, and you get a bottle of water.

Yes, people, you heard that right. A bottle of water. A five-gallon bottle of water.

Given our drought that's lasted for months, you'd think any water would be valuable—but $300 worth of valuable? This water, however, isn't just any water. This water is very, very special. This water could be from the…wait for it…Fountain of Youth.

OK, disclaimer. The proprietor of the shop, Lorelei Cassidy, 60, looked shocked, *shocked*, when I asked if this was the claim made for this supposedly miraculous liquid, as I had heard from a reliable source. "It's just water," she said defensively, "like Vitaminwater."

Her assistant, Sharleen Robinson, 60, taking her cue from her boss, jumped on the Deny Everything bandwagon. When I asked what made this water so "special," Sharleen replied with some mumbo jumbo about it having no chemicals, then proceeded to claim that it came "straight out of the ground, from a well."

Well, well. A magical well. That seems to have run dry just as I arrived to seek out the truth of this fantastical tale.

(A question for my attorney readers: They're only giving this stuff away, ostensibly to build sales. Would selling a product with such a claim create legal complications, whereas giving it away wouldn't? And isn't this a kind of end run around those problems?)

But...to the rescue, just in the nick of time, came...well, he refused to give me his name, but I'll just refer to him as The Bottle Man—very hunky in an assisted living way. He sauntered in with a cart loaded down with bottles of water (cutesy label—Spring Chicken), looked around as if he had made a wrong turn on his way to Hippie Haven and had wound up in Bedlam instead. There was a mad rush from the ladies to pay their $300, claim their water, and load up their stash. "Happy ending," as Lorelei assured me. "End of story."

I sense that this is just the beginning, despite Lorelei's announcement that the promotion has ended. Apparently the promise of magic water created too much of a scene, so Ladybug Lingerie will only offer moderate sized cups in the future to desperate customers who, inspired by Lorelei and Sharleen's youthful appearance (they don't look 60, and yes, I checked, they are), will hold out hope that the trickle of water they'll be allowed in the future will work for them. And keep them coming back again and again.

So what's with Lorelei and Sharleen's back-to-the-future youthfulness? Plastic surgery, exotic creams, water from a fabled source? Or is this just a promotional stunt, designed to increase sales? In short, is this "fountain of youth" claim a scam, or is it for real? Stay tuned.

• • •

"Assistant? I'm not your assistant!" Sharleen slams Maya's article onto a display table, disturbing its can-can array of hiphuggers. "And now everybody knows how old I am."

Sharleen's dismay is the least of Lorelei's problems. She had hoped that things would return to normal after yesterday's debacle, but no such luck. She's already gotten calls from local TV stations who want more information. One alert and eager intern from Channel 7 has been waiting at the door since she arrived this morning, begging Lorelei for an interview to advance his position at the station. Lorelei denied him with as much grace as she could manage between clenched teeth. He's still there.

Waiting with the intern is a rapidly growing crowd of women, plus a few men of the gay and metrosexual persuasion, apparently early risers and *Herald* readers. "Is the special promotion still on?" a guy with gravity-defying spikes of hair calls out. Lorelei confirms that the promotion is over, and all customers could expect will be one, repeat one, cup of water as they shop, repeat shop, in the store. The guy holds his ground but agrees to go with the one cup, although Lorelei wonders just what he would buy in a lingerie store.

Despite their pleas, Lorelei insists that the door won't open before ten, hoping to discourage them from waiting outside for another hour. No such luck. The crowd has only increased in size, their voices background to Lorelei and Sharleen's arguing as they put the shop back in order after yesterday's debacle, a chore they were too exhausted to perform last night.

"Nobody cares how old you are," Lorelei says, re-folding a stack of teddies that Sharleen has sloppily laid out on a shelf. "Unless you're worried about your boy toy at Staples."

"That's mean," Sharleen says, smashing several bras into a drawer. "Besides, it's over. I haven't seen him for a week." She slams the drawer shut, leaving a stray pink bra strap hanging out like a tongue. "And that's not the point anyway."

No, there are other points. Aside from the unwanted publicity, Lorelei has a more personal problem with Maya's article, namely the reference to Ladybug being a fading decades-old shop that catered to the girdle-and-flannel-nightie-crowd. She doesn't mention that to Sharleen, whose anger concerns only herself. No need to fuel that fire by pointing out that Maya insulted, not just Sharleen, but the shop's image, which, thanks to their VaVoom line, has, instead, been elevated to a more contemporary level and deserves better.

"I think we should forget about giving out any water at all," Lorelei says. "I just want to go back to selling lingerie, period. This has been nothing but trouble since the start."

Sharleen jerks her head around from the rack of nighties slipping off hangers she's ramming together in frustration. "Are you kidding me? Without the water, we're just another underwear store." The crowd is pressing against the door, spike-hair guy in front, pointing to his watch. It's after ten, and there's no time to argue with Sharleen, who is wrong, wrong, wrong, which Lorelei says as she brushes by her to open the door.

"We'll talk about this later," she says, and leaves her to the nighties, several of which have fallen on the floor. Lorelei doesn't even care.

Before she opens up, she needs to figure out how to handle this water distribution. One per customer, that's all, but how can she limit that? "Sharleen!" she calls. Sharleen's head pops up from her place on the floor where she is rescuing fallen nighties.

"What?"

"You've got to man the water bottle. They can't help themselves, or it'll be total chaos. Just stand there, fill the cups yourself, try to remember who's already had one..."

"Who's going to help customers find stuff? Who'll be at the front desk at the cash register? Who's..."

"Me. I'll do it. We've got to deal with this the best we can right now." Lorelei has no real answers for this. All she wants to do is get through the day. She'll think about it tomorrow.

She takes a deep breath and opens the door just wide enough for her to step outside, where the crowd eagerly awaits. "Thank you all so much for coming to Ladybug Lingerie," she begins in her best manager's voice. "We're happy to help you find the items you're looking for." She takes another deep breath. "While you're shopping, you're welcome to a cup of the water which I'm sure you've heard about, but please understand that we make no claims about its..." she hesitates, "properties. We're offering one complimentary cup per customer as a courtesy, which you can obtain at the water cooler in the back of the store." Optimistically, she adds, "We hope you enjoy shopping at Ladybug."

The crowd shifts restlessly during Lorelei's speech. When she opens the door, they pour through like a Black Friday crowd at Walmart, almost knocking her down in the process. They stream to the back of the shop, where Sharleen awaits, a fearful smile frozen on her face.

Several customers have emerged triumphant, cups clutched possessively in their hands, and actually start looking through the merchandise. But Lorelei knows that Sharleen can't keep up with the demand, and the bottle will have to be changed soon. Much as she hates to do it, she calls Juan. She needs a third person to quell any disorder that might arise. She dials. No answer. She leaves a message: "Help! We need you at the shop."

Disorder has arisen. Apparently Sharleen has noticed that one customer—the spike-haired guy–has butted in line for a second cup, and Lorelei can hear Sharleen from across the shop. "Whoa whoa whoa," she hears her say, "one per customer, sir, I think we made that clear."

"I didn't get a full cup," the guy says. "You gave me half a cup."

"Everyone gets the same amount. Step aside please and let the next person in line get her cup." Sharleen's voice rises, getting that ragged edge to it that Lorelei knows all too well signals that Sharleen is on her way to meltdown. "Next!" Sharleen calls.

"I'm not moving," the guy says. "I didn't come here to get ripped off."

Lorelei swims through the crowd to rescue Sharleen, who is looking quite flushed and sweaty, not a good sign. She notices that the ends of the guy's spiked hair are carefully tipped in purple, and the completely irrelevant thought flashes through her mind that hair today seems to come in all colors and why is that? "Is there a problem?" she asks.

"Yeah. I want a full cup. I got a half cup. I got ripped off."

"It's *free*, you greedy prick!" Sharleen yells. "You're supposed to be shopping, not drinking."

Okay. Code Blue! Code Blue! Lorelei steps between Sharleen and Spike. "I'm going to have to ask you to leave," she says to him. *And what if he doesn't? What then? Where is Juan?*

The next woman in line pipes up. "Yeah, leave," she says in aggrieved support. "What are you doing here anyway?" Her frizzled gray hair oscillates with umbrage. "This is a ladies' store. You're not shopping. You just want the water." She eyes him up and down. "And you don't even need it! What are you—forty?"

"Thirty-five," Spike snarls, and on closer inspection, Lorelei realizes he's probably forty-five or more, with some work already done around the eyes, judging from the faint scars above his eyelids. "I have just as much right to be here as you, Granny."

Granny and Spike, Lorelei realizes with a start, are being videotaped by the Channel 7 intern, his long pale face serious behind his camera as he records their escalating altercation. Where did he come from? She thought he left, but no, he didn't leave, he must have been swept in with the crowd, the little sneak, hoping something exciting will happen here that he and his cohorts at Channel 7 can edit into a distorted news bite. First Maya, now this. Where will it end?

Like a welcome apparition, Juan's face appears at the front window of the shop. Lorelei hopes she's not hallucinating, and yes, she's not, because here comes Juan, parting the sea of customers like some kind of Cuban Moses. While a hush doesn't exactly fall upon the crowd, there is a discernible settling down as he proceeds to the back of the shop, the only male among the few there who wears his age with dignity. He takes over the distribution of cups from the water bottle, his lowered brow and pressed lips the only indication of what Lorelei knows is consternation. She is sure she'll hear more about this when they are alone.

At least he gets rid of Spike, who, once he sees that Juan is in charge, crumples his empty cup and stalks out of the shop. Lorelei notes with dismay that he's followed by Intern Guy, camera rolling.

But sales are happening. Lorelei's attention swings to those customers who, between careful sips of water, are actually buying. Sharleen mans the cash register, the zip of credit cards seeming to lull her into a welcome calmness. The shop has settled into a kind of rhythm: Juan handing out cups of water, Sharleen ringing up sales, Lorelei helping customers find what they need and commenting on the wisdom of their choices. It almost feels like a normal day, even when a muscular guy with a rainbow tattoo on his furry forearm asks if there are any extra-larges in the red bikini panties he's holding. So normal, in fact, that Lorelei feels that the worst is over and the craziness has come to an end.

It isn't until later that she notices when customers leave the shop that they're lingering outside. Now what? She goes to the door and understands: they're being interviewed. The Channel 7 intern has posted himself on the sidewalk, and customers, apparently happy to be on TV, await their turn. She can't hear what they're saying beyond the glass door, but represses the impulse to go outside and stop this. She can see where that would go: onto the Channel 7 evening news. Her appearance would be the highlight of that segment, and she's not going to give them that.

Sharleen, however, will. "What's going on?" she asks, leaving her post to join Lorelei at the door.

"This has gotten out of hand," Lorelei says. "If we don't end this fountain of youth hysteria, our shop will never survive it."

Before Lorelei can stop her, Sharleen is outside. The intern shifts the camera from Ruby Braithwaite, of all people, to focus on Sharleen.

"Hey," Sharleen yells. "What's going on here?"

"I have every right to be here," the intern says. "I'm on public property." He taps his sneakered foot on the sidewalk to make his point. "Public property. Paid by taxes."

"You're harassing my customers. I'm calling the cops."

"Interviewing is not harassment," the intern says. "It's journalism."

Ruby Braithwaite, apparently peeved at having her interview interrupted, turns on Sharleen. "He's just asking questions," she says. "I have a few myself, like why are you so stingy with that water? We're supposed to come back every day for a measly cup? I'm running out! I need more!" The camera swings back to Ruby, who lifts her chin in both defiance and proof. "Look!" she cries. "No more turkey neck! It *is* the fountain of youth!"

"It's just water," Sharleen protests. "And water's *wet*. The drought's dried everybody up. You get a little water in you, you look better, you feel better. All those shriveled-up parts of you get, like, plumped."

"Plumped?" the intern asks, homing in for a close-up of Sharleen.

She pats her hair and stares into the camera. "Yeah. Like pouring water on a sponge. Wet water. Dry sponge. Plump!"

"Where's this water from?" the intern asks. "You told Maya it was from a well."

"It's from... a supplier. The supplier has a well."

Lorelei cringes from her position behind the door, cracked open enough so she can hear. "Shut up shut up," she mutters, but Sharleen does not shut up. Instead, she gives Lorelei a look as if to say, "I'm doing great, right?" and continues: "It's just plain old water from a plain old well..."

"So where is this plain old well?" the intern asks.

"...that, because of the drought, we bring in as a courtesy for our customers who may be experiencing a water shortage." Sharleen flashes a grin for the camera.

"Where's the well?"

"Oh, up north somewhere," Sharleen says, flicking her fingers in that general direction. "Where there's no drought."

Okay, Lorelei wills her, *end it there.*

Which maybe she would have, had Ruby not thrust herself into camera range. "Who cares where it comes from? It works. Right, ladies?" she cries to the women outside the shop awaiting their turn with Channel 7. "All I want to know is, how can I get more?"

"Yes, more, more!" the crowd chants. "We want more." The camera takes it all in.

• • •

The next day, Lorelei's first call comes from CNN. Then NBC, ABC, CBS, Fox, and "The View"— calls triggered by the Channel 7 news segment the evening before. Now the news is ubiquitous on Facebook, Twitter, and all points internet: the clamor for access to the fountain of youth. Maya's column told of the frenzy; Channel 7 showed it.

The intern no doubt locked down a job there. He captured desperation, hope, and greed in a three-minute segment, narrated in his own nasal voice.

Lorelei can't deal with this barrage of crazy publicity. She won't grant interviews, but the news rolls on in a media blitz. Sharleen is unhappy with the way she was edited—bad angle, not her good side—but the lure of fame overrides her dismay. She wants to do the interviews. "It'll be good for the shop," she rationalizes. "We'll keep it classy. How about Dr. Oz?" She pauses. "Oh, yeah. He's gone. How about..."

"The shop doesn't need any more publicity." Lorelei points to the crowd outside. "We're a freak show now. I just want to go back to being what we were before all this started, just sell lingerie, that's all, no water, not for sale, not for free."

Despite Sharleen's objection, Lorelei declares they're on vacation. "Let's take a couple of weeks off," she says. "Go away with your guy or whoever. I think we both need a break from all this." She turns off her phone and puts the "closed" sign up. This doesn't stop the curious from gathering in front and snapping selfies.

When she arrives home, the first thing she needs is a nice hot mind-numbing bath. She strips down and tosses her lingerie on the floor, rather than her usual habit of placing it in her hand-wash laundry bag. She turns on the faucet, sprinkles her bubble bath crystals, and waits for the scented foam to rise.

It doesn't. At least not with the luxuriousness she has come to expect. Have the bath crystals gone flat? She holds her hand beneath the faucet. The water is gushing out, but its energy seems to have dissipated somewhat. What is going on?

Once the tub is full—taking longer than usual—she slides in and tells herself that it's just her imagination. The water is hot, the bubbles are fine, her bath is doing its job. She relaxes into its soothing liquidity and tries to stop thinking so much.

Juan hasn't returned her calls since he left the shop yesterday. He stuck it out until closing time, then took the empty bottles and went home. Did he see the Channel 7 bit? Was he angry, disgusted, sympathetic?

She doesn't know. He hasn't called. She needs a drink.

WINONA

Well, the price was cheap enough. The house is a disaster, unlived in for several years, right next door to Lorelei's, lucky for me. The owner, who had moved to the Keys, was only too happy to sell it to me for peanuts. The faded "For Sale" sign, wrapped with vines, had been up so long that his phone number was almost illegible. When we met to sign the papers, he seemed leery of me, even though I wore the boring pantsuit and looked, to the best of my ability, conservative. But, given that the house was such a wreck, I'm sure he would have sold it to a serial killer if his check didn't bounce.

If it hadn't been for the serendipity of this house for sale, I might be doomed. Whatever deep source that's supplying Lorelei's well is probably flowing beneath this house, untapped by the shallower wells of the neighborhood, like this one, that still function despite the drought. The water splatting from the faucet is tinged a faint ochre, the same color that stains the plumbing fixtures in the kitchen and bathroom. The owner assured me that it's passed inspection, and whipped out some official paper to prove it. I didn't plan to drink it anyway, but it was a great opportunity for me to negotiate a drastic price reduction.

My instincts were right, as they have been through the centuries, but before, they led me to the spring without needing to drill for it. My plan is to extend this pathetic excuse for a well and bore down until I hit the spring—my spring—that supplies Lorelei's well, then divert it to this house. I asked the engineer who manages the water supply of the casino to figure this all out, with the excuse that I'm unhappy with the water here. He's got connections, and when I confided that I needed some creative and discreet well-digging, he agreed to send out someone who might be willing to work under the table: Fred the digger. Actually, thanks to being maybe a little *too* creative in his approach to his work, Fred had run into some career problems of his own. So under-the-table worked for him. But, the engineer assured me when I hesitated, Fred knows wells, so I agreed. If he succeeds in diverting the spring, I should be guaranteed an uninterrupted supply. I don't want to live here. I just want to live.

I've never felt so mortal in all my years as I have in the past few weeks. All these symptoms—hot flashes, achy joints, the inability to remember things like who was the last guy I slept with—are warning lights on a dead-end street. There is nothing uplifting about any of this, and I am beginning to have empathy for all those menopausal women whose lives have seemed so stunted to me. I now relate to their escalating crabbiness, and I don't intend to travel that path. Some may argue that 500 years is a long time to hang around, but to me, it's just the beginning.

I agree to meet this Fred at the house today, around back where the well pump is, overgrown with weeds and thick with spider webs. "You Winona?" he asks, then answers his own question, "Must be. You fit the description." His squeaky voice is a strange mismatch with his simian physique—small head, thick neck, broad shoulders supporting arms so furry he has to part the hair to read his fake Rolex. "Whaddaya need me to do here?"

"I understand that somewhere beneath this turf is some very good water," I say, "and what I want you to do is tap into that."

He explains he's happy to do it, not necessarily as a favor for our mutual friend, the engineer at the casino, but as a means of covering some pretty heavy debts he's incurred at poker during his recent, shall we say, unemployment. His face elongates with sorrow as he admits this, but his bad news is good news for me. I want this endeavor to be as secretive as possible, so his need to do it under the table is a plus. I'm paying him a hefty fee, making him more than willing to take on this job, which, he says, compared to the complicated process involved in oil drilling, should be no big deal. But, he adds, who knows? Maybe there's oil under here, which, if he hits that first, he says, would be "way more profitable."

"Wait. What?" I ask. "Are you talking about fracking?" That's all I need, someone who could contaminate my spring. "I need someone who can drill for water, not oil or gas."

"Water's a piece-a cake. I done that before I went into fracking, which is more complicated, plus they're trying to stop it in Florida, good luck with that. So this'll be a easy job." I eye him skeptically. "Don't get your panties in a knot," he says, amending that at my scowl. "Don't worry. Oil and water won't mix here. I guarantee it."

I don't really trust this guy, but I have to. What's the alternative?

He nabs a fallen dead palm frond and sweeps away a big web, rips out some weeds and peers at the pump. "Huh." He bends down for a closer look. "This thing work?"

"It draws some pretty scummy water, if that's what you mean by working."

I swat at a swarm of mosquitoes released from their home in the puddle leaking from the pump. "That's why I need it to go deeper. Much deeper. Until it hits someplace where there's really good water. Pure uncontaminated water."

Fred gives the cap on the pump a good thump and shakes his head. "Don't matter how deep you go. I'll betcha there's nothing better, water-wise, anywhere under here." His laugh is a high-pitched giggle.

"What makes you say that?"

"It's not like water around these parts has been so great to begin with, not for a long time, anyway. The government dug canals to drain the Everglades way back when to make farmland—flood control, they called it—and now everybody complains that all that farming with its fertilizers and pesticides contaminated the groundwater." He shrugs. "It's a trade-off."

I know. I remember the Everglades before the canals, when water flowed clear and free through the tall grass. Before the land was carved and sliced and the water was tamed. Before so many birds and animals disappeared. Before the pythons proliferated— muscular, slithering shadows devouring whatever is in their path.

"Yep," Fred goes on. "Water's gonna be a problem everywhere." He ruffles the dry earth with one hand, releasing a puff of dust. "We got the drought now, but then there's too *much* water, like sea rise flooding the streets in Miami Beach." He giggles at the irony. "Florida's sitting on porous limestone that's solid as swiss cheese. Salt water's eventually gonna infiltrate what fresh water there is, and then, you wanna talk about trouble? But you gotta keep building. It's progress," Fred proclaims. He clamps his knees with furry hands and rises with some difficulty. "Now they're complaining about the oil."

I haven't paid much attention to whatever talk I hear about drilling for oil in the Everglades, mostly chatter from some of the employees and tourists. The constant cacophony of the casino erases any real conversation. I work late, don't watch the news, don't concern myself much with what's going on in the outside world. My survival depends on the spring, and anything else is incidental.

"Bet there's oil under here," he says, stomping the ground. "We've found tons of it in Big Cypress in the west Everglades. My guess is if we fracked right under our feet," he kicks at the dirt with a steel-toed boot, "we'd hit the motherlode."

"I'm looking for water," I say. "I can't drink oil."

But Fred's on a roll. "There's a underground formation not far from here called the Sunniland Trend that's just begging for fracking. 150 miles long, 20 miles wide, a whole stretch of oil field from Fort Myers to Miami that's hardly been tapped." His voice rises to operatic heights. "It's those tree-hugging nutcases holding up the works."

"Not my problem," I say, resisting the urge to hammer him into the ground. "I need clean water."

"Yeah, clean water, like we're trying to poison everybody, kill those fuckin' panthers, whatever." He gives the pump another thump. It responds with a hollow echo. "We take *precautions*. It's a *process*. I mean, when you go horizontal, which is what fracking is, you gotta inject maybe five to 20 million gallons of water and chemicals under pressure...."

"Wait. Five to 20 *million*?"

"...to hydraulically fracture the rock and extract the oil and gas."

"Where's all that water coming from?" The thought that those huge quantities of water might be from my precious spring makes me want to kill this guy.

"Surface aquifers," Fred says. "Where city water comes from." He gives an annoyed sigh. "Yeah, so people complain that we're drawing that water away from them, 'specially with this drought, but, hey. It's to their benefit. Finding oil just adds to the value of the land."

"*Surface* aquifers," I repeat, just to make sure that all that water for fracking isn't taken from deep within the earth, where I suspect the spring lies. "They're upset that those aquifers might be depleted?"

"Well, that. And also that what's used for fracking isn't drinkable any more." I sigh with relief, which he mistakes for dismay. "So maybe it's a little contaminated afterward," he confesses. "It can't be returned to the water cycle, lotsa chemicals, no secret there. So we treat it like toxic waste, dump it into these deep pits so's it stays away from the aquifer, but they say yeah, the pits aren't lined, nobody monitors them, bla bla bla." He waves his hand in the air, erasing such nonsense. "They say the fracked water seeps into the aquifers and wells and it's poisoning their kids and such. But you gotta look at the big picture. You can't let that black gold just sit there. You wanna think about the kids? Well, kids are gonna need gas and oil in the future so think about *that*, I say."

Right now I have my own future to worry about. "Look, I don't care about oil, I don't care about fracking, all I care about is whether or not you can find the water I know is there, deep down."

"I'm the best," he says.

"Fine. When can you start?"

WATER, A MEMOIR

Does water have memory?

Does it recall the spark that heralded its birth, the conjoining of elements flung from a newborn universe to a home in a molten earth? The primordial fluid hid in vast deep pools as the planet cooled like an oven-hot muffin. Its surface gradually crusted over, cracking and shifting, layer upon layer that jostled for space, thrusting into peaks and valleys, forming hollows to cradle the embryonic liquid that nestled in its earthly womb. With time, the water burst free, its youth a roiling rush inside earth's crust, carving mammoth caverns with waterfalls so steep they seemed to pour into the center of the earth.

Does it remember the stirrings of life that disturbed its virginal state? The tickle of bacteria, the energy of algae giving breath to the air—early life forms that kick-started the evolution of creatures that swam in, crawled out of, drank from, and in countless ways, despoiled the purity of earth's first water.

Is there memory of ascension, of being lifted as vapor to the sky, of transformation from liquid to cloud and back again? The cycle promised a future of eternal rebirth. But in and on and above this earth, eternity is just an illusion.

So water recalls how to hide: in recesses and crevices that reduced it to a trickle, invisible as it morphed into mud, emerging in a safe place to gather its strength. Its force restored, it escaped to the freedom of an undiscovered waterfall. Or to a sapphire lake in the heart of a dead volcano. Or to a secret stream deep beneath porous coral rock.

Escape. This is the dream of water. This is the hope of the Spring.

THIRTEEN

Lorelei checks her phone again. Still no message from Juan despite the numerous messages she's left. He's never done this before, shut her down without an explanation. She even drove to his house to see him face-to-face. He didn't answer her repeated bell-ringing, so she slipped a note under his door. Receiving no response after several days of angst, she tries not to think about it. But she does. The shop has been closed since the media barrage, so there's not much else for her to do but obsess over his absence.

With the shop temporarily shuttered and no more news on that front to report, the media's fortunately short attention span has turned to more lurid happenings on the Kardashian front. Now that the insanity seems to have come to an end, Lorelei thinks it's time to re-open the shop. Without the water. After all, there's rent to pay, vendors to satisfy, and customers who, she hopes, are more interested in lingerie than water. And working will keep her mind off Juan.

Sharleen, whose days without work have seemed empty and without purpose, is happy at that news, but needs reassurance that even if the water to the shop is terminated, her own supply is guaranteed. "Just enough to maintain. It's okay if I stay right where I am."

"I'm sick of the whole thing. I'd just as soon drink mud at this point."

"Is that asking so much," Sharleen persists, "considering you have an endless supply coming out of your faucet?"

"It's not endless. It might even disappear." Lorelei stops to let that sink in before adding, "We're going to have to ration the water, even for us. It seems to be dropping in pressure and quantity."

"Can't Juan fix it?" Sharleen asks, her hands clasped in dismay.

Lorelei shakes her head. "I don't know where he is. I haven't heard from him since he left the shop a few days ago."

"But...he's *got* to fix it. What'll we do?"

The recent decline in the water, though barely noticeable, has created mixed feelings in Lorelei. She almost hopes it disappears. And yet. She does appreciate the way she not only looks, but, more importantly, feels. If that evaporates along with the water, it would be an adjustment. And not a happy one.

She has caught herself looking in the mirror and wondering if, without the water, she would revert back to the old Lorelei, not just in appearance, but in attitude. She wants to believe she would gracefully accept the decline of her looks, but hopes that, whatever happens, her newfound openness to life and her ability to love will remain. She can't imagine going back to the person she was before. She can't imagine life without Juan.

Closing the shop temporarily has made Lorelei a reluctant homebody. Intent on her business, oblivious to the day-to-day doings of the populace of Melaleuca Lakes, she had little interest in the comings and goings of her neighbors. In all the years she has been in her house, she has befriended only one neighbor, if "friend" means they exchange Hello's and perhaps a brief comment on the weather if they happen to be outside at the same time.

Like now. Corabelle, her elderly neighbor, has spotted Lorelei sitting on her porch in the middle of the week—an event so rare it draws Corabelle away from her usual post on *her* porch where she observes what little action there is on the street. Eyes closed, her mind turning over and over the question of Juan's whereabouts,

Lorelei is unaware of Corabelle's presence until she hears her scratchy voice in her ear: "I saw you on TV."

Lorelei keeps her eyes closed, feigning sleep. She just can't deal with Corabelle right now, especially when Corabelle's subject is one which Lorelei would just as soon forget.

"Saw you was peeking around the door of your store," Corabelle persists. Lorelei hears the porch swing squeak. Corabelle has settled in for the duration, making herself comfortable. Lorelei opens her eyes and acknowledges her neighbor with a resigned sigh. Corabelle, who was middle-aged when they bought their homes across the street from each other nearly thirty years ago, has shrunk considerably over the years. Her tiny orthopedic shoes dangle from the swing, which she keeps moving with rhythmic thrusts of her body. *Squeak. Squeak.* She punctuates each thrust with commentary.

"I never been to your store. I don't wear fancy underwear." *Squeak.* "What all that fuss about?" *Squeak.* "Water? I don't need to go to no underwear store to get water." *Squeak.* "But you famous. On TV." She pauses in her thrusts. "I was on TV once." The squeak stops as Corabelle waits for Lorelei to ask about Corabelle's TV experience. She doesn't.

Undaunted, Corabelle segues to a new subject. "We got a new neighbor. That house next to you, been empty for years." Lorelei had noticed that a "Sold" sign had gone up, and she had heard some rumblings from what she had assumed was some kind of work going on there, invisible from behind the overgrowth of trees and foliage between their houses.

"Well, I hope whoever bought it will clean it up and mow the lawn."

"It's one a them lady-mans," Corabelle says. "You know, a transylvanian."

Lorelei can't resist. "A vampire?"

"I didn't say nothing about vampires. Why you think I was talking about vampires?"

"Transylvania. It's where the vampires live." Lorelei frowns in seeming puzzlement. "Now why would a vampire want to move here? I'm sure there's better blood in Miami Beach."

Corabelle stares at her. "Why you talking about vampires when I'm talking about a lady-man?"

"You mean a transsexual?"

"Whatever."

"How do you know she's a transsexual?" Lorelei is so happy that the conversation has changed from her TV exposure to this that she's curious about Corabelle's answer. "Did you meet her?"

"No. I just saw her out fronta her house, talking to a guy with a truck. But I could tell. She was tall, really tall. With all this black hair, coulda been a wig. Those lady-mans, they wear a lotta wigs. And boots. What kinda girl wears boots here?" She shakes her head in disbelief. "Also, she had these big boobs. You know they ain't real when they're that humunguous, sticking out like that."

Lorelei was enjoying this. A transsexual neighbor. That would liven up the neighborhood for sure, as well as improve the appearance of a neglected house that was rundown and overgrown with weeds. "What else?"

Corabelle lowers her voice. "And. She looks like a Indian."

Lorelei feels as if the breath has been sucked out of her. "Indian?" she manages to say.

"Yeah. One a them Semmyoles or Missakusees. Only she didn't dress like them, with the quilty dresses and all. She dress like a lady-man. Boots."

Winona. The casino manager. The girl of Juan's dreams.

Lorelei doesn't bother excusing herself, but jumps up to go inside, leaving Corabelle swinging and squeaking, a confused look on her face.

She dials Juan repeatedly, each time leaving the message that he must call her, it's important, call her right away. Her last message sounds frantic, but she doesn't care: "Winona has moved next door to me. What's going on?"

When she doesn't hear back from Juan, she decides to see for herself what's going on. "Where you off to?" Corabelle wants to know when Lorelei reappears. Receiving no answer, she hops down off the swing and follows Lorelei on her march to the house of Winona.

"Whoa," says Corabelle when Lorelei pounds on the door. Receiving no answer, Lorelei circles the house, Corabelle trailing behind. The weeds have taken over the lawn, surrounding the house with a tangle of knee-high growth broken only by a flattened area where it's clear that a truck has ridden. When they arrive around back, there it is: a digging rig, seemingly unmanned, and a pile of slurry that's been excavated, apparently to no avail, where the well was. It's a familiar scene to Lorelei, giving her a sense of déjà vu from her first encounter with Juan. She's relieved to discover that the rig isn't Juan's, but from another company, "Fred's Digging and Rigging."

What's going on here? Is Winona so menopausally desperate for the water, as she had claimed to be when she purchased $1200 worth of lingerie to obtain four bottles, that she'd resort to buying a house for its proximity to Lorelei's well? Or—she speculated as her jealousy kicked into high gear—did she also buy it for its proximity to Juan?

She calls and leaves a message for Juan again, not caring that she sounds hysterical because she is: "Winona is digging a well right next door to my house. Why? Why don't you call me back?" She hangs up and stares at the phone as if doing so will force him to pick up.

"You ladies looking for something?" Lorelei swings around, expecting a pubescent kid from the sound of the voice, not this furry hulk who is bearing down on them from around the corner of the house. His steel-toed boots clomp indentations in the weeds as he makes his way, pointing an unlit but well-chewed cigar in their direction. "I leave here to have me some lunch and a beer, and what happens? I come back to trespassers." He jams the cigar in the corner of his trapdoor mouth, and glares at Lorelei and Corabelle with tiny eyes shaded by caterpillar brows.

"You be careful who you talking to that way," Corabelle says, her indignation expanding her body to its full five-foot height. "We neighbors. We got every right to be here so just watch your sassy mouth."

Lorelei, inspired by Corabelle and fueled by her own roiling emotions, picks up the pace with her own accusation. "What are you doing, anyway? Do you have a permit?" And the questions she really wants answered: "Who hired you? And why?"

"What is it your business?" The cigar migrates from one corner to the other as he contemplates this fiery opposition. "The lady just wants better water, is that a crime?" he says, adding, "Bet your water is pretty pukey, too."

"Nothing wrong with my water," Corabelle says. "Perfeckly good, just a tad brownish, but perfeckly good."

Lorelei says nothing. Her own water isn't just perfectly good, it's perfect—something no one needs to know, especially those in her immediate vicinity.

"Well, with this drought you're lucky to have any water at all," Fred the digger says, mollified. "I'm coming up dry here, but it could be 'cause it hasn't been used for, I don't know, years?" He chews the cigar thoughtfully. "I'll go down maybe another 20 feet, and then I might just tell this lady to forget it. Don't know why she bought this dump anyway. Lots better places to go than this godforsaken place," he says, then backtracks at the stricken look Corabelle gives him. "No offense."

"I been here 30 years, and no complaints," Corabelle says in protest. "Lookit the trees, the lake, alla that. Don't you call my home 'godforsaken.'"

Lorelei isn't here to defend her place of residence, although she has questioned it more lately: the toxic melaleucas, the now-desiccated lake, the general decline of the area itself, not to mention the dereliction of this house next door. But now that she has this wonderful water, why would she want to leave?

The person who should leave is Winona.

"So," she ventures, "just why do you think this lady hired you to do this, anyway? Seems to me if it's got such problems, she'd look elsewhere."

"Beats me," he says. "From what I can tell, her house—my guess is most of these houses—have wells deep enough to get potable water, even through this drought. But for some reason this area has some kinda erratic rock formation. It's mostly limestone, but I've heard that here and there you can hit a plate of weird rock that don't belong here at all." He kicks at the rocky soil with a boot. "She was pretty damn sure there was good water under here. Don't know about water, but I betcha there's oil here, and I sure would like to find out."

"Oil? What you talking about, oil?" Corabelle says. "Where you get such a crazy idea?"

"You'd be surprised what they've found in the Everglades," he says. "I know. That's what I do, when I'm not digging wells for crazy Indian ladies who don't know what they're talking about." He makes a regretful face and retracts that: "Don't mean it that way. Just that I don't expect much here. Water-wise, that is."

"I'd quit while I was ahead if I were you," Lorelei suggests hopefully. "Why not be honest with her?"

"Well, she's paying me. Paying me good, and that's the bottom line." He shakes his head. "Don't get it though. She acts like she knows something I don't know, but I'm not the one to question that. I'm just a digger, not a psychic."

Neither is Lorelei, but she's beginning to suspect there's more to this than she had thought. She feels there's another dimension to this that she can't fathom, as if she's watching someone else's dream.

"Okay, ladies. Back to work," says Fred, shooing them away with his furry paws. "I gotta get something done today before Pocahontas comes to check on me."

"She a lady-man?" Corabelle asks.

"What?"

"She one a them trans...trans..." Corabelle looks to Lorelei for the word.

Lorelei just shrugs, although she knows, from close inspection during her own encounter with Winona, that she most definitely is all woman. But she sees no need to share that fact, given her animosity towards Winona, and simply says, "Transsexual."

"Well, hell." Fred chews his cigar thoughtfully. "Could be," he concedes. "She's a pretty tough cookie, that's for sure. Guess I really don't want to cross her if that's the case. She could be trouble."

That, Lorelei thinks, is probably the truest thing that's been said today.

She and Corabelle trudge back through the weeds. When they reach her house, Lorelei says a firm goodbye, with one request: Let her know if she sees Winona. Lorelei doesn't know what she'll do if she has that information, only that she needs it. Somehow, she's got to keep a handle on the situation, whatever that might be. What if Fred the digger does manage to sink a well deep enough to infiltrate the source of the water? Life, as she's known it lately, would never be the same.

●　　　●　　　●

Lorelei is awakened from a restless sleep by the ringing of her phone. It's Juan, calling from the airport, and he's on his way to her house. She thinks she's dreaming, but no, it's Juan. He'll explain when he sees her.

When she sees him at her door, she flings her arms around him, neither reprimanding nor questioning why he disappeared from her life. He holds her close for a long time, then tells her his story.

True, he left in anger the last time he saw her. Between the craziness at the shop and the media barrage, he wanted out. Afraid he would be sucked back into the drama, he didn't answer her calls or respond to her note. He secluded himself, emerging only to go on jobs or pick up groceries. He spent the rest of his time online or in the library, researching the story of Ponce de Leon's search for the fountain of youth. While he felt that it was just a myth, still, he was disturbed by his own experience—the dreams, the unnerving connection with Winona, the effect the water had on those who drank it. Although the science was sketchy, it still raised questions about the properties of the water and the possibility of genetic memory. Most importantly, the wisp of family legend he remembered from his father began to obsess him, and he realized he would have to travel to Puerto Rico to unravel that mystery.

That's where he has been since he last saw Lorelei. No cellphone, no contact, just immersion in a family history he had never known before. He found a slew of cousins whose family tree led back to Ponce, who had four kids: three daughters and one son. "My cousin Carlos, who's the oldest surviving descendant aside from me, is keeper of the family history," Juan tells her. "He has a journal Ponce wrote for Luis, Ponce's son, who came to Cuba with his mother who attended to Ponce after he was wounded. After Ponce died, his wife—the mother of Luis—saved the journal and gave it to Luis when he was old enough to understand."

"A journal? Why hasn't it been made public?"

"Carlos tried. He found it when he was rummaging through some stuff his family had taken from Cuba before the revolution. He took it to some historians at the University of Puerto Rico, but they dismissed it, said it was unreliable. It's kind of a mess, really, hard to translate and even harder to figure out what's truth and what's fiction."

"Did you see it?"

"My cousin has it. He took me to see it. He keeps it in an air-conditioned vault because it's so fragile, but had it professionally translated from the original Spanish into English. He's trying again to contact historians to see if they'll reconsider its authenticity. He gave me a copy, and I brought it with me."

"I'd like to read it." Lorelei's curiosity is laced with anxiety. She senses that this document might reveal more than she wants to know.

"I thought you might," Juan says. He reaches into his leather bag and hands her a sheaf of papers. She begins to read.

JULY 1521

Let me begin where it all began: in a jungle deep in the heart of Timucuan territory. It was my second voyage to the New World, one intended to obtain the riches that abounded in that territory, as well as to convince the savages to change their heathen ways. During my first trip, I had heard rumors of a magical spring that could bestow eternal youth. At first, I dismissed that story as a myth, but the rumors persisted, and when we landed once again on the shore of the Timucua, I heard the beating of drums indicating there was a meeting of the Tribal Council. This, I determined, would be my opportunity to have an audience with the Chief, Cacique Athore, who had evaded me on my last excursion into his land.

We arrived at their meeting, unexpected and unwelcome, judging from the array of knives and arrows suddenly aimed in our direction. Apparently we had interrupted a ceremony of some sort, but I persisted, offering, through gestures and sign language, the many treasures we had brought from Spain in exchange for their gold. The Chief disdained this, but in a moment of brashness, of which I've been accused, I indicated my curiosity about the whereabouts of the spring. His disdain became anger, and he ordered us back to our ship. Convinced by his arsenal of arrows, we departed.

But I am a persistent man, as my soldiers well know. My suspicions about the spring were confirmed when I saw the youthful appearance of the savages, in particular the Chief himself, who had supposedly been Cacique of this village since the Timucuans occupied this territory hundreds of years ago. How was this possible? There had to be some truth to the fable. I decided to find out.

My return the next day was surreptitious and unannounced. Accompanied by my most trusted and agile soldiers, we crept silently through the jungle and waited. Far off, we could hear the tinkling of bells, the trumpeting of horns. Then, floating above the tangled mass of foliage, there came into view a dazzling sight: the Chief enrobed in royal splendor, and a woman of such ferocious beauty that I thought I might be dreaming. They moved and swayed, and as they emerged from the jungle onto a path, it became clear that they were being transported on litters, surrounded by an entourage of tribespeople. Stunned, we secretly watched as they journeyed down the path. Fearful of discovery, we nonetheless followed, until the procession stopped in a hidden cove. Here, the Chief and the woman descended from their litters amidst a rising crescendo of chanting and drums.

They knelt, but not in prayer, as I had first assumed. Before them glimmered a placid pool of clear blue water so crystalline it looked like glass. Taking what seemed to be cups carved from large conch shells handed to them by two tribesmen, they filled them with water from the spring, and drank.

This must be the fabled spring, or why would their drinking be so ritualistic?

The entourage departed. I waited until the tinkling of bells and the sound of horns faded into the forest. The spring, luminous in the near distance, lured me with its promise. I had to sample the waters for myself. I signaled my soldiers to stand back, and I crept to the water's edge. Although its size was only that of a small pond, its clear depths seemed endless, as though it were a diamond that ended at the center of the earth.

As I bent down, I saw my face reflected in the spring's smooth surface, mirroring the creases and folds of my age. I cupped my hands, cradled the water and drank. It was like no other liquid that had ever passed my lips, not even the finest wine. I drank and drank, much to the astonishment of my men. Once I was sated, one thought filled my mind: I must have this.

"Follow them," I ordered my soldiers, and pointed to where the entourage had disappeared down the path. They stared at me, reluctant, but I insisted. It was my intent to confront the Chief and offer him great riches in return for a modest amount of water from his spring.

I presented myself boldly before him on the path. There is little I fear, having crossed the ocean twice now, a voyage rife with storms and disease. This man, fierce as he appeared, was no match for the violence of nature and man I have encountered. But when I mimed the drinking of water from the shell cup, and presented the jewels I had hidden in my armor as barter, the Chief signaled his bodyguards. An array of arrows was aimed at me. My soldiers automatically reached for their weapons, and for one frozen moment, our deaths seemed imminent.

A piercing cry shattered the stillness. It was the woman, the glorious beauty who accompanied the Chief. In language I couldn't fathom but somehow understood, she pleaded with the Chief, who regarded what she said with anger at first, then acceptance. He signaled his bodyguards to confiscate our guns and swords. The arrows lowered at his command, and I bowed in deep gratitude to this woman, this angel who saved our lives.

As we were rudely escorted back to our ship, I turned for one last look at the woman. She stood tall and proud, a being such as I had never seen, adorned with tattoos, lips stained blue, wearing nothing but a loincloth, feathers in her waist-length hair, and ropes of gold and pearls around her neck. She was a creature of the jungle, and I was her slave.

Our eyes met. Her eyes were the color of the water from the spring. Something passed between us, a lightning bolt that stopped time in a place of no beginning and no end.

The moment ended with the prodding of a knife in my ribs from one of the Chief's henchmen who accompanied us to the shore, where we climbed into our rowboats and returned to our ship.

The story does not end there, for I am persistent, and, some may say, foolhardy. The lure of the water was compelling, overwhelming. And, in some inexplicable way, connected to the woman.

Disregarding the objections of my soldiers, I ordered them to return to the spring under cover of darkness. Each carried a wooden barrel which he then immersed in the spring until it was full, then sealed. Weighed down, we crept back through the jungle, elated at our success, until the arrows flew. They seemed to come from nowhere and everywhere. It was miraculous that we managed to clamber aboard the boats without more damage than we received. My soldiers are good men, and I am a bold leader.

We were fortunate. The arrows struck a few of my men, but did little harm. It was the barrels of water that were pierced. Enough was salvaged for my own needs, which, I explained to my grumbling crew, I was taking for myself as an experiment. If it did indeed perform the fabled miracle, then we would return with enough force to overcome the savages, and claim the spring for ourselves. There would be enough for everyone.

Upon our return to Puerto Rico, I drank the water several times a day for weeks. At first, there was little difference aside from a general feeling of well-being and an increase in energy, which, I was loathe to admit, had been diminishing. But then there were other signs. My hair and beard regained their lushness and color; my skin was tighter, my body lighter, and the accursed width about my middle disappeared. Most pleasurable was the return of my virility, which escalated to the point where my wife grew exhausted from my lust. Her complaints soon turned to happiness when she discovered she was with child—our fourth, our only son: Luis.

My delight soon faded as the water was depleted. The signs of decline from my 47 years were returning. The brief respite from age made me crave a lifetime of youth. I had to go back to the land of the Timuqua to claim the spring, now that I had proven that the myth was real. So I requested another voyage from the King.

Not knowing my real purpose for returning, he instead gave me another mission: to explore the western coast of the place I had named La Florida. The west was the land of the Calusa, who were not only in need of conversion, but were said to have a wealth of gold for the taking. I agreed, but my intention, once that deed had been accomplished, was to return to the eastern land of the Timuqua, where the spring was found.

We never reached the east. Though we came to the western land with the best of intentions, our approach as we disembarked from the ship and made our way to shore was watched by enemy eyes. The Calusa were fierce warriors, giving us no chance to meet with their Chief before we were attacked in force. Many of my men went down, myself being one of them, grievously wounded in the thigh by a poison arrow. As I crawled to safety over the sand, a most arresting vision overcame me. I thought I saw, hidden in the jungle surrounding the beach, the glorious Timucuan woman who saved my life. Was I hallucinating in my fear and pain? She was here, in a land so far from her own, peering at me through the tangle of foliage.

My eyes locked on her crystal gaze, and I froze in my interminable crawl across the sand. In that moment, she was by my side. She unclasped a pouch that hung from her waist, and extracted the same shell cup I had seen at our last encounter. She put it to my lips, and sweet water filled my mouth. Time stopped, it seemed for an eternity. Then the Calusa turned their attack on her, so she fled. She was gone, elusive as a dream, leaving me only the shell cup which I have kept to this day. Somehow, I made it back to the ship. I survived the harrowing voyage to Cuba, but to no avail, for my death is fast approaching.

So this is for you, my little Luis, to read when you are older. Perhaps I am foolish, now dying because of my folly. Before you dismiss me as a demented old man, you must know this: if not for my foolishness, my son, you would not exist.

FOURTEEN

Lorelei is silent, processing what she's just read and what it could mean. She smooths out the papers in her lap, and looks up at Juan. "Do you believe it?" she asks.

"I believe Ponce wrote it," he says. "But do I believe that his story is true? He may have been delusional. I'm still working on figuring it out." He opens the bag and retrieves a tissue-wrapped bundle. "There's something else. Carlos gave me this."

Lorelei unwraps the bundle. Inside is what appears to be a large conch shell, etched with faded markings. "What is this?"

"Remember the shell cup Ponce wrote about? Carlos found this in the package of family possessions, and this may be it. He wanted me to have it." Juan picks it up and studies it. "It could just be some souvenir, but why else would Ponce keep it?"

Lorelei takes the shell from Juan. It seems to grow warm in her hands. She puts it down on the table. "What will you do with it?"

"I don't know. Maybe donate it to a museum, if historians verify the journal." He laughs. "Or sell it at a garage sale."

Lorelei is not amused. She hands it back.

"I brought it for you," he says. "A peace offering. For disappearing like I did with no warning."

"I don't want it," she protests. "It's yours."

He places it up high on a bookcase. "Keep it for now," he says. "I'll take it back once I decide what to do with it." He steps back to admire it. "Actually, it looks good there. Like it belongs."

Lorelei is in no mood no argue. She's happy he's back, and that's all that matters.

Juan takes two glasses and fills them with water from the sink. "Still clear as crystal," he says, then adds with a frown, "it seems to be running much slower. I'll have to check it out."

Lorelei brings her glass to her lips and drinks what, she realizes, may be the very same water from the very same spring Ponce drank from.

"It's strange," Juan muses, "to think I wouldn't be here if Ponce hadn't stolen the water from the spring." He takes a long drink, and then another. "Maybe it's true. If he hadn't had that Viagra reaction to it, then Luis—my great-great-times-twelve grandfather—wouldn't have been born. No Luis, no generational succession of Juans, no me."

"No you." If the woman hadn't saved Ponce's life, if he hadn't returned to steal the water, there would be no Juan. Impossible. She can't imagine her world without him.

But...she *can* imagine now who that woman really is.

Juan lifts his glass in a toast. "To Ponce and his crazy obsession."

"To the woman who made it all possible," Lorelei says, raising her glass. "To the woman on the path. To the woman in your dream. To..." She takes a deep breath. "...Winona."

Juan sets his glass on the table. "What are you talking about?"

"It's true, isn't it?" She takes a gulp of water to fortify herself. "The journal. Your dream. I don't understand it, but somehow they're all Winona."

After a long silence, Juan agrees. "That thought has crossed my mind, too." He takes the journal and slowly turns its pages. "It's not only the parallel of the journal to my dream. It's the déjà vu feeling I had when I read the description of the woman in

Ponce's journal. And—don't freak out here—it was the same feeling I had each time I saw Winona."

"I'm freaking out here."

"Don't. It's not the way it sounds. It was more…like there was some inexplicable connection. I dismissed it because it made no sense, and was beyond the realm of what I considered rational." He smacks the journal with the back of his hand. "This is like a road map to where we are today."

"Well, here's where we are," Lorelei says. "Winona's hired someone to tap into the water from my well. She's figured out where it comes from and she wants it." Her voice rises to a pitch she hasn't reached since she saw an iguana in her kitchen last year. "What does she know, and how does she know it?"

Juan stands, takes the glasses, now empty, and goes into the kitchen. Instead of re-filling the glasses, he puts them down and goes to the window, where he stands, staring at his reflection in the black glass. "I wish I had never tapped into the well," he says. "Or, at least, just found plain old water. Not this."

Lorelei walks over and joins him at the window. Their images glimmer back at them. Lorelei links her arm with his and leans her head on his shoulder. Her window twin mirrors the gesture. She seems even younger than the real Lorelei in the forgiving darkness. "If you hadn't, then where would we be now?" she asks.

"Maybe right here, right now," he says. "Just a little older, but still here."

Juan reaches over and brushes her hair away from her face. She looks up at him. "How do you know that?" she asks. "If nothing had come of your digging my well, if all you hit was dust or just plain water, that would have been the end of it." She shifts her gaze to her mirror self. "You wouldn't have returned for the cranky old lady who met you at the door that first time." She cringes when she recalls how she looked then—face smeared with night cream, hair hanging limply to her shoulders. Even worse, she remembers how she behaved. "It's a wonder you didn't just turn around and leave."

"Well, you *were* cranky," he says with a grin. "But 'old'? That didn't factor into my decision one way or the other. I just thought you were attractively feisty. I liked that."

"Attractively feisty? What does *that* mean?"

"I don't know. There was something about you that lit up in your determination to get your well fixed. I knew you wouldn't take no for an answer, so that made me even more resolved to solve the problem. Also, you're cute when you're mad."

"I wasn't mad," she protests. "And nobody's ever called me 'cute.'"

"Well, now they have." He cups her face in both his hands. Their kiss lasts a long, long time. "There's something else," he murmurs in her ear.

"Mmm?" she asks dreamily.

"I know you were looking at my butt when I was checking under your sink."

"I was not!"

"I saw you. It happens. Plumber's crack, it's an occupational hazard. At least you didn't squeeze my butt cheeks, like one lady did. Talk about a shock." He puts his arms around her, takes her butt in both his hands and gives her a little squeeze. "Like that," he says with a wicked grin.

Lorelei's face turns red in recollection of their first encounter, when he was looking for the reason her well had run dry. She did have that moment when she wanted to reach out and touch the furry patch above his butt, that moment of insane desire, so unfamiliar at the time, but so commonplace now, when she often absently stroked his back, his butt, and yes, the soft furry patch above his plumber's crack. She was a different person now.

Or was she?

All those years she spent emotionally locked away from her true self: it was there all along. She might have turned to stone had Juan not freed her from the tangled snarl that encased her heart.

Was it the water? Or was it that the right person came along who saw beyond her frigid veneer to the woman she really was. She hoped that was the case, because if and when the water vanished, she didn't want the person she was now to disappear as well.

WINONA

Fred is quitting. He says he's gone as far as he can, that he's hit some kind of rock that's damaged his drill bit, and now I owe him for that.

"I *what?*"

"Owe me. $375. You're lucky I wasn't using my $850 bit, so you're getting off cheap. There's some kinda kryptonite down there. Bent my drill like a pretzel. I never seen anything like it." He wipes his forehead with a ratty bandana, and hands me his bill. "I added it on to the usual charges."

I look over the bill, crumple it, and bounce it off his nose. "Not only am I not paying for your damned drill," I tell him, "but I'm not paying for your incompetence." I could easily slam this creep into the ground, but I refrain. Instead, I grab him by his sweaty T-shirt and pull his face next to mine. "You will get another, better drill, and you will drill through that rock. It's possible. It's been done." I hesitate before divulging what I know and what he doesn't. "Next door. That house has a well that was driven through that rock to good water. Someone has done it. And so will you."

"So get that someone to do it for you. I ain't gonna try no more."

I'm obviously not going to hire "that someone," since it's Juan, so I'm stuck. Then it occurs to me: Fred's a fracker. He's got a horizontal drill. Could he possibly access Lorelei's well that way? Just dig a tunnel to her pump and suck it out?

"That's crazy," he says when I suggest it. "You got no idea what you're talking about."

"Well, do you have a better idea?"

Fred pauses in what I assume is his version of thought before saying, "Y'know, I betcha there's oil and gas here, just under our feet. What d'ya say I do a little borehole, just to see what's what."

This guy has a one-track mind. "You're not helping."

"Stay with me. If I come upon something promising, oil-wise, it could possibly open the gate to some serious drilling in these parts. I mean drills that not only could suck up what oil is in this field, but major drills that could poke right through your kryptonite to the water beneath it." His eyebrows spring up with revelation. "Two for one!"

"Well, good luck with that," I say. "That's some pie-in-the-sky fantasy you've got cooking in your head, but even if it somehow worked, it would take years. And I need it now."

"Not true. There's precedent." He rolls the word around his mouth like a toothpick. "If I do find that there's the possibility of oil here, then the next step would be to find out who owns the mineral rights beneath these houses."

"Mineral rights? What does that have to do with anything?"

"Everything. Because if the homeowners here own the mineral rights, then each one could benefit if there's oil under their homes. Who wouldn't sell those rights to an oil company in this dumpy development? It could be their ticket out."

"What do I care if my neighbors get rich? I just want water. Is that too much to ask?" I know I'm sounding desperate, but I am. Just this morning I felt a twinge in my lower back and a crick in my neck, pains I've never felt in all my 500 years. What's next? Hip surgery? I'm deteriorating fast, and this Neanderthal isn't helping. "Do something!" I say, intending it as a command, but it emerges as a plea. I am not myself.

"Okay," he says. "Here's the deal. The permit I got to drill for water ain't the same permit I need to drill for oil. Till I get that, I'm gonna bring in a borehole drill and just kinda explore a little, maybe in a different spot. See what's what down there."

"You know what's down there. Rock. That you have to drill through."

"I tried that already. What I'd like to do is just bore down far as I can get, then go horizontal and take some samples. If I find there's some indication of oil or gas, then we'll go for it. The big companies know what to do from there, but meanwhile, they can bring in heavy equipment that can smash through that layer—mine ain't gonna do it—to do deep exploration, and, in the process, get to that water you say is there."

"I don't like the idea of smashing anything. What happens if there is oil or gas there. Won't that pollute the water that's beneath the rock?"

"Not a chance, not a chance," Fred says. "We got ways to separate alla that, no problem. It's all geological, complicated stuff, but I'm an expert. Trust me."

I *don't* trust this guy, but what choice do I have? I'm not feeling as sharp as I used to, when I might have questioned him more, but I neither have the time or inclination right now. Besides, there are other considerations. "Is this legal?" I ask. I don't want trouble.

Fred gives an exaggerated eyeroll. "Legal. You know what's legal? Whatever makes money. That's legal." He rubs his thumb and fingers together. "I've played this game before. I know how it works."

I'm too tired to argue. That's another bad sign. Too tired. I've always had an abundance of energy, sometimes maybe too much, where it's gotten me into circumstances I've had to extricate myself from—the incident with those hunky construction workers comes to mind—but in retrospect, not such a good idea. Now the thought of such gymnastics just exhausts me, and I'm fearful that I'll never feel that way again.

"Okay," I agree. "See what you can do, but don't ask for trouble, and don't do anything to contaminate the water. Bear in mind: it's just the water I want."

"Sure, sure," Fred says. "There won't be any problem. I know people. It'll all be on the up and up." But he's got a manic look on his face that belies what he's saying, and I immediately regret our agreement.

"Let me sleep on this," I say. "This is a little too sketchy for my taste. I need to think it through."

"Don't think too hard." He pokes at his temple with his dirt-smeared forefinger. "Thinking. That's how nothing gets done. You can think something to death." He grins and adds, "You know what they say. Just Do It."

Just Doing It isn't hard. It's Undoing It that could be the problem.

●　　　●　　　●

Too tired to head back to work at the casino, or even to go home to my apartment near there, I lie on the bare mattress in the house, contemplating the dead-bug-freckled light fixture overhead and Fred's offer. What's the alternative? He does have the know-how and network to make this happen, but I don't want to get mired in some shenanigans that could have far-reaching consequences having nothing to do with my request to just dig the damn well.

I jump up with a sudden burst of energy, compelled to return to Lorelei's well. Maybe I can figure out some way to divert it myself, without Fred. I've tried this before, but I can't help myself. It's the same desperation of losing something, yet returning to the same spot time and time again in the hope that somehow, this time it will magically appear.

Juan and Lorelei are standing at her kitchen window, seeing their own reflections, not me creeping around outside. I strain to listen to what they're saying, but my hearing has gone even further downhill. It's frustrating, being right outside, seeing them, not hearing them, like watching TV with the sound off.

They touch each other in a way I've never been touched. Softly. As if caressing something precious. And. They kiss like they're melting into one another. How would that feel, I wonder?

I'm overcome with a sense of loss. It's not jealousy. Jealousy, like love, is an emotion I've observed but never felt. As I've come to realize, what I thought was love for my Chief was really teenage lust. What shatters me now is knowing that I've never been in love, and chances are I never will. Maybe in my weakened state I'm vulnerable to sentimentality, but seeing their happiness exposes a nerve I didn't know I had. Five hundred years of chasing the spring may have leached all emotion from me. I've had great adventures, great experiences, great sex—but no friends. I feel like a skipping stone across life's pond, never going deep enough to feel what others seem to feel. What is love? What is hate? Just words, as far as I know.

For the first time, I realize my life has been one long scavenger hunt with clues that constantly change. The reward is ephemeral— the promise of eternal youth—and then the spring moves on. So I hop back on the treadmill: search, find, search, find, on and on forever, whenever forever is.

Do I want 500 more years of that? When it's fueled by fear that it could all be finite, is life without end really living at all?

FIFTEEN

In the lull after Ladybug Lingerie was temporarily closed, without work to fill her time, Sharleen had pursued a repeat of the brief moment she had felt she was a star, by reviving the fountain of youth story for the media. Her fifteen minutes of fame as self-appointed spokesperson for Ladybug Lingerie had flared, then flamed out quickly, most notably after she was invited to appear on a local TV lifestyle show, "SoFla, SoGood." Lorelei, after failing to disabuse her of that notion, had forced herself to watch.

Sharleen teetered onto the set, waving at the audience, thrilled at the applause. Lorelei had a flash of "Huh?" as she watched Sharleen wiggle into her seat facing the host, the relentlessly vivacious Roxy Rodriguez, all wild red hair and whooping laugh. Someone had clearly done a professional make-up job on Sharleen, softening her Dolly Parton persona to more of a Lindsay Lohan look. But, yes, it was Sharleen, evidenced by the first words to come out of her mouth when asked by Roxy if she really believed she had drunk from the fountain of youth. "Decide for yourself," Sharleen squeaked in a nervous voice.

Roxy leaned forward to peer at Sharleen's face, now frozen in a terrified grin. "So who's your plastic surgeon?"

Sharleen's grin collapsed into a pout of denial. "I've never had surgery," she declared, "unless you count my appendectomy."

"Peel?" asked Roxy. "They do great peels these days."

"No peel!" she shot back. "No peel! No nothing, anywhere!" To Roxy's open- mouthed delight, Sharleen bounced up out of her chair and did a little spin. "Check it out. Tight and firm." She gave her butt a good, sound smack. "No Spanx here!"

"Okay!" Roxy patted Sharleen's chair. "Sit down, *chica*. You've made your point."

Sharleen, clearly rattled, sat. The camera's closeup revealed she was perspiring beneath the makeup which, upon meltdown, uncovered flaws in her skin's perfection.

"Looks like you might need another dose of that magic water," Roxy said. "I'm seeing some serious crinkling here."

"I know," Sharleen wailed, fingers flitting across her cheeks. "I'm being *rationed*."

"Sounds more like rationalization," Roxy said, and the audience laughed along with her. Suddenly serious, Roxy retracted her wide mouth and pursed it in contrition. "Really," she said, nodding with practiced sincerity, "you do look marvelous, for whatever reason." With an athletic fling of her arm, she flipped into full Roxy, flashing a brilliant smile. "Let's hear it for Sharleen and the fountain of youth!"

Slinking off-stage to the patter of applause, Sharleen bumped into Roxy's next guest who had a parrot on his head that glared at her with beady bird eyes. She fled, forlorn, the feeling of celebrity she had enjoyed at the beginning of the show now erased in a very public way.

With that, the story lost its value and dropped into the abyss of yesterday's news. The Internet keeps it alive, YouTube clips rising like video zombies from the social media muck. There's even a GIF of Ruby proclaiming "No more turkey neck! It *is* the fountain of youth!" Over and over and over, like a nightmare that won't stop recurring. But even that is lost in the avalanche of cat videos and food hacks, so it's just another irritating grain of sand on the Internet beach.

With the shop reopening after its three-week hiatus, Lorelei welcomes the distraction as well as the challenge of reviving the business after the tumult of bad publicity. Witnessing Sharleen's public humiliation had melted away any resentment Lorelei felt toward her, and reignited the underlying affection that has held their friendship together after all these years.

Hopes dashed for her fantasied dance with fame, Sharleen agrees, chastened, when Lorelei asks her to return for the re-opening. The only water in the bottle will be Crystal Creek once again, so without the allure of Spring Chicken, Ladybug Lingerie needs an upgrade to bring customers back. Lorelei has restocked with a greater depth of inventory—sassy and sexy for the young and chic; elegant and Bacall-ish for the midlifers; formidable and practical for those in need of such support. She has spruced up the décor to make it more contemporary, but most important, convinces Sharleen that her presence is crucial. "You're the attraction," Lorelei says to a sulking Sharleen. "It's your personality, your spirit, that makes customers return again and again. I can't do it without you."

And with that, Sharleen is back.

• • •

As with all things media, the world, in its voracious greed for novelty, had chewed up Ladybug Lingerie and spit it into the Google gutter. But Ladybug has risen from the ashes, transformed in the eyes of its core of loyal customers. In retrospect, they look upon the water-guzzling phase of their shopping experience much as they might look back at some shared teenage mischief, embarrassing but harmless, worth a giggle before moving on with life. The water, they concede, was probably just a placebo that induced the hallucination of youth, something they imagined but didn't really happen.

What did happen, at least for the more reflective among them, was a recognition that beauty can have its stages and is not degraded by age. With the exception of Ruby Braithwaite, whose petulant boycott of the shop was actually welcomed by Lorelei, all of her former customers returned, as well as a young, hip influx. Initially attracted by the media blitz, they stay when they discover that what they assumed was a staid, fusty girdle emporium has what they are looking for in sexy, fun fluff. With something for everyone, Ladybug endures.

The resurrection of the shop has helped to blur Lorelei's obsession with Winona and what's happening practically in her own backyard. She hears the sound of the drill early each morning, a sound that seems to follow her all the way to work. She can only surmise that Fred is having little success, and wonders if it's an indication that something is happening with the water itself. She still has an adequate supply, but the force and quantity of what's coming out of her faucet is noticeably diminishing. Juan has been tinkering with the pump to see if that could be the problem. The pump is fine, he says. Let's just keep an eye on it.

Corabelle keeps her posted on Winona's comings and goings. According to Corabelle, Winona seems to have disappeared for the most part, showing up for some kind of consultation with Fred now and then. Apparently, something happened a few days ago, Corabelle reports. "Don't know what the problem was, but it looked like Fred and the lady-man got to yelling at each other."

Lorelei doesn't know if this is good news or bad news. Think positive, she tells herself. Maybe it's a sign that Fred has had no success at drilling through to the water, and that Winona will just give up and disappear. Or, she realizes with a start, maybe he did hit water, and now they're just fighting over money.

"Oh," Corabelle adds, "and it looks like he's got a new kinda rig, from what I saw pulling backa her house a few days ago. I'll tell you, it makes some terrible noise I got to listen to all day. You lucky you're at work. That sound can drive you batshit."

Propelled by a synthesis of rage and fear, Lorelei pushes past Corabelle and runs to Winona's house. She takes the front steps two at a time and pounds on the door, its bile-yellow paint peeling in flakes that scatter on the rotted wood porch. She tries to peer through a window, but the tattered shades are drawn, hanging at odd angles that reveal only darkness within. The house seems to emanate mold from every crack and crevice. Nothing has changed here since Winona purchased the place, aside from the mauling of the weed-choked back yard.

Receiving no response, Lorelei dashes to the back of the house to see the well itself up close. What will she do next? She has no plan. She only knows she's got to do something.

What awaits her is not just one well, but two. The first well seems to be abandoned, its slurry pile melting into the mud and weeds that landscape the yard. The second well has been bored near the edge of the property where Winona's neighbor's cyclone fence begins, and seems to be narrower and of a different purpose from the first. The rig is poised above it like a bird of prey, but there are no clues as to what this is all about.

"You again?" She recognizes the voice before she whirls to see its source: Fred the digger. He's advancing on her, his barrel-chest leading the way, simian arms ending in tight furry fists. He removes the unlit cigar from his face to point it at her. "What're you looking for?"

"What's that all about?" Lorelei points to the new excavation, fearless in her anger. "You've been disrupting this neighborhood for weeks now," she says, channeling Corabelle's complaint about the noise. "Maybe it's time to just give up and leave us in peace."

"This ain't your house." Fred jams the cigar between his teeth and chews it like gum. "You're trespassing. What this is about is none-a your business."

But it is my business, Lorelei wants to say. It's my water she's after. Instead, she asks, as calmly as she can muster, "Did you hit water yet?"

The cigar goes still. Fred's insect brows quiver with suppressed glee. "I think I found something better."

Better? What could be better than the water? But, "What's that?" she asks, sensing a truce—as well as a truth—in the making.

Fred's eyes ping from side to side, as if someone else might be listening. "I can't say right now." His voice lowers to the pitch of a teenage girl telling a secret. "But you guys might be very very rich very very soon." He nods knowingly. "Very *very* rich."

Lorelei's mind hovers between relief that the water is still safe, and disregard of Fred's promise of wealth. She doesn't care about the possibility of riches.

Fred can't contain himself. It's clear he is bursting with information that just needs sharing, so he does. "I think I hit the motherlode," he says.

"What are you talking about?"

"Ya see that borehole over there?" He points to the rig at the edge of the property. "It's an exploratory well, dug down deep— way deeper than I thought I could, given that rock ledge I hit before. But my drill kept going and going, so I'm thinking the rock I run into was just some kinda freak thing, cause mosta what's under here is what's under almost every place in Florida: limestone."

This, Lorelei knew from what Juan had explained to her, was true. The rock he had to drill through to get to the water was like nothing he had ever encountered before. Thankfully, it hadn't stopped him, as it had Fred. But, what had Fred discovered as he drilled deep through limestone?

"Oil," Fred says with a smug smile. "The sample I got from the borehole shows there's traces of oil under here." His smile stretches into a tobacco-stained grin. "We're gonna be rich."

Lorelei feels as if something has shifted beneath her feet and she's not quite sure where she stands. "You didn't hit water?" she asks, fearful that his drill contaminated her source.

Her heart stops at his "Yeah, I did," but recovers when he adds, "It's that same crappy stuff you all been drinking anyway, specially since the drought. Just at a lower level, but not the kinda water Pocahontas thinks is here, for some reason." He chews thoughtfully on his cigar. "She's got some notion that there's great water under there. Well, dream on." He shakes his head. "You'd think she'd be happy about all this—I mean, gas, oil, she's gonna be rich, fer Pete's sake. But no, she almost tore my head off the other day when I told her."

Lorelei nods sympathetically. "Hmm," she says.

"So. You own your house?" he asks.

"Why do you ask?"

"If you do, lucky you. You own your house, you own the mineral rights." He points his cigar in a sweeping gesture that encompasses the vista of Melaleuca Lakes. "Alla you guys that own the mineral rights are gonna get a visit from someone you're gonna think of as your fairy godfather: a 'land man.' He's gonna make you a offer you can't refuse." He jams the cigar back between his teeth and gives her a satisfied grin.

"And what if I do refuse?"

Fred's face compresses like a flat truck tire. "You won't," he says. And with that, he stalks off, leaving Lorelei to wonder what lies beneath, and what it all could mean.

● ● ●

Ruby Braithewaite is back. She bursts through the door of the shop, bellowing, "Where's the water, I'll pay anything, name your price!" Lorelei had hoped that she had seen the last of Ruby, but that was wishful thinking. It was rumored that the effects of Ruby's brief experience with the water's rejuvenating qualities had retreated, thus requiring the services of Dr. Rollie, who had welcomed her return with a mid-week special. Ruby was freshly, if temporarily, revived with laser planing, cheek injections and some serious Botox, which brought her to the unhappy conclusion that, without regular infusions of the water, her future would entail this kind of perpetual enriching of the coffers of Dr. Rollie. The reversion back to her dependence on surgical upkeep has apparently ratcheted up her neurosis to the point where here she is again, brashly demanding access to the water.

Several customers browsing through merchandise raise their heads like meerkats sniffing trouble. Sharleen retreats behind a rack of poufy negligees, leaving Lorelei exposed at the counter to deal with Ruby on her own. She is not in the mood to confront Ruby. She hasn't been in the mood for very much at all since Fred informed her of the potential for fracking beneath her house, and what that could mean for the future of her water. And now, here's Ruby to complicate her life even more.

She won't allow it. "What are you talking about?"

Ruby frowns, a difficult post-Botox task. "You know what I'm talking about. Look at you! Hardly a wrinkle in that sneaky face of yours. You're hoarding Spring Chicken for yourself."

At that, Sharleen peeks through the hanging negligees, attracting Ruby's attention. "And you," Ruby says, jabbing a gnarled finger at her. Sharleen retreats but it's too late. Ruby stalks to Sharleen's hiding place and shoves the gowns out of the way to scrutinize her face up close. "Ha," Ruby says. "So, she's not sharing with you, either."

Sharleen shoots Lorelei an I-told-you-so look, then shuts it down at Lorelei's warning glare. "There's nothing to share," she says. "We're not in the water business."

Lorelei has recovered enough to assume her manager persona. "We do have a new Donna Karan shipment that might interest you." She forces a smile. "I know how fond you are of her line."

Ruby responds with a blank stare, then croaks, "It's not here?"

Lorelei feigns misunderstanding. "No, the shipment just arrived, a lovely selection of silk robes." She notes with perverse satisfaction that Ruby's latest foray into the world of Dr. Rollie has been less than successful. Her cheeks are puffed out like a squirrel's storing nuts. "Would you like to see them?"

The audience of customers has frozen into watchful apprehension, merchandise they had been handling delicately now clutched in sweaty hands. Lorelei knows she has to not only defuse this situation, but cancel out any thoughts of the water and what it had brought to the shop and its reputation.

Ruby, however, is not cooperating. "I saw you on 'SoFla SoGood,'" she says to Sharleen with a sneer. "Roxy really called you on that one, didn't she? You just wound up with egg on your saggy old face." She dismisses Sharleen's attempt at protest with a flip of her wrist. "It's obvious. Lorelei's got it all to herself. Just look at her."

All eyes turn to Lorelei. She wants to duck behind the counter, then reappear looking her true age. But she knows she doesn't, and for the first time, wishes she did.

How can she put a stop to this potential reopening of what she had hoped was a closed book? All she wants is to put that nightmare behind her, enjoy the newfound success of her shop, and just live her life. Happily ever after, however long "after" might be.

The shop seems to hover in an airless void as the customers await her response.

And then it comes, with the inspiration of Ruby herself.

"I had plastic surgery," Lorelei says.

A collective sigh arises from the gathering, whether of relief or acknowledgement, Lorelei doesn't care.

"Omigod," Sharleen breathes. "So, that's where you were when you closed the shop."

Lorelei gives a little shrug and an embarrassed smile she hopes confirms her impromptu lie.

Ruby is silent. Then, "Who did it?" she demands. "Dr. Rollie?"

Lorelei shakes her head, no. "I can't tell you that," she says, knowing there's nothing to tell. The mystery will remain, and with that, she assumes, the question of the water should end.

But it's not over for Ruby. She pushes her face close to Lorelei's, grabs hold of her shoulders with claw-like nails. Lorelei feels as if she's been attacked by an eagle. "You have to tell me," Ruby rasps in a voice that combines pleading with a threat. She releases one hand, which roams first over Lorelei's face, then descends to examine her breasts. "He did a great job on your boobs," she mutters. "They feel *real*." Lorelei recoils, horrified. No one has ever physically invaded her space like this. She is left speechless.

But Sharleen is not. Fists clenched, shoulders hunched, she clomps out on her platform heels and yanks Ruby away from Lorelei. "Get out," she commands. "You're not welcome here." Too startled to fight back, Ruby squawks feebly as Sharleen marches her through the shop, pushes her outside, and shuts the door behind her. Lorelei is stunned at the applause that follows.

• • •

Later, as Lorelei and Sharleen close up shop, Sharleen is uncharacteristically quiet. She carefully folds bras one into the other and lines them up in their drawer, seeming to study each one for flaws like a stage mother inspecting her daughter for the Little Miss Universe contest. Finally, she speaks. "Did you really have surgery?"

Lorelei knew this was coming, but hadn't prepared an answer. If she admits her confession was a lie, then she's back to square one with Sharleen and her feeling that Lorelei is hoarding the water for herself. If she compounds her lie by insisting it's true, it would be the first time she has ever outright lied to Sharleen. She doesn't know if she could live with that. As erratic and rocky as their friendship has been through the years, there has always been a baseline of trust that has never been broken. It's as if the water has found a fissure to breach that could expand into a canyon between them.

She hedges. "What do you think?"

Sharleen closes the drawer and faces Lorelei. "I don't know," she says. "But what I do know is that it doesn't matter. If you had surgery, fine. You look great. Nice job. If you didn't, then you still look great. I don't really want to know if it's because of the water or not."

"It's not that..."

"You know, seeing Ruby in all her craziness did something to me. I felt like I was watching a version of myself." Sharleen busies herself with re-folding teddies on a shelf. "I'm never going to ask you about the water again. I realize now I've held a grudge because of it, and I don't like feeling that way about you."

Before Lorelei can think of a response, Sharleen continues. "What I realized when I watched Ruby implode was that I've depended all my life on what people thought of me, especially how I look." She sighs and re-folds a teddy. "Obviously, I loved how much better I looked when I drank the water. But do you know when I felt really *good* about myself?"

Lorelei had never thought about Sharleen's feelings about herself. She was too busy thinking about her own feelings.

"That was when I wasn't even caring about how I looked. When I started using parts of myself that I didn't even know existed. Like when I came up with ideas, and felt I had a brain that worked, and could even call myself *creative*, which is something no one ever said I was." Sharleen's look of defiance unnerves Lorelei. She *had* told Sharleen good things, hadn't she? Hadn't she encouraged her to come back to the shop by telling her that she was the one who attracted customers with her personality and spirit? Hadn't she praised her for her creativity in designing the label?

Lorelei realizes with a start that perhaps all that praise came across to Sharleen as condescending. To be honest, she *had* been surprised that Sharleen proved herself to be more than the two-dimensional person she had always considered her to be. She realizes that there had been glimpses of a deeper level which she had ignored, abetted by Sharleen herself, who had seemed to thrive on the persona she had created. She was, certainly, a wacky, fun-loving hedonist on the surface, but had Lorelei, in a way, helped foster Sharleen's low self-esteem by presenting herself as the opposite—a serious, pragmatic, smarty-pants? With the discovery of the water, Lorelei has discovered aspects of herself that she hadn't known existed. Why shouldn't Sharleen have, too?

Lorelei's sudden guilt attack provokes a blurted confession: "I didn't have plastic surgery."

Sharleen shrugs. "Doesn't matter." She begins to collect empty cups left by the customers around the shop. "Not so many of these lately," she observes, tossing what she's got into the trash. "I'm guessing the ladies aren't drinking so much because they know the water's not miraculous. So, more for you at home."

"It's running low," Lorelei says, and confesses, "I filled six bottles, just as a backup. You can have as much as you want," hoping the offer will counteract what looks like her own selfish greed. Has she become a water hoarder, keeping it from Sharleen, her partner and friend? With the incremental slowing of water from her well has come an undercurrent of anxiety about it. She finds herself rationing it, taking quick showers instead of allowing herself the luxury of long soaks in the deep, scented water of her tub. Nevertheless, she has seen indications of withdrawal. Lines she had forgotten are surfacing on her forehead, and the flexibility she had been taking for granted was gradually diminishing, evident when she stooped to open a drawer or climbed a ladder to reach high shelves. The changes were minimal but noticeable to herself until her denial of the fact became a nagging fear. Combined with her fixation on Winona and Fred and his machinations, she's allowed these things to run a constant narrative in her head. This, she knows, is not good.

"No thanks," Sharleen says to Lorelei's offer, to her surprise. "What's the point? We both know it'd just be temporary, and then I'd have to work my way back to the way I feel now, which is not caring." She pats at the soft bulge of muffin top which has reappeared recently, a portent of bigger things to come. "Well, I guess I do care, but I'm trying to find something beside the way I look that'll make me feel good about myself."

Before Lorelei can compose a response to that, something that will sound sincere and uplifting, Sharleen has disappeared. She returns with her purse to say goodnight, and is out the door. "'Night," Lorelei calls, but Sharleen is gone.

Lorelei is baffled. Sharleen seems to be undergoing some kind of evolution before her eyes. Is she really accepting the inevitable, or is it just a coverup and the old Sharleen is still in there, plotting and planning some way to retrieve the youth she had enjoyed, if briefly? After all, Sharleen had come to work this morning looking like the old Sharleen—mini-skirt, platform sandals, bouffant and all. Now, it's as if someone has siphoned her brain and replaced it with common sense.

Then again, Lorelei's own behavior, she must admit, has at times seemed as if someone else were controlling her actions. Perhaps the water was really a catalyst that revealed what was there all along, just beneath the surface—sensuality, awareness, the ability to love—frozen in time. She surprised herself, sometimes happily, sometimes not, but she knows she's not the same person she was before. She has no explanation for any of it, any more than she can understand what happened to Sharleen.

Right now, it's not the water—or its loss—that is primary in her thoughts, although Winona's search for it has created unexpected complications. No, irrational as it seems, what concerns her is Winona and her connection to Juan.

•   •   •

When she gets home, Juan is there, tinkering once again with the pump, which he said might be the cause of the water problem. Lorelei isn't surprised to see him; they had noted the decline in both pressure and quantity for a while now. She hadn't expressed her alarm at this to Juan, but it was evident by her frequent comments on its decrease, her efforts to ration what was there, and the knowledge that the six bottles she had filled in case the water ran out would only prolong the agony. Juan dismissed her occasional reference to how this was affecting her—her appearance, her energy, her minor aches and pains—by saying she looked fine to him, still beautiful and full of life. But something was happening that was out of the ordinary, and his fussing with the pump indicated his own concern. Now his tinkering has resulted in a pronouncement: nothing wrong with the pump. It's the water that's receding.

"Why is this happening?" Lorelei asks, trying not to sound panicked. "Does this mean I won't have any water at all?"

Juan shakes his head. "I can't explain it. Maybe its source has dried up. Maybe it's found another path. Or," he adds with a touch of optimism, "maybe it's plateau'ed, and all that'll happen is that you'll have less pressure, but it'll still be there."

Lorelei goes to the sink and pours herself a glass. The water comes out slowly, but what gradually fills the glass is as clear as it's always been. She takes a long drink, savoring it as if it's the last time water this good will ever pass her lips. She almost wants to cry—not because the potential for loss means her rejuvenation may be ending, but because this new lease on life might end as well. That thought is too much to absorb, and her sadness turns to anger.

"It's all Winona's fault," she declares.

"What?" Juan looks baffled. "What does she have to do with this?"

"If she hadn't hired that obnoxious well digger, none of this would have happened." What she doesn't add is the fear that there's more to Winona's interference than her desire to tap into Lorelei's well. Winona's connection to Juan, though indefinable, intensifies Lorelei's grievance against the well-digging and its unexpected turn into exploration for oil.

"True, Winona hired him, I guess to find the spring," Juan says. "If he thinks there's oil and gas under here, then his real purpose for digging might not just be questionable but illegal. That aside, I doubt if he's responsible for what's going on with your water. Look: he hasn't come near your well. What he's done is dig a borehole right past the aquifer, down deep to where he thinks there's gas or oil. If what he's looking for is just water, he would have stopped at the aquifer."

This doesn't satisfy Lorelei. "It's too coincidental," she says. "All that digging and pounding…it has to have had some effect." She tips the glass back to drink the glistening teardrop of water that remains, letting it settle on her tongue before swallowing. "I think she's put a Miccosukee curse on it." She laughs to show she's kidding, but somewhere deep inside, she's not. She knows there's a connection. She just knows.

* * *

Corabelle is at her door, rapping like a woodpecker. Lorelei debates answering it, but it's too late to hide. Corabelle's squinty eyes—all that's visible of her through the glass—have spotted her. Her rapping accelerates until Lorelei opens the door and Corabelle is inside, reporting the latest news. "One-a them 'land men' been making the rounds of the neighborhood, offering people all kinds a money to sell them mineral rights, you know what that is?"

Lorelei says Yes, but Corabelle's going to tell her anyway. "That means they can buy up alla whatever's under your house, and you know it's not just dirt." She nods wisely. "He come to your house yet?" When Lorelei says No, Corabelle humphs. "Well, he came to mine, offered me a shitload of money, but I said to him, I said, 'You just get your fat ass outta here 'cause I am *not interested.*'" She crosses her arms and waits for Lorelei to ask why, and when she does, Corabelle pronounces, "I have my principles!"

"Well," says Lorelei, "that's certainly admirable." Alongside her sudden trepidation at what this latest development could mean, comes a new appreciation for this feisty little person, white hair tied in a bandana, tiny eyes squinting with righteous fury, sturdy little legs planted on the floor. "What are the other neighbors doing, do you know?"

Of course Corabelle knows. She has taken this up as her cause, quizzing the other residents of Melaleuca Lakes as to their opinion of this new development. "Oh, I am stirring stuff up," she says with pride. "It's war, is what it is." According to Corabelle, she has rallied the troops, awakening their normally soporific response to neighborhood events. This has divided the residents into two camps: one, the Corabelle Camp, against selling rights, are mostly long-time residents prone to inertia, resistant to any change in their lives that might create uncertainty, the same ones who had argued against removal of the offending melaleuca trees because it would cost too much and it was too much trouble to change the name of Melaleuca Lakes. The other camp, the Why Not? Camp, sees, despite the prospect of danger to their property and water supply, only the economic upside to selling rights to the land beneath their feet for a fee—amount undisclosed as yet but promised to be huge. "Those greedy bastards are going *down*," Corabelle declares.

Lorelei's trepidation turns to alarm. "Is this actually happening?" she asks. "How could it come to this without proper permitting and review by...I don't know...some kind of local committee?"

Corabelle shrugs. "Beats me. I think that Fred guy is pushing it through, maybe he's got some kinda pull around here, I don't know." Her features compress into the heroic face of a Ninja turtle. "All I know is I'm gonna put a stop to this crap before it goes any further."

Lorelei senses that it will go further. Now there's war on the horizon. Plus, the water is disappearing, along with her youth.

And then there's the mystery of Juan and Winona. It's all too much. A weariness overcomes her. She wants to take a nap.

"You gonna sell, too?" Corabelle asks, perturbed. "You got that look on your face."

"No, no," she says. "I'm not selling. I'm just tired." She sends Corabelle off to continue her mission. "Good luck," she calls after her. And she means it.

* * *

One drop plunks onto the multicolored heap of dry beans in her soup pot. It sinks, leaving no sign of having been there. Not a bean is dampened. Lorelei turns the faucet on full blast, but nothing emerges, not even a sigh.

She runs to the bathroom and turns the faucet in the tub. Again, a lone drop emerges, hovers, and falls onto the white porcelain. She touches it with one finger, then places it on her tongue. It is her last taste of the spring.

Juan arrives soon after her call, his demeanor funereal, his tools at the ready. "It's gone, isn't it?" Lorelei asks. She knows the answer. But Juan is willing to attempt a resurrection. She watches, hands clasped, as he works, disemboweling the pump and laying parts on the ground. Eventually she stops surveying the scene, and goes inside to mourn.

She knew this was coming. Now that it's here, her dismay is tempered by a strange feeling of dissociation, as if it's happening to someone else. The water may be gone, but she is still here. Everything, and nothing, has changed.

When Juan finally emerges, she's not surprised at his diagnosis. The pump is fine, but the well is an empty hole, ending in nothing. It will have to be sealed.

"What will I do for water?" she asks. After all, she is a practical person, and despite her loss, she's already thinking pragmatically.

She needs to drink, to bathe, to make soup. She needs to go on living.

Juan lowers himself onto the couch with a grunt. "I'll dig you a new well down to the aquifer. It'll have to be closer to your property line, away from the rock. With the drought, the water may be kind of puny, but you will have water." He reaches over and touches her hand. "I'm sorry it won't be water from the spring."

The next few days are filled with the sight and sound of destruction and construction. She watches from her window as Juan removes the pump, then fills the well, first with bentonite chips, then cement. He crowns it with a metal cap to seal it. It's almost as if it never existed.

His rig appears in her yard the next day, and the new well is dug with no obstruction. It's up and running with, predictably, the same ochre-tinged water she had before. So it's back to big bottles of Crystal Creek for drinking and cooking, and baths in cloudy water. Rather than use the six bottles she's kept in reserve, she decides to save them for some future emergency. She may not have the fountain of youth, but she does have something better: she has Juan.

•   •   •

She's dreaming. She knows she's dreaming, but it's so lovely she wants it to be real. She and Juan are at home—not her home, but his. The fish tanks have blended into one, and they are inside of it, as if they were living in an endless aquarium. Miraculously, they can breathe underwater. Hand in hand, they drift pleasantly along, accompanied by aquatic creatures both familiar and fantastical who seem to consider them as equal beings. They swim in their own private universe; they have always been here and will be here forever. Time has no meaning as they float along in a perpetual Now.

A rattling noise penetrates the reverie of her dream, low at first, then escalating until she awakens to the reality of rain beating on her window. She looks out on a charcoal landscape already dotted with puddles. Unlike other passing storms that teased the brittle dryness with a few meager drops, this time it's for real.

WATER, WHEN IT FALLS
AS RAIN

Nebulous in its embryonic state, cradled in warm air, the vapor wafts heavenward, abandoning the sun-baked earth. It ascends into cooler air, gains substance until, saturated, it evolves from mist to cloud, condensing, taking form, multiplying into countless droplets. In the rapidly-cooling air, droplets collide and mate with each other to coalesce into bigger drops, pregnant with themselves. Gathering strength, they swell and mushroom into a towering cloud that rises high and wide, blanketing the land below with darkness.

Rogue drops ascend higher, freeze into ice particles that smash into falling soft hail to create electrical polarization: lightning. Its sharp crack accompanies a drum roll of thunder, and the show begins.

The drops gather behind the curtain of cloud, awaiting gravity's cue. They rapidly expand in the turbulent air, their weight increasing until they can no longer be contained. Hesitant at first, the tentative drops fall into the atmosphere, their path to earth paved by flashes of lightning. Encouraged by the applause of thunder, the waiting drops follow, frenetic in their escape, ecstatic in their free fall.

The land below, dehydrated and thirsty, fervently awaits their arrival.

SIXTEEN

Kippy the Channel 9 Weatherperson has been promising, with balletic sweeps of her Ann Taylor-clad arms across the computer-generated map, that the cold front moving southeastward from the Mississippi Valley would soon bring "much-needed rain to our drought-stricken South Florida." By the third day of such promises, Kippy's arms are windmilling in her desire to dislodge the cartoon clouds that seem to be stuck somewhere over Alabama.

On the fifth day of unfulfilled promises, Kippy is looking pretty fierce. She glares through disheveled strands of her once-tended coiffure; her long graceful fingers are balled into fists that punch at the cut-out clouds inching over a happy-face sun. But at last, on the seventh day, Kippy can rest, for rain has come to Miami.

The first drops arrive unheralded from a restless sky, its few smudges mistaken for smoke. One drop plops on the visor of a golfer too busy cursing his luck on Doral's ninth to notice. Another dents the sand next to a receptionist from New Jersey napping on Crandon Park beach. Still another pings off the hard hat of a crane operator at a construction site in Bal Harbour. None of the above takes note.

But the first dark smudges are mere advance troops for the army of thunderheads that lurks beyond the Everglades. It moves stealthily eastward, rumbling and rolling over the parched and cracked land, releasing an artillery of rain upon the startled inhabitants. Alligators raise their beady eyes heavenward; egrets and herons spread dessicated wings to the sky; snakes slither from dusty burrows. Mosquitoes find their buzz again, and a panther remembers his prowl.

The deluge begins at dawn, sweeping through the city in a wet gray curtain. Gardeners rejoice, kids stomp through puddles, ground water rises and fills lakes, ponds and wells. The world seems suddenly greener; the air, soft and alive. The only dark notes are the laments of tourists who curse the timing of their vacations, and the predictions of pessimists who forecast that another plague of hurricanes will follow this torrential cascade.

WINONA

Okay, I've had it with Fred. He's telling me he's not looking for water any more, that the incessant rain has raised the water level and my well is full. He dismisses my argument that I want water that's *below* this well, but I'm not about to tell him why. It's gas and oil he's after now, he says, he's gotten mineral rights from half my neighbors, so if I'm not interested, they'll be more than happy to let him dig up their yards. Great, I tell him, just get your greedy ass out of my yard and take your rigging with you. You're fired. No more exploration on my property, and I wish you the worst of luck.

Now what? I'm back to square one. It's getting harder and harder to go to work at the casino every day. I have to resort to coffee to get going in the morning, and while I pick up steam during the day, by closing time it's evident that I've wound down. Even Susie Billie has noticed, taking advantage of my distraction by insisting she be promoted back to Poker. When I object, she threatens to quit, claiming discrimination since there are very few Miccosukees hired at the Miccosukee casino, and she's one of them—as am I, as far as they know. It's not worth arguing, so she's out of Bingo and back at Poker once again, creating havoc since she never really mastered the game. Do I care? No.

I haven't had the heart to go back to the house for a few days, but tonight, when I return to resume my watch on Lorelei's well, something is different. I can't see the pump, and it looks like a new well and pump have been installed at the edge of her yard. What's going on?

I have to find out.

I part the jungle of foliage and bushes that separates my property from Lorelei's, and creep cautiously into her yard, aware that the full moon is probably putting me in the spotlight. I keep one eye out for that vicious possum that has attacked me before. I'm in no shape to have to wrestle him again, but so far, so good. Hopefully, even if he sees me, he remembers our last encounter and is keeping his distance.

When I reach the spot where the pump once stood, all that remains is a dull metal cap locked over a pipe sticking out of the ground. I tear at it in disbelief, trying to pry it loose. My spring! Where is my spring? It's under here, I know it's under here!

I find a rock and bang repeatedly at the cap, not caring that the thud of rock upon metal may alert Lorelei to my presence. It doesn't budge, and then I notice that there's a rim of cement that seals it to the pipe.

Is it sealed? Did Juan fill the well with cement? Is my spring buried forever beneath the earth? I throw myself over what is now a gravestone marking the death of my spring, and do something I haven't done for centuries. I sob.

I am so immersed in my despair that I don't notice the feet planted in front of me. Bare, long-toed and muddy, they emerge from worn jeans that, I see as my eyes rise from feet to jeans to black T-shirt to their owner, are worn by Juan. His arms are crossed over the white drop of water emblazoned across the shirt, but despite his confrontational stance, his look is less stern than it was at our last encounter in Lorelei's yard. It is more a look of puzzlement, confirmed by his question, "What's going on?"

I can't answer at first. I'm so overwhelmed by grief that to put it into words might diminish it. My loss is too great. I've spent my life seeking and then finding the spring. The thought that my energy is at such a low level that I may be incapable of continuing that search is overwhelming. What will I do if it's beyond my reach?

At last I find my voice. I put my hand over the capped well. "Why did you do this?"

He studies me for a moment before answering. "The well was dry. I sealed it." He pauses. "It's gone. The spring is gone."

Hearing it said out loud makes it all too real. I struggle to my feet and summon up the formidable woman I once was and intend to be again. "You knew what you were doing," I accuse. "You know who you are, you know who I am, and you know how to find where the spring is."

Juan backs away, shaking his head. "I don't know what you're talking about."

"You owe me," I say.

"What?"

"You owe me," I repeat. "If not for me, you wouldn't be you."

Juan's shocked silence confirms my suspicion.

It's all coming together now. Juan isn't Ponce, but Ponce is within Juan, and I think I know why. I'm so sure that I say it: "You're a descendant of Ponce de Leon."

"How did you know?" he blurts.

So. It's true. That explains the connection I felt the first time I saw him, the moment I touched him. Like this.

I reach out. My hand rests on the water drop on his shirt. Time collapses. I am back on the jungle trail, pleading with the Chief to spare Ponce's life. My eyes meet Ponce's, and I am thrust forward in time to another place, the land of the Calusa. Hidden in the depths of foliage, I see Ponce crawling along the sand, clearly wounded. Once again, I relive that moment when I offer him water from my shell cup, then, pursued by Calusa, leave the cup behind in haste to escape into the jungle. From there, I witness his comrades scoop him up, drag him into the breaking waves to a rowboat, then onto the ship that awaits.

I feel a hand on my arm, and spin forward into the present. Juan is steadying me with a worried look on his face. "Are you okay?" he asks. "You seemed to go somewhere else, like a trance or something."

"I was somewhere else," I say. "In another time, in another place."

"Are you hypoglycemic?"

How do I explain this? How can I expect him to believe who I am, who I was, who I hope to be forever? How do I tell him I'm 500 years old, I knew his ancestor, and, by the way, I really need to find the fountain of youth that Ponce died searching for?

Well, I'll try.

"Maybe you've noticed I'm Native American," I begin.

"What does that have to do with your spacing out?"

"Actually, I'm a very *old* Native American." He blinks. "500 years old." He frowns. "Let me continue. I'll start at the beginning."

He crosses his arms and eyes me skeptically.

"I first met Ponce, your..."

"...ancestor," he says. A wry smile plays along his lips. He's humoring me.

"...on a jungle trail. He was blocking the path of my wedding entourage, offering jewels in exchange for water from our spring. My Chief was so angered that he ordered his men to kill him, but—because I didn't want murder to mar my wedding day—I begged him to let him go." I pause modestly. "I saved Ponce's life."

Juan's smile fades. He's suddenly more focused on what I'm saying.

"That was a mistake," I continue. "Trusting Ponce to just go and not come back. Instead, he returned with his men to steal water from the spring. Of course, our warriors attacked, but Ponce managed to escape, taking many barrels of water with him."

Juan nods, as if he knows what's next.

"After that, the spring began to disappear. My Chief blamed me, since I pled for Ponce's life. Had Ponce been killed, he wouldn't have returned for the water, and my Chief was certain the spring would still be with us, untainted by the Spanish invaders. I was exiled and left to wander the jungle with nothing of my own except my shell cup."

Juan's eyes widen. "Shell cup?"

"It was my only possession. And once I found the spring again—much later, when I traced it to the land of the Calusa to the west—my shell cup served me well, not just for drinking, but as a reminder of who I was and still am: a queen."

And then I tell him it wasn't a trance I just had, but a flashback in time: giving Ponce my shell cup to drink from, being pursued by the Calusa and leaving the cup behind.

Juan stares at me with an almost frightening intensity. "Tell me about this cup. What does it look like?"

I close my eyes and conjure up the memory of the shell cup I held so many centuries ago. I can almost feel its heft in my hands, the rough ridged exterior, the silky smooth interior. My fingers trace the whorl of protrusions that ascend until they reach its finial, the crown I cradled as I drank from it.

"It's a conch shell, about this big," I say, indicating its size with both hands, "the color of sunwashed sand on the outside, sunrise pink on the inside."

"Is that it?" he asks. "Just a conch shell?"

"No. It was a ceremonial cup, so its opening was enlarged for drinking. What made it sacred were the carved designs on its exterior. My cup was originally made for the Chief, but he was unhappy with the design, so he gave it to me and had a more perfect cup made for himself." I smile at the memory. "I much preferred the design, flawed as it may have been, of my cup."

"Describe it," Juan says. It's a demand, not a request, and I have to wonder why.

It takes me a moment, since it's been hundreds of years since I've seen my cup, and these days my memory isn't what it used to be. I close my eyes, and then it comes to me: Etched into the exterior are two doves with flaring tails that fan out around the curve of the shell. The birds face each other, their beaks seeming to kiss behind the column that separates them. They each have one round eye, a circle with a dot in the middle. One of the birds has a smile on his beak and a glint in his eye, an untraditional aberration that made my Chief reject the design and give the cup to me. He ordered another design for himself: a fierce warrior with a bird-beak mask, arms like long-feathered wings, legs spread over an elaborate bird's tail.

When I describe my shell cup, Juan is silent for a long time, arms crossed, staring down at the ground in thought. I see, superimposed on the real-life Juan, my memory of Ponce as he stood his ground on the trail. They look nothing alike—Ponce was short and sturdy, his features broad and lined with determination; Juan is tall and lanky, seemingly more easygoing. They do have the same stride, a certain attitude, and, of course, those panther eyes. Still, I feel there's a deeper connection, that they share some intrinsic quality that links them through the ages. Curiosity? Daring? Foolhardiness? I don't know either of them well enough to guess.

Juan emerges from his pensive state, and studies me long and hard. Whatever he's thinking, he seems to have come to some acknowledgment. And then he says something I never expected to hear.

"I have your shell cup."

SEVENTEEN

It's late. Lorelei is dozing off on the couch next to Juan, who seems compelled to read, once again, Luis's journal recounting Ponce's story. She can understand his fascination with his famous ancestor, but she wonders if he's not reading too much into the ramblings of a delusional old man.

She is startled awake by a loud banging coming from the backyard. Juan throws the journal aside. Not bothering to put on his shoes, he rushes outside. "Stay there," he orders Lorelei as she scrambles to go with him, "in case you have to call the police."

She retreats to the window. In the moonlight, she sees Juan approach a woman sprawled out on the grass next to the capped well of the now-defunct spring. When the woman stands to confront Juan, Lorelei realizes with a start that it's Winona, in all her six-foot glory. Now the two are arguing. To Lorelei's chagrin, she sees Winona reach out and put her hand on Juan's chest. What is she doing?

For a long moment, Winona and Juan are frozen in what looks like a romantic tableau, Winona's hand unmoving from Juan's chest, Juan seemingly mesmerized by her action. And then the moment ends. Juan is holding Winona's arm and looking searchingly into her eyes. Furious, hurt, and confused, Lorelei is torn between wanting to yell out the window or actively doing some serious damage to one or both of them.

Now Juan is listening as Winona talks. He seems intensely fascinated by whatever it is she's saying, nodding and frowning as she speaks. Then he seems to soften, saying something that causes Winona to stand back, throw her hand over her mouth, and stare in wonderment at Juan.

Okay. That's it. Lorelei slams out of the house and stalks to where Juan and Winona are standing.

"What exactly is going on here?" Lorelei knows she sounds like a fishwife, but she doesn't care. This is such a blatant display of... she doesn't know what. But she's owed an explanation.

Winona looks, up close, less formidable than Lorelei remembers her. She seems to have diminished somewhat, not in size, but in manner. Where before, she had been Amazonian in her presentation, now she seems more like an off-duty Wonder Woman. Juan, too, seems stunned by something that apparently has nothing to do with Lorelei's sudden appearance on the scene. Lorelei's anger is morphing into bewilderment. "What's going on?" she repeats, this time more puzzled than accusatory.

"It's complicated," Juan says.

"I'll bet," she says, then, realizing she sounds snarky, adds, "I'm listening."

"Can we go inside?" Juan asks. "It's a long story, and my feet are cold."

Lorelei tips her head toward Winona. "Her, too?"

"Her, too," Juan says. "She's part of the story."

Lorelei is shaking, not from the chill, but from a premonition. Up to now, Winona has been a dark shadow lurking in the background, and now she's moved front and center. This can't be good.

Once inside, Winona appears, at first, not to know where to put herself, and stands uncomfortably until Juan offers her a seat on the couch. She sits stiffly, her bare feet apart, a muddy match to Juan's, who sits opposite her on a rattan chair he has found too uncomfortable in the past. Lorelei perches on the edge of the matching rattan chair. Between them is the coffee table, and on that, Luis's journal of Ponce's story, thrown there by Juan when the banging sound outside began.

Juan picks up the journal and smooths out its pages, their edges bent and ruffled from his multiple readings. "Until now," he says, "I wondered if this were really true, or just the deathbed hallucinations of a monomaniac."

"What is it?" Winona asks.

"It's Ponce's story," Juan says. "It's your story, too."

Juan opens the journal and begins to read. As he proceeds with the description of Juan meeting the woman on the path, Winona seems to dissolve into herself. "That's me," she says in a hoarse whisper.

"It can't be," Lorelei says, but somehow she knows it is. Pieces of a puzzle separated by time are joining in a moment of truth. Still, "Do you believe it?" she asks Winona.

"Believe it?" she says. "I *lived* it."

"I was skeptical, too," Juan admits. "But this is what made me believe you." He reads: *She unclasped a pouch that hung from her waist, and extracted the same shell cup I had seen at our last encounter.*

Lorelei's eyes travel to the shelf in her bookcase where Juan had placed it after his return from Puerto Rico. She rises slowly to retrieve it, and, cradling it in both hands, brings it to Winona. "Your shell cup," she says. Winona hesitates, then, with a look of wonder, takes it and briefly holds it to her lips.

"My cup," Winona breathes.

"It was given to me, along with the journal, by a cousin in Puerto Rico," Juan says. "I thought it was just a memento, and didn't realize its significance until I read the journal."

Juan continues reading, but Winona seems to be somewhere else, caressing the cup with a faraway look. When he reads the journal's last line: *if not for my foolishness, my son, you would not exist,* Winona nods in agreement, her energy restored with the telling of the tale.

"And if not for *my* foolishness—saving Ponce's life—he wouldn't have returned to steal the water. Luis wouldn't have been born, and neither would you. So," she concludes, "if not for *me,* you wouldn't be here."

"I know," Juan says. "What can I say? I guess 'thank you' doesn't quite do it."

"Uncapping the well and giving me the water would." Winona grips the shell cup expectantly.

Juan shrugs and shakes his head. "It's gone," he says. "I told you. It ran dry. I don't know why, or where it went."

Winona is on her feet. Before Juan can react, she reaches over and grips his arm so tight that he winces. "You found it before, and you'll find it again," she growls. "You're a well digger. So *dig.* It's under there. You know it's under there."

Juan attempts to pry himself loose, but Winona, powered by anger, hangs on. "It's gone," he protests. "Why would I lie to you? It's just not there."

Winona releases her grip. Juan backs away, warding off any future attacks with a raised hand. "Really," he says, "if I could bring it back, you could have it. Every drop. I do owe you, but there's no way to repay you."

A wave of resentment passes through Lorelei at Juan's presumed generosity. Who is he to say Winona could have the water? And then another wave, this time of regret, washes over her: aside from the six bottles she has saved, there's no more water to be had.

Lorelei is still sorting out her feelings—resentment, regret, jealousy, guilt—when the complete preposterousness of having a 500-year-old woman sitting in her living room overwhelms her. This is crazy.

And yet it must be true.

Juan, the would-be scientist, believes it. Ever the skeptic, he has proof. The journal. The cup. The rejuvenating effects of the water from Lorelei's well.

But...can he explain what Winona was doing in his dreams? Why he seemed to dream what Ponce had lived? And then she remembers what Juan had explained to her about epigenetics—the genetic memory of something that happened to an ancestor.

Winona interrupts Lorelei's contemplation of the strangeness of things by knocking over a chair in her rush to the door. Juan runs after her, but Lorelei is stuck in place, stunned by the sudden noise of the clattering chair and Juan's shout to "just stay there, okay?" Lorelei rushes to the kitchen window and sees Juan, crouched down, talking to Winona, who is creeping along the ground, head tilted, seemingly listening to the dirt. One hand grasps the shell cup, and that, too, is turned downward, as if it could hear what the earth is saying.

Juan's head jerks up as Lorelei approaches. "I can't talk any sense into her," he says. "She says she has to find the spring, and this is how she does it." He spreads his hands helplessly. "I told her that she's got as much of a chance of finding it as someone who's dowsing for water with a stick." He pauses. "Actually, dowsing might even work better."

Juan rises to his feet. "This is pointless. I'm going inside." He turns to Lorelei. "You coming?"

Lorelei shakes her head. "Not yet. In a minute."

Juan shrugs and heads back to the house, but Lorelei stays put. She's mesmerized by Winona and her gritty determination.

Winona freezes in her tracks. Presses her chest to the ground, as if she were listening with her heart. She moves the cup around in a slow circle, making whorls in the dirt. "It's here," she says. "Faint, far below, moving away fast." She points westward. "That way." She rises painfully. "Knees. Getting worse," she comments, "but not for long." She laughs, a short, rueful bark. "I'll find it again. I always have."

Lorelei has her doubts, but what annoys her is Winona's certainty of her own infallibility. Sure, for 500 years she's been successful at tracking the spring through time, but Lorelei hopes that this time she's wrong, that the spring is lost forever and Winona just dries up and blows away. Far away from Juan.

She can't help herself. She's still jealous, even though she knows that Juan and Winona's relationship is a tenuous one, rooted only in the connection between Winona and Ponce. Still, Winona made Juan possible. And Lorelei has Winona to thank for that.

Which she can't bring herself to say. Instead, what she says is, "There are worse things than not living forever."

Winona rises to her full six-foot height and glares down at Lorelei. "Really?" she says. "What's worse than getting old and dying?"

That's easy, Lorelei thinks. "Not living the life that you have," she says, a bit more smugly than she meant.

"What makes you think I'm not living my life?"

"I don't know," Lorelei says. "It just seems like you're so obsessed with getting to the spring that nothing else matters." She thinks of Sharleen, whose obsession almost devoured her until she came to her senses, and repeats Sharleen's admonishment: "You need to find something that makes you feel good about yourself."

Winona's nostrils flare at the affront. "Who are you to tell me how I feel about myself?" she says. "I've got plenty going for me. What have *you* got?"

It slips out before Lorelei even realizes the truth of it: "Someone I love who loves me back."

She braces herself for what she expects to be a sarcastic retort, but Winona remains silent. She seems to examine the shell cup she's holding, running her fingers lightly over the engraved birds.

"I thought I had that, once." Her fingers pause in their exploration. "But I was wrong." She turns abruptly, then ducks into the foliage between their houses and disappears into the darkness.

WINONA

I never confused love with making love, although I do love that. There were many, many men that I came to know as the centuries went by, and each one had his virtues. Although I am discriminating in my selections, most were chosen for their virility, not their depth. Call me shallow, but I was in it for the pure sensuality. I didn't want to invest myself again in someone who could cause me such pain. Once in a lifetime—even a very long lifetime—is enough.

But now and then I wonder about what I may have missed. The feeling is fleeting, lasting perhaps the length of a romantic movie, or the time it takes for an adorable kid to turn into a screaming little monster. The desire for marriage and kids can disappear in a moment, and then I'm happy to be independent me. Eternally ageless, eternally searching, eternally...eternal. That's my life.

When the spring has been easily available to me, I've had few worries. I've found work to support myself, men to seduce, ways of entertaining myself in the time in-between. I never concern myself with health. Eternal youth has its benefits aside from knowing you'll live forever. Looking good, feeling good, having boundless energy—those are givens I've never had to work for, or even think about.

Over the centuries, I've observed how much time and effort people put into the act of just surviving. This century—war and deprivation aside—survival has become a business: health food, fitness centers, diets, spas, drugs to build you up, drugs to slim you down. Every week there's some new revelation: Kale! Fitbits! Running shoes with toes! As if any of this makes any difference in the greater scheme of things. I'm just glad I don't have to deal with it.

At least, until now. In the past, the spring has moved on, but I easily traced it to its new location. It always turned up somewhere in nature—a hidden nook, a secret pond, a stream flowing beneath a rock. Heart to the earth, sensing, not seeing, I trusted my instinct to lead me to it. As it did, when it led me to the Everglades.

And then, as it always has, the spring began to diminish. I put my instinct to work, but to no avail. Even with my heart to the earth, I could not track where the spring was flowing. I was just beginning to feel the effects of deprivation when fate interceded in the form of Sharleen, Lorelei—and Juan. Without really understanding my connection to him, I knew I had found the spring...but this time, not in nature. It was deep underground, separated from me by steel. For the first time, I was afraid.

I don't know if my fear was evident to Lorelei when I left her last night, or if I exhibited something deeper—something so unfamiliar to me that I still don't know what to do with it: emotion.

I guess that's what overwhelmed me when she told me she had something I did not: Someone to love who loved her back. Maybe that wouldn't have struck me to the core as it did, if I hadn't been holding my shell cup in my hands. Touching the long-lost etchings of the birds brought back the past in a rush, and I was swept into a black hole of loss. I made my way back to my house, clutching the only remnant of what was once the possibility of a happy life.

Now all I can do is lie down beneath a spidery palm and watch a scattering of stars drift slowly across the night sky. When dawn breaks, I find myself covered in dew. The dampness revives me, but I still lie here in the flattened weeds, reluctant to resume what I now feel is a finite life devoid of any meaning.

I force myself to my feet and look around. What was I thinking when I bought this place? I certainly wasn't going to live here. The house is a wreck, the yard is a dump, and the only thing flowing underground is the ominous promise of oil. I see nothing but trouble ahead, in the person of Fred and his minions. I want no part of it.

What's the point of keeping the place now? It serves no purpose. I thought it would be the path to the spring, but it's nothing more than a liability. Sell it? Who wants it? Let the bank have it. Maybe give it to Corabelle. She's a fighter. I like that.

One thing I know. While I still have the strength, it's time to move on. I sensed last night at Lorelei's that the spring was moving, too. Far below, heading west, it's taken a new path. I'll find it. I must. What else can I do?

When I climb into my Jeep to continue my quest, I see sunlight glinting off objects in the back seat that weren't there before: six bottles of water with "Spring Chicken" labels. Six sexy chickens seem to wink at me. Attached to one is a note.

May you find what you seek, wherever you go. Hope this helps you on your way.

EIGHTEEN

Lorelei can't explain the empathy she felt when she saw the effect her words had on Winona, but she recognized Winona's loneliness, and saw herself as she once was. Like Winona, she hadn't known what she was missing, but unlike Winona, she was fortunate to find it. Was it guilt that made her willing to relinquish the last of the water, or was it acknowledging that she didn't need it anymore? Was it gratitude for Winona's role in Juan's existence? Or, on a selfish level, was it just a guarantee that Winona would go away, never to return.

She doesn't want to analyze her motives. Giving Winona the water put an end to it all, and for whatever reason, she feels that a burden has been lifted. All she knows is that now that the water is gone, she feels lighter.

Funny how something that seemed so important, that crowded out the things that really do matter, can evaporate and not even be missed. Lorelei gives the water full credit for taking her life on a different, if complicated path, but it's done its job, and it's over. The question she has to ask is, Where does she go from here?

Her musings are interrupted by the now familiar woodpecker-rapping of Corabelle on her door. Corabelle brings bad tidings, as she has so often of late.

"Okay," Corabelle begins when Lorelei opens the door. No "hello," no preface, no need for exposition regarding her mission today, which is to update the progress of the disaster about to befall the residents of Melaleuca Lakes. Just a question: "You ever hear of 'forced pooling'? It's a law that says if a certain percentage of our neighbors signs away their mineral rights, then the rest-a us gotta go along, like it or not." Corabelle leans close to Lorelei's face, close enough for Lorelei to smell the bacon Corabelle clearly had for breakfast. "You didn't sign on with one-a them land guys, did you?"

Lorelei shakes her head, no, eliciting a sigh of relief from Corabelle. "Good. 'Cause if we're outnumbered by those creeps that sold out, the drillers can suck up gas and oil from right under our *feet.*" She stamps her tiny foot for emphasis. "They got these horizontal drills that'll sneak under your house and you won't even know it until, BAM, you got poisoned water plus all kindsa stuff crumbling below you." She pauses in contemplation. "I think that Merle Beadle sold out. I saw a Vizio 60-inch TV box in her trash pile yesterday. Now where'd *that* come from, I'd like to know."

Lorelei senses danger. Corabelle is rallying the troops, and Lorelei doesn't intend to volunteer. Corabelle, however, thinks otherwise. "That means we gotta amp up our game. Go house to house, get everybody who hasn't sold out to slam the door on those guys." She whips out a notebook, flips to a list that apparently includes Lorelei's name, and announces, "You got Monday, Wednesday and Friday, ten to noon." She ignores Lorelei's head-shaking protest, as well as her claim that she works, she has to be in the shop, and there's no way...

"It's your civic duty," Corabelle interrupts. "We got to nip this thing in the bud before Big Oil comes at us with all their legal whoop-de-doo. We get enough numbers, they won't mess with the Melaleuca Mob."

"Melaleuca Mob?"

"Yeah. That's us. The good guys." Corabelle flips the page. Lorelei sneaks a peek and sees in big block letters: MEDIA. Beneath that is an indecipherable list which Corabelle scans with a finger. "Okay, here," she says when her finger comes to a stop. "You handle this one."

With absolutely no intention of handling anything, Lorelei looks anyway. "Miami Herald Neighbors Section," it reads. Lorelei notes that 'Neighbors' is spelled 'Naybors,' which gives her a clue as to what Corabelle's next order will be, since this is obviously not Corabelle's strong suit. "Write them a letter," Corabelle says. "One-a them letters to the editor. Tell them all about what's going on here, so the world will know."

Aside from the fact that the *Herald*'s "Neighbors" section is hardly the world, Lorelei has no desire to contribute to Corabelle's crusade. Now that her focus is no longer on the water, life can take a fresh, new path, and it's not going to be in the realm of proselytizing. Even for a noble cause like saving the planet (or whatever part of it is in Melaleuca Lakes).

But she does have to give Corabelle credit. She has reinvented herself into this little political dynamo, ready to take on the big guys. Lorelei wants to be supportive, even if she's not willing to pound the cracked pavement of Melaleuca Lakes, so she agrees to write the letter. Who knows? It could shine, if not a spotlight, at least a flashlight on Fred's shenanigans in a corner of Miami-Dade County that no one pays attention to.

• • • •

The letter unfurls on her computer, increasing in intensity as Lorelei types away, detailing the progression of Fred's crimes and misdemeanors to lay the groundwork for fracking beneath their little community. She doesn't immediately respond to what has now become commonplace: Corabelle's woodpecker-rapping on her door. She rises to answer it, annoyed at the interruption to her train of thought by Corabelle's frenzy to impart the latest disastrous news. What now?

"You know they been marking spots on the property of alla them neighbors that sold out?" she asks. Lorelei has a vague recollection of Corabelle reporting that. "Well, guess what they marked them for?" Without waiting for an answer, Corabelle grabs Lorelei's hand, steers her out the door, then drags her to Winona's house. There, on the line separating Winona's property from her backyard neighbor's, is a big tank-like truck manned by two men in orange helmets.

"*You* talk to those guys," Corabelle demands. "They ignoring me like I'm some kinda invisible person."

Lorelei masks her shock with what she knows can be a stern school teacher demeanor, and approaches the men with a determined stride. "What exactly is going on here?" she demands.

One man, his eyes shaded by his helmet, stares mutely at her. The other tips his helmet back, revealing a barbershop quartet mustache. "Who are you?" he asks.

"I live here," she says, pointing in the direction of her house. "I want to know what you're doing and why."

"Is this your property?"

"No, but..."

"Then it's none a your business." He turns and busies himself with what looks like a rotary drill on the machine. "We got permission from the property owner, and we got work to do."

"I don't think so. My neighbor wouldn't do that," Lorelei says, certain that in her haste to leave, Winona hadn't sold out.

"Well, lady, she did. Go ask her." He points, not to Winona's house, but to Winona's backyard neighbor, who Lorelei sees peeking out at the goings-on between two slats of her blinds.

Corabelle sees her, too, and trots over to yell, "I see you, Merle Beadle, you sneaky sellout bitch. I hope your Vizio breaks right after the warranty runs out." The blinds snap back into place and Merle Beadle is gone.

"See? We got a right to be here," he says.

"You're on her property, too," Lorelei says, indicating Winona's weedy yard. "You can't just roll over anybody's yard and do what you want."

"We're not digging on her property. We're digging here." He thumps a booted foot at a marked spot. His partner revs up the engine, and the drill revolves ominously.

"Wait! Stop!" Lorelei cries, but Corabelle goes into action. She grabs a downed palm frond and begins to beat at the drill.

"Hey, hey!" The drill operator makes a grab for the frond, but Corabelle is too quick. She swipes it across his head, knocks off the helmet and exposes a flattened head of hair that resembles a well-used Coco Mat door mat. His partner rushes to his rescue.

"I'm calling the police," he threatens, mustache bristling with indignation.

"No, I'm calling the police," yells Corabelle. She whips out her cellphone and dials 911. "We're being attacked," she reports, and Lorelei can hear the faint response of the 911 operator, asking where she is. Lorelei, thinking this is going over and beyond, tells Corabelle to tell the operator Never mind, it's a mistake, everything's okay, we can handle this. Reluctantly, Corabelle does.

The two drillers exchange glances. "Okay," says Coco Mat, "let's just cool down and talk about this."

"Okay," Corabelle agrees. "You're poking a hole in the ground and I want to know why."

"It's no big deal. It's called a shot hole, only 5 inches across and 25 feet deep. It'll be filled in and covered up when we're done so you won't even know it was there."

"What're you doing it for in the first place?"

"No big deal," he repeats. "It's just a test."

"Seismic testing," Mustache adds, and despite Coco Mat's signal to shut up, Mustache goes on, apparently proud of his knowledge. "Geokinetics. It's done so we can figure out what the subsurface geological layers are."

"Yeah," Coco Mat reassures them. "Just a little hole in the ground. You'll never know it was here. You're lucky we didn't have room to use the thumper truck instead." He and Mustache exchange a knowing look. "*Then* you'd have something to complain about."

"What's a thumper truck?"

"It's this monster diesel truck, 'bout 67,000 pounds or so, with these huge vibrating steel plates that pound the ground to create sound waves." He pauses. "*Huge* steel plates, eight by four feet wide, seven inches thick."

"Wham, bam..." Coco Mat begins.

"...*thank* you, ma'am," Mustache finishes, and they guffaw with mutual glee. "That mother will mow down everything in sight, so be happy we're just digging these little holes instead."

"Hold on," Lorelei says. "Why do you need to know what the geological layers are, and what does this hole have to do with it?"

"Well, actually, it's going to be more than one hole. See those markers?" He points at little blue flags that march down the property line, past Lorelei's yard and on down the block. "We got permission from those people all along the line to dig shot holes where they're marked."

"But you'll never know they were here," insists Coco Mat.

"Sellouts!" Corabelle yells in the general direction of the offending neighbors.

"And then what?" Lorelei's bad feeling is magnified by the look on Corabelle's face.

Ignoring Coco Mat's signal, given with a finger drawn across his throat, to quit, Mustache pontificates. "After the holes are dug, we drop dynamite in the holes..."

"*DYNAMITE?*" Lorelei and Corabelle cry.

"*Little* dynamites," Coco Mat corrects.

"...which we explode..."

"*EXPLODE?*"

"...to send acoustic waves into the rock layers. Then these bounce back to the surface and are recorded by receivers called geophones that'll let us know whether or not there's oil or gas in the rock formations."

"Oil. I knew Fred was behind this," Lorelei says.

"Yeah. Fred," Corabelle snarls. "But if there is oil, no way is anybody going to go fracking to get at it, not if you want a fight on your hands." She sets her face in a grim mask of determination. "We are the Melaleuca Mob!"

Coco Mat shrugs. "And we got a job to do. So let's do it." They return to their positions. The engine revs up, the drill spins. With a terrifying roar, the ground is penetrated.

For the next week, the sound of drilling fills the air. Lorelei is grateful she can escape it while she's at work, and is equally grateful that Sharleen's transformation into a more even-keeled partner hasn't changed her effervescent personality, which continues to draw customers. While her wardrobe and makeup have remained pretty much Sharleen, she is revealing fewer of her attributes—skirts a little longer, necklines a little higher—than before. And though the signs of age have returned, she wears them without complaint.

With the return to normalcy, as well as customers, the shop has become a sanctuary away from the noise, chaos and anger Lorelei experiences when she is at home. The constant hammering drives her outside in search of Fred. In her imagination, her dire threats (she hasn't yet figured out what they might be) force him to back down. She combs the neighborhood, but Fred is nowhere to be seen. With time on her hands and hate in her heart, Corabelle has parked herself wherever the drilling is going on, figuring Fred will eventually show up. But he seems to have vanished behind the curtain of activity that now roils the once-peaceful neighborhood of Melaleuca Lakes.

Juan has tried to help. He's explored the legality of Fred's process, found that what he's done is questionable, but can find no real answers from the tangled bureaucracy and politics that Fred has apparently mastered. Since Melaleuca Lakes is in the unincorporated area of the county, he is told that regulations that would apply within the city of Miami don't apply here.

Corabelle has riled up enough angry neighbors to file a complaint with the police, but their response has been negligible, with a backlog of murders and maulings taking priority. Juan would confront Fred himself if he could find him. All he can do, at this point, is sympathize with Lorelei and be there as much as possible, reassuring her that chances are, all this exploration will yield nothing. His suggestion that she just give it up and move in with him has met with stubbornness. She seems to have caught Corabelle's determination to defeat this at any cost.

One day, the drilling stops. The weight of anticipation is in the air, as if the day—a hot, humid day, smothered with bloated rain clouds ready to burst—were holding its breath. Lorelei decides to stay home from work. Her suspicion that something ominous is about to happen is correct. Mustache and Coco Mat are unrolling an orange plastic temporary fence in a wide perimeter along the location of the shot holes they had dug. They then unravel something red at the end of a long yellow cord into the shot holes, one of which is at her property line, visible from her window.

Dynamite.

The first explosion rattles her windows and shakes her floor. Beyond the scrambled mass of weeds and brush that separates Winona's yard from Lorelei's, a plume of dirt and rock shoots high into the air, pauses, then retreats.

The men proceed to the hole behind Lorelei's house, and repeat the procedure. Ignition, *boom!* Something seems to shift beneath her feet as if the earth tilted off its axis and left the floor of her house not quite level. The plume rises, a fountain of debris. Shattered earth rains down on the little bromeliad-dotted rock garden Juan had started for her—easy upkeep for the gardening-challenged. The drillers move on to the next shot hole to repeat the procedure.

Lorelei pushes the orange fencing aside and cautiously approaches the blast area to survey the damage, stepping over chunks of dirt-encrusted limestone. The cups of the bromeliads are clogged with pulverized earth; several were flattened by the explosion. Lorelei mourns them briefly, propping up the fallen, picking dirt clots from the survivors. It's not so much their demolition that dismays her, as it is a premonition that something even worse could be on the horizon.

The next boom, from her neighbor's property line, is not so much heard as felt. She has that same disorienting feeling that the horizon has tipped just a bit. Maybe her eardrums were damaged, she thinks, upsetting her equilibrium. She watches, a little dazed, as her neighbor's plume rises and falls, a mini Yellowstone that repeats down the block as the day wears on.

When the rains come in late afternoon, thrumming the ground with a tom-tom beat, Coco Mat's promise that she'll "never know it was here" of the hole in the ground, while exaggerated, is somewhat true. The rain has pummeled the excavated area, leaving a muddy swath of mush that conceals its exact location. The dismal scene only adds to Lorelei's feeling of doom.

"Come on. Let's get out of here and go to my house," Juan says later that evening as he surveys the scene of destruction. "This is too depressing. I'll come back tomorrow and help put things back in order."

Lorelei can't bring herself to leave. She feels compelled to stay as an act of defiance, as well as a reluctance to abandon her wounded home. Corabelle is already a whirlwind of action, banging on doors to either castigate those neighbors who sold out to Fred, or to instigate a rebellion among the like-minded. Lorelei doesn't have the energy or the inclination for such activity, but she has penned another email to the *Herald*'s "Neighbors" section detailing the latest disaster in Melaleuca Lakes, and how it has personally affected her. She feels oddly satisfied when she hits "send," even though she knows that even if the letter makes it into print (which her previous letter failed to do), it'll have no effect whatsoever. Just another whiner complaining about progress, some will say if they bother to read it, while others may sit and nod in agreement over their morning coffee, then turn the page to see what's on sale at Macy's. The only readers who might react viscerally to her letter are those of her neighbors who either (a) are members of the Melaleuca Mob or (b) sold out.

Corabelle's call to arms has divided the community and, in a way, enlivened it. The negative effect of neighbor pitted against neighbor is balanced in a positive way by people actually getting to know each other, for better or for worse. Two bridge games and a mah-jongg group have sprung up as a result, and there is talk of a march on city hall with a bagel brunch to follow.

Since Lorelei insists on staying put until they hear the results of the seismic testing and what that might mean, Juan stays with her despite his reservations about the condition of the house. He, too, senses that something is awry, but it's more a feeling than a certainty. He's spent days inspecting the house for damage: checked the foundation, the floor seems level, the walls show no signs of cracks. "It seems okay," he reports as they get ready for bed. "Are you okay?"

She slides under the covers and stares at the ceiling. "It's probably just psychological," she says.

"What is?"

"I feel like I'm sleeping on a sailboat on calm seas. It's not a rocking motion," she tries to explain, "but more like..." She frowns in thought. "...what a rubber duck might feel like in a bathtub while the water is going down the drain."

Juan gives that a moment. "I think I know what you mean," he finally says. "Bad vibes."

"Bad vibes," she agrees sleepily. "You're right. It's been a nerve-wracking week. Let's stay at your place tomorrow night. I'd like a little normal for a change."

• • •

A distant rumble, like the sound of a train going by. Lorelei and Juan are jolted awake as it gains in velocity to a roar that fills the room with thunder, ending in an earsplitting *CRACK*. Too stunned to scream, they find themselves sliding downward, bedcovers tumbling with them, mattress plunging into what appears to be a jagged hole in the floor, pitch-black and expanding into a fathomless pit. Juan scrambles upward, pulls Lorelei with him, grasps at what remains of the floor and hangs by both hands at its edge, Lorelei wrapped around him. The bed is swallowed up, disappearing in a fluttering farewell of white sheets and tumbling pillows.

Lorelei clings to his waist as he grips the splintered remains of floor that shreds beneath his fingers. She feels herself slipping down his sweaty hips, screams *Juan, help me!* but he can't, it's all he can do to hang on, and they both sway over the infinite inkwell beneath them. The floor tips even further, bringing with it Lorelei's dresser, its drawers regurgitating her collection of lingerie as it tumbles out in chase of the vanished bedcovers. Last to go is Lorelei's favorite, imbued with the nostalgia of the first time she and Juan made love: VaVoom's crimson teddy, made of the finest silk, deceptively delicate with the strength of a parachute's canopy.

As the teddy exits the drawer, it seems to pause. The dresser spins wildly. Its drawers slam shut before it stops, wedged in the doorway of one still-standing wall. The errant teddy is partially wrapped around one leg of the dresser; the rest stretches provocatively just beyond Juan's reach where he grips the floor's edge. Afraid to release his hand, he creeps his fingers in a crab crawl beyond the edge, oblivious to the splinters they're collecting along the way. The teddy teases him with its proximity. Centimeter by centimeter, he makes his approach. In an adrenaline surge of power, he reaches out and grabs the teddy's silky folds, wrapping them around his wrist before releasing his other hand to pull Lorelei up to the floor's edge, which she grips in terror.

"You've got to hang on until I get myself up," he says. "Can you do that?"

Lorelei nods, fearful that her fingers will succumb to the splintering wood beneath them.

Juan takes a deep breath, yanks on the teddy to make sure it's secure, then hoists himself up, one hand on the teddy, the other pushing hard against the floor's deteriorating edge. He levitates to chest level, takes several more breaths, and with another adrenaline surge, pulls himself up and out, causing the floor to tip even more precariously and Lorelei to scream in alarm.

One hand gripping a leg of the dresser, he grabs Lorelei's forearm and yells for her to *push, push, push*, with her other arm, which she does with a strength she never knew she had. With one final thrust, she is on the floor next to Juan, his arms wrapped around her. It's a momentary reprieve, for the floor continues to tilt. Gathering what strength is left, they hustle around a fallen wall, up a vertical hallway, through the door before it falls flat behind them. They scramble away from the house as it folds in upon itself like a house of cards. It disappears in a deafening roar into the bowels of the earth.

They huddle together across from the site where the house once stood, staring at the cloud of dust and debris now settling into the jagged hole in the ground. Shivering, more from fright than the nighttime chill, they are oblivious to the crowd of neighbors, several video recording with cellphones, gathered in awe at the surrealistic sight before them.

"Sinkhole," one whispers.

The word bounces from person to person, gathering in volume until it becomes a chorus of certainty, verified by the sight before their eyes.

Animated with righteous anger, Corabelle emerges from the crowd, pink chenille robe flying, bunny slippers flapping in the dewy grass. "It's alla that dynamite," she accuses. "I *told* you those guys were going to destroy us, and here's the proof." She points to the site of destruction before changing the direction of her finger, aiming it at the crowd. "You guys that sold out, you did this." She squinches her eyes in search of her main target, and spies her at the edge of the crowd. "I see you sneaking away, Merle Beadle. Was your 60-inch Vizio worth this?" All eyes turn to Merle, who defiantly shifts the blame to her fellow sellouts.

"Yeah?" Merle counters. "Well, it's not just me. It's him." She points to Lorelei's neighbor, "and the Farbers and the what's-their-names—the ones with the bratty kids, and..."

"Stop it!" Lorelei shouts. The crowd's noisy reaction falls to a hush. "I don't care who's to blame," she says. "Right now, I'm just glad we're still alive." For the first time, the crowd turns their attention to Lorelei and Juan, whose bloody and battered appearance elicits gasps. "I need to figure out what I'm going to do next. I'm cold, and I'm scared, and I just lost my house." At that, Lorelei's state of stunned shock melts into sobs. Juan folds her into his arms, where, covered in dust, they look like figures from Pompeii, frozen in time.

Corabelle rushes to them, removes her robe and throws it over their shoulders. "You come home with me," she says, a commanding figure in her flimsy nylon nightgown. She shoots a venomous look at Merle Beadle, and dismisses the crowd with the sweep of a crepey arm. "Go on," she orders. "I'll take care of this." They disperse, some slinking away in guilt, the rest with looks of worry on their faces, for, as several opined when reality set in, "What if our house is next?"

More time is spent with paramedics and cops who arrive on the scene, exhausting Lorelei and Juan to the point where they agree to stay with Corabelle for the few hours left until morning, rather than making the trip to Juan's house. After showering and drinking cocoa Corabelle has prepared to soothe them, Lorelei and Juan spend a sleepless night on Corabelle's foldout couch in the living room. While Lorelei is grateful to Corabelle for her kindness, as well as her transformation from annoying pest to savior, she declines her invitation the next day to stay on. It's not that the couch is as comfortable as sleeping on a rolling pin, but she can't bear another night in the vicinity of the devastation. She has nothing left now, and wants to get back to some semblance of a normal life.

•   •   •

By the next day, the sinkhole has gone viral on social media. While uncommon though not unheard of, sinkholes make news. Thanks to Corabelle and her newfound talent for publicity, as well as the videos recorded by their neighbors, this one is a sensation. Not just an ordinary sinkhole, which can be the result of the sudden collapse of porous rock beneath the surface, "This sinkhole was man-made!" says Corabelle when interviewed by Channel 7. "Caused by alla that dynamite that they do before they do their *fracking!*"

Fracking. The F word itself—sharp, harsh, threatening—calls up all the anger, fear, and defiance of those who oppose it, as well as conjuring up the disasters that may follow in its wake. Fractured physically as well as socially, Melaleuca Lakes remains split between those who stood their ground, and those who sold the ground beneath their feet, with the latter being excluded from Melaleuca Lake's annual Pot Luck Picnic and Hacky Sack Fest.

Corabelle has been elevated to new prominence due to her outspoken opposition to Fred's operation, as well as for her success: Fred is now being investigated for his circumvention of the law, and is under suspension for breach of the tenets of his profession. Several of his cohorts, both political and bureaucratic, have joined him in public disgrace. There is talk of banning fracking in Florida. Corabelle has done what Fred would have considered impossible: she stopped him in his tracks.

A geological study conducted by the state has assured the residents that their homes are safe. Apparently, says a spokesperson when questioned by the media, it was some inexplicable space that existed beneath a rock of unknown origin that possibly would have remained undiscovered, if not for the dynamite explosions. These may have opened cracks in the limestone that caused it to shift, thus dislodging the status quo and causing the cave-in beneath the house. But that was a freak occurrence and should not recur, assuming no further damage is done either by shot holes, horizontal drilling or fracking.

That, at least in Melaleuca Lakes, is something they can guarantee.

•   •   •

Lorelei has returned to work, if only for the distraction. Her first day back is disorienting, a Rip Van Winkle day where time seemed to have gone on while she slept. The shop is the same as she left it the day of the sinkhole. Sharleen has stepped up and taken over, managing to fill both of their roles while Lorelei recovered from the shock.

Lorelei senses a change in Sharleen the first moment she enters the shop. Gone is Sharleen's flibbertijibbet approach to organizing the merchandise. It's displayed as Lorelei would have wished, but even more so. Sharleen, engrossed in draping a mannequin in a lacy black negligee, doesn't notice Lorelei's entrance. Her attention is focused on the flow of silk over the mannequin's waxy arms, making sure the spidery lace is shown at its best as it falls in layers to the mannequin's impossibly thin ankles. The old Sharleen would have tossed the negligee over the mannequin as if it were a ratty old bathrobe; this new Sharleen is a perfectionist.

Lorelei murmurs a word of approval: "Lovely."

Startled, Sharleen turns, almost knocking over the carefully couture'd model who sways tipsily on her stand. "You're back!" she says.

"I told you I'd be returning today," Lorelei says. She senses that Sharleen had either forgotten (the old Sharleen), or was assuming she'd continue to be running the show (the new Sharleen). Right now, Lorelei wasn't sure which one she preferred.

"Welcome home," Sharleen says, and, to Lorelei's surprise, rushes over to give her a hug. Sharleen was never a hugger, but then, neither was Lorelei. She hugs her back, and realizes: things are different now.

As the day goes on, Lorelei becomes aware that Sharleen has morphed into a fuller version of herself. Still outwardly the same in appearance, she seems to have added layers of depth so subtle that customers are unaware of the change. Beneath the wacky charm she still projected, Sharleen exudes a confidence she had never exhibited before. Their partnership, while equal on paper, had always been tilted toward Lorelei as the dominant decision-maker. As Lorelei settles back into the rhythm of working again, she realizes that the balance has shifted, and they are, at last, truly equal.

One of Lorelei's concerns about returning was that her customers would be uncomfortable in her presence, not knowing how to react to the bizarre way in which she lost her house. But one by one, as they enter the shop, each seems genuinely happy to see her, greeting her with a hug (she'd never been so huggable in her life), and never once mentioning the circumstances that preceded her return. The fountain of youth and its consequences have slipped into vague memory. They return to the shop, loyal customers all—not because of an artificial lure, but because they like the owners and their merchandise. Things have returned, not to normal, but to a new normal—one far more satisfying than the old.

.   .   .

Where her house once stood is a small pond, roped off by police tape. Lorelei and Juan have returned to the scene to give it one last look after a month of procrastination. Although the sight of the pond is startling, Juan understands what happened: ground water seeped through the limestone until it gradually filled the hole. How deep it was, he couldn't guess, but the intense blue color indicates that it descends to great depths. Lorelei tries to picture her house and all its contents at the bottom of the pond, but it's beyond her imagination. Somewhere. Far, far below. It would forever be a mystery.

Lorelei hears the familiar patter of tiny orthopedic-shod feet. Corabelle.

"So, you're back," Corabelle says, clearly happy to see them. She peers into the depths of the pond. "Still hard to believe. Alla that aggravation, and now this." She shakes her head mournfully, but then perks up. "Anyways, we been talking about turning this into a plus 'steada a minus. Melaleuca Lakes has a new lake! A kinda *small* lake, but still. Once it's approved and alla that yellow tape is gone, we think it could be a little park. Or something."

Lorelei is at a loss for any words but, "That'll be nice."

"It's really *blue*," Corabelle notes.

"It's really deep," Juan adds. "That's why."

"Well, anyway. Look what's still here. Your mailbox, kinda." She points to the spot where the mailbox once stood, only now it's lying on the ground. "They still delivering your mail and papers, you know that?"

No, Lorelei didn't know that. She had requested a change of address, but a month later, apparently no one has gotten the message. The toppled mailbox seems pretty stuffed, despite its demise, indicating the determination of her mailperson to fulfill the motto of the USPS: neither snow nor rain nor heat nor gloom of night nor sinkholes would stay her courier from his appointed rounds.

"I threw away lots of it, some junk mail and alla them *Miami Heralds* you got, but I saved what looked like some important stuff—bills and whatnot—I'll fetch you from my house." She trots across the street while they wait.

Juan bends to retrieve what's in the mailbox—more junk, and today's *Herald*. While they wait, Juan idly skims through the sections. He stops, startled, at one headline, adjusts his glasses and stares at the page. "Look at this," he says. Lorelei does, and catches her breath.

WEEKI WACHEE SPRINGS
HIRES NATIVE AMERICAN MERMAID

In a first for the 60-year-old roadside attraction, Weeki Wachee Springs in northwest Florida has hired a Native American to perform as one of its legendary mermaids. Winona Ibi, whose ancestry, she says, goes back to the ancient Tequesta tribe, has achieved the dream of every little girl who has ever watched the mermaid show. Having passed the rigorous audition and scuba test, Ibi has reached mermaid status, earning her tail in record time, due, not only to her outstanding performance, but to her striking appearance. Standing (without tail) at 6 feet, "she is star quality," says head mermaid Trixie McGillicuddy. "We are planning a show around her: 'The Little Mermaid Meets the Indian Queen.'"

Ibi turned down their original suggestion, a reprise of their late '90s show, "Pocahontas Meets the Little Mermaid." The new show will be more to her specifications, says McGillicuddy, which is to present Native Americans in a noble light, as befits their heritage. It will also showcase Ibi's formidable swimming skills (which include breathing through an air hose, and smiling,

eating and drinking underwater), as well as
her endurance. With a current of five miles
an hour, Weeki Wachee's chilly 74 degree water
is fed into the limestone cavern by numerous
underwater springs, some at depths as yet
uncalculated. Ibi seems quite at home in this
environment, and plans to stay on, she says,
"forever."

> As the mermaid's signature song puts it:
> *We're not like other women,*
> *We don't have to clean an oven*
> *And we never will grow old,*
> *We've got the world by the tail!*

The photo accompanying the article shows Winona behind the glass of the underwater theater, arms outspread in a queenly pose. More surprising than her glittery turquoise tail, her seashell bikini bra, or the crown of conch shells atop her flowing hair, is her wide, happy smile.

"She's smiling!" Juan says.

"I never saw her smile." Lorelei studies the photo closely. "Good teeth," she notes.

"You think she found the spring?"

Lorelei shrugs. "I don't know. But it looks like she may have found herself."

• • •

"It's weird," Lorelei says to Juan as they snuggle on his couch, the room dark but for the glow from the aquariums. "I don't miss my house."

"Well, this is your house now," he says, then corrects himself. "Not just your house. Your home." He holds her closer. "*Mi casa es su casa.*"

She knows that's true. She feels more at home here than she ever felt in her own house. She had coasters on her coffee table; Juan's rustic table invites her to put her feet up. She had a dry-clean-only bedspread; Juan's bed is covered in a homemade quilt.

Her house reflected the old Lorelei; Juan's welcomes the new. While the loss of her home is devastating and traumatic, it is, in an odd way, liberating. She doesn't know yet what to do with that freedom, but the door behind her has slammed shut, leaving an empty landscape ahead to fill with her future.

Aside from dealing with the practical aftermath of the disaster—insurance hassles, a possible lawsuit against the fracking company—Lorelei is still sorting out the emotional overload of it all. Narrowly escaping death leaves scars. She has nightmares about that, where she is falling interminably into the center of the earth with no end in sight. But then she wakes up in Juan's arms and sinks into a sense of security that balances out her fear.

The terror of that night has receded, but still clings in shreds of memory. In the comfort of Juan's embrace, she watches two brightly hued rainbow fish dart in and out of the windows of their underwater castle. "It's surreal," she says, "the thought of my house just swallowed up, like a big cookie eaten by the earth." The rainbows, bored with their chase, flit to another part of the tank to tease a Siamese fighting fish. Its lavish tail swirls like a matador's cape as it fends off their attack. "Now and then I try to list what I lost, but nothing of real value comes to mind. I did splurge on a set of good silver, thinking maybe someday I would have company for dinner. But I never did."

"Wasn't I company?" He fakes a pout.

"You're not company. You're family. Besides," she adds, "that *was* my good silver we ate with. You just didn't notice."

"I was too busy trying to digest all those beans."

"And those Baccarat glasses we drank from. My birthday gift to myself. Gone." She feels a twinge of regret for those, more for their symbolism than for their beauty.

"Anything sentimental? Like an old boyfriend's love letters?" He gives her a teasing look. "Maybe his socks?"

"I didn't have boyfriends," she says. Itzy's face flashes through her mind's eye, fades and disappears.

Then she remembers the box. The shrimp-pink shoebox that once held the silver Capezio shoes she had bought for the prom—a splurge she allowed herself since Sharleen had lent her the dress. In it she had placed the few mementos of her youth: her report cards, her spelling bee award, the A+ essay her English teacher had entered in a contest she didn't win. Her high school diploma, mailed to her, rather than presented on the stage from which she had been barred in disgrace.

The box had also contained photographs, faded black-and-white squares with scalloped margins: her mother, frail, pale, at the register of their grocery store; her father, burly, black-haired, lifting a box on a shelf. A baby picture of herself, fat and bald as a Buddha, the only photo of herself as a child until school pictures were taken years later. Those had been in the box, too, a collection of postage-stamp-sized portraits snapped in the annual school ritual, the only copies she had—her parents wouldn't buy the package offered by the photographer—that chronicled her evolution from a gap-toothed first-grader to a sullen high school senior. All gone.

Also in the box was a vertical strip of photos of Sharleen and Lorelei, shot in a carnival photo booth when they were both fifteen. She closes her eyes and conjures it up: out of focus in black-and-white, their fifteen-year-old faces mug for the camera, crossed eyes in the first shot, tongues out in the second. In the third, they turn to each other with big wide grins on their shiny, fresh faces. So young. So young.

A sudden sense of loss overcomes her. Not for her house, not for her things, not even for the sad collection in the Capezio shoe box.

"What's wrong?" Juan asks as she shrinks into his arms, eyes teary. "Something I said?" He holds her close and rubs her back. "I was just kidding about the beans. I *love* beans." She acknowledges his attempt at humor with a wry laugh.

"It's not that," she says. "It's just...I feel like I lived my whole life just going through the motions." She sniffs. "I don't know why it's hitting me now, but the remnants of what little life I had before are buried in that sinkhole."

They gaze in silence at the fish frolicking in their tank, seemingly happy in their watery world, oblivious that there are oceans beyond them. "When I came here on the boatlift," Juan says, "I came with nothing. I mean nothing, zero, nada. Just the clothes on my back and a canteen of water. Even that was empty by the time we made it to shore." He frowns in recollection. "But I was so grateful to have lived through the voyage that I felt I had escaped with all the riches in the world."

Lorelei sighs. "It's not the *stuff* I'm talking about. It's..." She sighs again. She doesn't know what she's trying to say.

"I know. It's not the stuff, or even the proof that you had a life. It's the life you think you might have had that you feel you missed." Juan shifts his position and rubs his shoulder. "Sorry. Getting a little numb there."

Lorelei shifts her position as well. She can't sit in one place for long without some ache or pain arising. She remembers how she felt when she drank the spring's water, the flexibility, the sensation of lightness where her body moved without thought. It seems like a dream now.

"Do *you* miss the life you might have had?" she asks.

"Miss it? I don't have any way of knowing what could have been, so how can I miss the unknowable?" He laughs. "Hey. Whatever happened, each step of it laid the foundation for the next step, and the next, and the next. Where would we be if none of those things happened? I wouldn't be here now, with you."

When did her life really begin—the life she has now, Lorelei wonders. Were all those years of dedication to the shop, denying herself the experience of the world, mere preparation for that moment when she dialed Juan's number in desperation? Was it just the water that created her transformation? Or was it reaching the age of 60 and realizing it was now or never. Had that willingness to change been there all along, just waiting, like Sleeping Beauty, for the kiss of fate to awaken her?

"What's past is prologue," Lorelei says, startling herself. "Shakespeare," she adds. *Where did that come from?* Buried in the abyss of memory (tenth grade, Miss Jackson's class, *The Tempest*), perhaps, like the Titanic shrouded in the ocean depths, it was merely awaiting the moment of discovery. Maybe none of what was gone was truly lost, not even mementos in a Capezio shoebox that fell to the bottom of time.

"What is the past, anyway?" Juan asks. "Facts, for sure—proveable facts, says the scientist in me. But we write our own stories around those facts." He reaches out his arm, stretching it, then circles it around Lorelei again. "Sometimes I wonder if what I think of as my story isn't a mash-up of truth, imagination, and wishful thinking."

And that, Lorelei realizes, is her story, too. While there's no way of knowing whether it will have a happy ending, she wants to fill each page to come with all the life and love she can.

The rainbows are frenetic now, chasing the Siamese fighting fish who taunts them with her agility, flirting with danger, darting over and under the rainbows as they bear down on her. Juan rises to watch them, a smile hovering at the corners of his mouth as if watching mischievous kids at play. He scatters flakes of food into the tank. The fish rush to the surface, mouths pulsating open, shut, open. The water roils with their hunger.

WATER, THE FOURTH ELEMENT

The spring escapes, rushing through deep rock unspoiled by mankind. Diverted into channels, losing its way, some of the spring remains, recycled in the eternal rotation of evaporation, condensation and rain. Reincarnated as ocean, river, lake or stream, it will fall victim to humans who will pollute it and fight over it, changing history in the process.

The water that descends to subterranean depths has never touched life. It remains as hallowed as its sisters: earth, air, and fire. Early alchemists believed those four elements formed the physical world, and, in the right combination, could turn base metal into gold.

Or create an elixir that promised eternal life.

The spring doesn't look back. It doesn't mourn what it leaves behind, but sees only the path before it. As pure as the virgin source which replenishes it, it flows on, wild and free.

END

About the Author

Photograph by Maggie Silverstein

Marjorie Klein's first novel, *Test Pattern* (Wm. Morrow Publishers, 2000; HarperCollins/Perennial 2001) was a Barnes and Noble "Discover Great New Writers" selection. *Boom! A Miami Beach Story* was published in 2021. Her essays and narrative nonfiction have appeared in various publications, including 20 years of writing for Tropic, the Miami Herald's former Sunday magazine. Recipient of a Florida Individual Artist Fellowship and an MFA from Florida International University, she served as a preliminary judge for the National Foundation for Advancement in the Arts for 13 years and is a member of the Flatiron Writers group in Asheville. She has taught in writing programs at the university level in Florida and North Carolina, and presently lives in the Asheville, NC area.

Note from the Author

Word-of-mouth is crucial for any author to succeed. If you enjoyed *Time in a Bottle*, please leave a review online—anywhere you are able. Even if it's just a sentence or two. It would make all the difference and would be very much appreciated.

Thanks!
Marjorie Klein

OTHER TITLES FROM
MARJORIE KLEIN

Test Pattern

BOOM! A Miami Beach Story

We hope you enjoyed reading this title from:

BLACK ROSE writing™

www.blackrosewriting.com

Subscribe to our mailing list – *The Rosevine* – and receive **FREE** books, daily deals, and stay current with news about upcoming releases and our hottest authors.
Scan the QR code below to sign up.

Already a subscriber? Please accept a sincere thank you for being a fan of Black Rose Writing authors.

View other Black Rose Writing titles at www.blackrosewriting.com/books and use promo code **PRINT** to receive a **20% discount** when purchasing.

CPSIA information can be obtained
at www.ICGtesting.com
Printed in the USA
LVHW091725140423
744393LV00005B/646